Wait for Me

CAROLINE LEECH

HarperCollins*Publishers*

First published in the USA by HarperTeen, an imprint of
HarperCollinsPublishers, in 2017
Published simultaneously in Great Britain by HarperCollins *Children's Books* in 2017
HarperCollins *Children's Books* is a division of HarperCollins*Publishers* Ltd,
HarperCollins Publishers
1 London Bridge Street
London SE1 9GF

The HarperCollins website address is:
www.harpercollins.co.uk
1

Text copyright © Caroline Leech 2017
The quotation on page 253 is reprinted courtesy of *The Scotsman*.
All rights reserved.

ISBN 978–0–00–821339–8

Caroline Leech asserts the moral right to be identified as the author of the work.

Typeset by Aurora Parlagreco
Printed and bound in England by Clays Ltd, St Ives plc

Conditions of Sale
This book is sold subject to the condition that it shall not, by way of trade or
otherwise, be lent, re-sold, hired out or otherwise circulated without the
publisher's prior consent in any form, binding or cover other than that in which it
is published and without a similar condition including this condition being
imposed on the subsequent purchaser.

MIX
Paper from
responsible sources

FSC
www.fsc.org   FSC™ C007454

FSC™ is a non-profit international organisation established to promote
the responsible management of the world's forests. Products carrying the
FSC label are independently certified to assure consumers that they come
from forests that are managed to meet the social, economic and
ecological needs of present and future generations,
and other controlled sources.

Find out more about HarperCollins and the environment at
www.harpercollins.co.uk/green

To my mum and dad,
Shirley and Jimmie Sibbald

Till a' the seas gang dry, my dear,
And the rocks melt wi' the sun;
And I will luve thee still, my dear,
While the sands o' life shall run.

from A Red, Red Rose
ROBERT BURNS, 1759–1796

❀ ❀ ❀

WAIT FOR ME

One

Lorna Anderson was ankle deep in muck and milk. And she was late. Again.

She really didn't have time to clean up yet another of Nellie's messes and still make it to school before the bell. Of course, this wasn't the first time that Lorna had somewhere important to be, yet here she was, broom in hand.

And to make Lorna's morning complete, her dad was raging at Nellie.

"What in the devil's name did you think you were doing, you *glaikit* girl? Can you not even carry a bucket without dropping the damn thing?"

"But Mr. Anderson—" began Nellie.

Lorna kept her head down and the yard broom moving. She tried to push the dogs away from the reeking, steaming mess, but Canny and Caddy dodged around her. They were determined to lick the spilled milk from every crevice in the farmyard's cobblestones, savoring this rare treat, and apparently oblivious to the shouting above their heads.

"If you'd been concentrating on the matter in hand, lassie," her dad continued, "you wouldn't have all these accidents. Particularly when the matter in *your* hand is a big bucket of *my* cows' milk."

The farmer's bulk cast a threatening shadow over Nellie, so petite even in her thick and unflattering Land Girl uniform, but Lorna wasn't too worried. Nellie was made of stronger stuff.

Right on cue, Nellie trilled cheerily, "Oh, Mr. Anderson, you know what they say about not crying over spilled milk!"

Nellie winked at Lorna, who smiled in spite of herself. Since Nellie had been posted to their farm two years ago by the Women's Land Army, Lorna had come to love her like the older sister she'd never had, though even Lorna could not deny that Nellie was as clumsy as clumsy came. Yet Nellie had an unshakable confidence that Lorna's father, and indeed every other man within fifty miles, would be putty in her hands if she flashed him her most dazzling smile. And she was usually right.

Nellie picked up the pail and sauntered back into the milking parlor with Caddy trotting in her wake, the border collie puppy following like a black-and-white shadow in case of further delicious catastrophes. Caddy's mother, Canny, gave a soft yelp, but the little dog still disappeared hopefully after Nellie.

Lorna's dad shook his head with an exasperated sigh, and Canny sniffed at his hand, as if to commiserate with him about the youngsters of today.

Lorna's dad gave his dog's head a quick pat, then took the yard broom from Lorna and starting sweeping ferociously.

A screech of brakes made Lorna turn. A truck was pulling into the yard, but it was not one of their regulars from the feed merchant or the dairy. This one was painted in army green, and a dozen men in dark uniforms perched on benches in the flatbed at the back.

Lorna's father stopped sweeping and raised his eyes heavenward. "Thank the Lord!" he said. "At last, someone to save me from all you women!"

"Dad?" Lorna said. "Who are—?"

Some of the men were looking around at the farm buildings, others stared at the floor. Some looked directly and unnervingly at her.

"They've sent a new man to work on the farm," Lorna's dad said, one hand squeezing her shoulder, "but it's nothing to concern you just now. Anyway, don't you have an exam this morning?"

Lorna opened her mouth to tell him that calculus could wait. She was almost eighteen, and when she left school in June, she'd be helping him to run the farm, so he ought to be telling her what this was all about. But before Lorna could say anything, a hugely muscled British soldier climbed down from the truck driver's seat. He had three stripes across the straining arm of his uniform. A sergeant, she realized, just like her oldest brother, John Jo. For a moment, Lorna wondered where her elder brother was right then.

As her father walked toward the sergeant and the truck, a thickset man whose head was closely shaven but whose chin was not called out. He waved at Lorna and said something to her, his voice harsh and guttural. Even if she didn't understand him, she recognized the language from the newsreels, and her heart leaped to her throat. He was speaking German.

He called again, and some of the others laughed. Suddenly Lorna felt exposed and awkward, and then the familiar burn of a blush began to creep up her neck.

The sergeant dropped the tailboard down with a clatter, startling the three cats sidling toward the milky cobbles.

"Army's been puttin' up proper fences over at Gosford for a week or so now," he said, "gettin' the camp secure for these blokes. I don't know why, though. It's not like they'll be chained up or nothin'. Too busy workin' for their keep, from what I hear."

He beckoned someone forward with a stubby finger. "Vogel! Your turn, Sunshine, down you come!"

Lorna grabbed at her father's sleeve while not taking her eyes from the men in the truck. Then her dad was growling in her ear. "Stop gawping, girl, and go!"

"But they're *Germans*," she said. "The enemy! You can't be

bringing enemy soldiers onto our farm, Dad. No!"

"They're prisoners of war now, not soldiers. Sure, that Mr. Hitler is the devil in jackboots, but the war is over for these chaps. And since they're fit and able young men, they can damn well do a man's work around this farm—"

"But Dad!" Her annoyance now obscured her embarrassment. "We're coping just fine—"

"—until your brothers come back."

"If they ever come back."

Even as she said it, Lorna knew she'd overstepped the mark, and she hoped her father hadn't heard.

He had.

"Do not tell me how to run my farm!"

He pointed deliberately in the direction of the village and the school. As Lorna began to argue, a prisoner—had the sergeant called him "Vogel"?—jumped down from the truck, stumbling as he landed, his back to them. He quickly righted his balance. Tall and skinny, his dark gray uniform didn't fit him. The pants were baggy and too short, and the jacket swamped his gaunt frame. He had the same haircut as the others, shaved close, and his neck was scrawny and pale. He was just a boy, and it looked as if a puff of wind would blow him away.

But then the boy turned toward them and Lorna could see a high cheekbone and strong jawline. All right, perhaps he was more a man, but still . . .

Then he faced them full-on, and Lorna's irritation was instantly extinguished, her shock catching her throat.

Half the boy's face was gone.

No, that wasn't quite right. His face was there, but from his left temple to his chin, across his cheek and down the left side of his throat, the pale skin had been burned away, leaving raw red scarring, tight and shiny. The flesh was puckered into the knotted remnants of an earlobe, and his left eye was stretched out of shape, round elongating to oval.

Lorna was horrified. What had happened? What had done that to him? She didn't know what she'd been expecting, but not *that*. And then an awful thought struck her. Had this terrible damage been inflicted by a British soldier like John Jo? Lorna felt sick at the thought, but still she could not look away.

"Christ Almighty!" her father muttered.

Then the sergeant walked in front of her, and the spell was broken.

"Don't look so scared, love, he won't bite." He seemed to find her discomfort amusing. "Well, not until he knows you better. Ain't he a horrible sight?"

Lorna glanced again toward the prisoner. Had he heard that?

The sergeant chuckled.

"Don't worry, love, he doesn't speak a word of the King's English. None of 'em do." He gestured to the German. *"Doo haff nine English, eh, Fritz?"*

Was that even German?

The prisoner stood straight and still. His expression—or as much of it as she could interpret from the undamaged side of his face—was impassive. A mask. Perhaps the driver was right, and he hadn't understood the insult.

As the sergeant gave them a mock salute and clambered back into the truck, Lorna struggled to remember what she had been saying before that awful scarred face had forced everything else from her mind.

As the army truck reversed across the farmyard, Lorna forced herself to look at the soldier again. He was glowering—*maybe*—the undamaged side of his forehead creased into a frown, but really, what expression could she ever hope to read there?

The rumble of the truck faded into the morning chill, and Lorna's father rubbed his hand over his face. For all his gruffness and bad temper with Nellie, he suddenly looked very weary. Had he been as shocked as Lorna?

Her father walked to where the German waited. "I'm John Anderson and this is my farm," he said, slower and louder than necessary. "I have two boys of my own away at the war, so you'll work in their place."

The prisoner appeared to be listening politely, even if he couldn't understand the words. He did, however, give Lorna's father a curt nod.

"You don't need to bow to me, son, just do your work. Oh, and this is my daughter," Lorna's father said as he saw she was still standing behind him, "who should be in an exam room *right now*."

But Lorna barely heard what he said. The German was looking at her, and Lorna shivered. His eyes were steel gray, glinting silver, hard and cold and angry.

Then his gaze fell to her school uniform and woolen stockings, her milk-and-muck-spattered shoes. The right, undamaged side of his face rose in a sneer.

Or was it a smile?

No, definitely a sneer.

He looked up again at Lorna and gave her one of those curt nods. Then, without another look in her direction, he followed her father, leaving Lorna alone in the yard.

The rooster crowed again, as if it were already time for—

School! The bloody exam! Lorna was late and Mrs. Murray would kill her. As she grabbed her coat and schoolbag from beside the gate, she scraped her knuckles on the wall and had to suck at the graze to stop it bleeding as she took off running toward the shortcut past the church. The path would be muddy, but her shoes couldn't get much filthier than they were already.

As she ran, Lorna resolved to forget about the German for now, to forget that her dad had invited the enemy onto their farm, into their home. But still, there was the way the German had looked at the mess on her shoes, his burned face, his angry eyes, and his distorted smile—no, his sneer—and somehow that made her run all the faster.

Two

BIG NEWS! Need to talk later.

Lorna waited while the ink dried on the scrap torn from the back of her exercise book, then slid it across the desk and under the page her best friend, Iris Robertson, was doodling her latest dress design on. The calculus paper hadn't been anywhere near as hard as Lorna had expected, and she and Iris had both finished it with plenty of time to spare. Now she was bored.

Iris glanced at the note and moved to slip it into her cardigan sleeve. Before it was hidden, however, long fingers reached out and took it from her hand, making Lorna and Iris both jump. Mrs. Murray stood over them, fanning herself with the note, then gave her head a quick shake of disapproval and returned to the front of the classroom.

Lorna had another twenty minutes of staring out at the heavy cloud that seemed to smother the high classroom windows before Mrs. Murray called an end to the examination. The teacher squeezed between the tightly packed desks to collect the exam papers into two piles—calculus from the older students like Lorna, and algebra from the younger ones. It had been close to chaos when the two classes had merged after Mrs. Duffy had run off to join the Women's Auxiliary Air Force the year before, but Mrs. Murray's rod of iron had soon brought an almost military discipline to the room.

As Mrs. Murray passed by Lorna's desk, picking up the papers, she paused.

"Would you join me in the hallway please, Lorna?" she said. "I need a quiet word with you."

Damn! It was only a note. It wasn't like she'd been cheating.

Lorna exchanged glances with Iris before reluctantly pushing back her chair and walking slowly to the front of the classroom. Esther Bell snorted loudly as Lorna passed her, but Lorna paid no attention. Esther got told off more than Lorna ever did, anyway, and it was because of people like Esther that Lorna was counting down the days until she graduated from school. Only then would she be spared the trial of seeing Esther each day.

"Class! Get out your English notebooks and start on the assignment on the blackboard," Mrs. Murray ordered as she opened her desk drawer and took out some papers. "We'll break for lunch at noon, as usual. In the meantime, I do not,

I repeat, *do not* want to hear one peep from in here."

She walked into the hallway, holding the door open for Lorna to follow.

Lorna glanced back at Iris, but she was gazing at William Urquhart with that ridiculous look on her face.

Lorna pulled the door closed behind her and faced her teacher. "Look, Mrs. Murray, I'm sorry about the note, but it's not like I was—"

"Oh, shush," said Mrs. Murray, waving away Lorna's defense with her hand. "This isn't about the note, this is about you. Now, I've been thinking again about you applying to the university for next year."

Lorna wanted to groan. It would have been better for Mrs. Murray to scold her for the note passing than this torture. "Mrs. Murray, you know that my father—"

"Yes, I know you've told me before that he's not keen on you continuing your education after you get your school certificate in June, so perhaps I need to go and talk to him—"

"No! Really, you don't have to do that." Lorna tried to calm her voice. "He needs me at Craigielaw, that's all."

Mrs. Murray studied her for a moment.

"Well, I'm not so sure," replied Mrs. Murray. "You have too bright a mind to rot on a farm your whole life, and I'm sure he knows that. Remind me of your birthday, dear. April, isn't it? That's when you'll legally become an adult. So you'll have to find a way to make him understand that you'll be responsible for your own choices after that. And who knows, perhaps your dad might just surprise you.

11

"Now, as I've said before, I'd love to see you at the university, but if you won't, I mean, if your father won't agree to that, what about Mr. Dugdale's Secretarial College?"

She held out the papers in her hand to Lorna.

"They offer all sorts of classes, like shorthand and typewriting, and I hear that Dugdale graduates are very highly regarded. You'd be able to go up to Edinburgh on the train each day, and the college is just a short walk from Waverley station."

The top sheet, with a fancy crest, was a letter thanking Mrs. Murray for her recent inquiry, and a printed brochure lay underneath.

"It's amazing what girls these days can do with good secretarial skills," Mrs. Murray continued. "And secretaries have all sorts of travel opportunities, you know. Glasgow, Aberdeen, or even *Birmingham*."

Lorna tried not to sigh. Mrs. Murray made it sound like Birmingham was the most exotic place on earth, but Lorna knew it wasn't even as far away as London, where Sandy, her other brother, worked in the War Office. And it certainly wasn't anything like Paris or New York, or Cairo or Bombay, or any of the other places Lorna and Sandy had talked about traveling to. But right now, Lorna couldn't think of going anywhere.

She knew she was virtually an adult now, and she would have to make some decisions soon about what to do with her life, but she couldn't even think about leaving her father alone at Craigielaw, at least not until the war was over and the boys came back. Then she might think about secretarial college. Maybe. But who could guess when the end might come? When the war was declared in September 1939, everyone had said it would all be over by Christmas. It was now 1945; six Christmases had come and gone since then. How many more . . . ?

And was secretarial college enough for Lorna? What about her dreams to travel?

"Lorna?"

Lorna realized that Mrs. Murray was still waiting for an answer.

"Lorna, have you got something on your mind this morning?" Mrs. Murray suddenly appeared concerned. "Is everything all right at home, dear? Are your brothers . . . ?"

Mrs. Murray's lashes were glistening wet.

"I mean," the teacher tried again, "have you perhaps had some news from the regiment?"

Then Lorna understood what she was really asking. Mrs. Murray's only son, Gregor, was one of John Jo's best friends—and Lorna's favorite by far—and was serving with him in the same regiment of the Royal Scots. Her husband had died when Gregor was quite young, so once Gregor joined up, she'd been left on her own.

"Oh no, Mrs. Murray, nothing like that. We had a letter from John just yesterday, and he's doing fine. He moaned about the cold and the food and all the usual stuff but seemed to be fine otherwise. I'm afraid he didn't mention Gregor in his letter, though."

Mrs. Murray's anxious expression shifted to relief, then to disappointment.

"But I'm sure Gregor will get in touch soon. I'll write back to John Jo this evening and I'll have him tell Gregor you were asking after him, if you like."

Mrs. Murray's mouth smiled, though her eyes did not.

"That would be kind, dear, thank you. Gregor never was one for writing, was he?"

Mrs. Murray gave a not very convincing laugh and dabbed at her cheeks with a white lace hankie she had drawn out of her skirt pocket.

"Come on then, Lorna, back to work, and please think about what I've said."

Lorna tried to hand back the college papers, but Mrs. Murray didn't take them.

"Keep them, dear." Mrs. Murray patted Lorna's hand. "You never know what might be around the corner. And if you would be kind enough to pass that message on to your brother, I'd be very grateful."

Mrs. Murray pulled open the door of the classroom and, squaring her shoulders, walked inside.

"George Brown! Sit down! Can I not leave this classroom for one minute?"

As Lorna returned to her desk, Iris tore her eyes away from William Urquhart to look at Lorna questioningly, but Lorna just shrugged back. The secretarial college papers crinkled inside her cardigan as she sat down. Her secret for now.

As Mrs. Murray wrote again on the blackboard, Iris nudged Lorna's elbow.

"*What news?*" she whispered.

Lorna shook her head and mouthed, "Later." As soon as they were alone after school, she would tell Iris all the details of that morning. After all, Lorna and Iris had shared everything since they were tiny.

It was strange, though; as the day wore on, Lorna became aware of an unfathomable desire to keep the arrival of that awful damaged stranger to herself.

Three o'clock finally came. William Urquhart stood up from his desk with an officious clatter. William was the son of the parish minister and was also Aberlady School's head boy. As such, he was responsible for ringing the big handbell by the front door to signal the beginning and the end of the school day.

As he passed by, William winked at Iris.

Iris giggled and blushed.

Lorna groaned.

What was Iris thinking? Of all the boys she could set her sights on, why did it have to be pompous William Urquhart?

As the first heavy peal of the handbell sounded from the front door, Lorna was on her feet, signaling to Iris to be quick. Iris clearly had other ideas. As everyone else surged from the room, she very carefully flipped down the lid of the inkwell set into her desk, wiped her pen nib on a cloth rag, and placed her workbook into her desk, lining it up carefully on top of the pile already inside. Then she took a hairbrush from her schoolbag and began tugging at the knots in her messy brown curls, pulling the hair straight down her shoulder with the brush, only to have them bounce back up again, looking no tidier than when she started.

"Come on, Iris, hurry!" urged Lorna.

"I'm coming, I'm coming," said Iris, stuffing the brush back into her bag. Suddenly, her eyes lit up as she looked behind Lorna.

William Urquhart was standing right there, uncomfortably close. He bowed at the waist—not a brief nod like the German's, but a full bow—and Lorna had to step back to avoid him touching her.

"Have a good afternoon, *ladies*," he drawled.

So full of himself!

He straightened up and brushed past Lorna. When he reached Iris, he lifted her left hand to his thick red lips and kissed the back of it.

Iris giggled again.

Lorna shuddered. Who did he think he was, Errol Flynn?

"Good afternoon to you, *William*," Iris purred. "I'll see you in the morning. I'm looking forward to it already."

William oiled his way out of the classroom. As they followed him out, Lorna glared at Iris but said nothing until they were on the street. There she bent double and pretended to retch into the gutter.

"What are you doing?" asked Iris.

Lorna stood up.

"*Oh, William, I'm looking forward to it already*," she cooed sarcastically, wiggling her hips in an impression of Iris. "Iris, you can't be serious."

"But he's so dashing."

Lorna scoffed.

"We've always said he looks like a young Tyrone Power, though."

"No, Iris, *you've* just started saying that." She glanced around in case William had reappeared. "*I've* always said that he looks like a snooty, stuck-up slug."

Iris pursed her lips in that infuriating motherly way, and Lorna knew what was coming—another lecture about how Lorna didn't appreciate William's better traits.

"No, you're wrong, he's not stuck-up. He's very intelligent and really, very mature."

"Did he tell you that?" Lorna didn't want to sound nasty, but sometimes she despaired of Iris, she really did. William had only asked Iris out for the first time the other day, but she was acting like they'd been an item for years.

"Actually, it was his mother who told me," Iris said without irony, ignoring Lorna's snort of derision. "And he's already been offered a place at Edinburgh University for September to study law. And then he'll do his postgraduate doctorate in theology so he can become a minister like his father. Of course, William has ambitions beyond a tiny parish like Aberlady. He'll have one of the big churches in Edinburgh, even St. Giles Cathedral, perhaps. He's very driven, you know, and

I very much admire that in an honorable man."

Lorna had heard enough.

"An honorable man? Iris! Listen to yourself. Don't you remember how upset you were just last year when he was so mean and patronizing about your Jane Austen project? And about your singing, and my drawing? Are you telling me he's really changed that much?"

"He has, Lorna. You're just not giving him a chance," Iris muttered through pursed lips. "He's changed since then. And you are being quite mean and patronizing yourself right now."

"I am not. I'm just trying to get you to see sense," Lorna retorted. "Anyway, what about John Jo? My brother will be heartbroken when he finds out you're not pining for him anymore."

"That was just a girlish infatuation," Iris said haughtily. "This is true love. William and I will be together forever."

"Forever?" Lorna scoffed. "But won't Saint William be called up when he turns eighteen in June? Chances are that by September he'll be off to the army, not to university."

Iris looked uncomfortable.

"Yes, possibly," she conceded, "but his mother seems sure that with his poor eyesight and foot problems, he won't have to go. A deep mind like William's would be much more suited—"

Lorna snorted.

"Poor eyesight? He doesn't even wear glasses. And I don't think having stinky feet can keep you out of the army. It certainly didn't work for my brothers."

"Stop it, Lorna! His eyes are very sensitive, Mrs. Urquhart says. And apparently, the Urquharts know a colonel up at Edinburgh Castle, and she'll have a word with him when William's call-up papers arrive. And for your information, William does not have stinky feet."

"Did Mrs. Urquhart tell you that too?" Lorna tried not to snap. "Come on, Iris, can you not see that his mother would do anything to keep her little baby at home instead of letting him out to play with the rough boys?"

Lorna couldn't stop the bitterness creeping into her voice. She didn't mean to pour scorn on a mother's fears. Lorna knew what it was to lie awake at night imagining every bomb or shell or bullet that might hurt John Jo or Sandy, and she wouldn't wish that on anyone else. But if her brothers were risking their lives, then why should William-bloody-Urquhart stay safely at home?

"Lorna, that's not it at all."

Iris sounded hurt. Lorna didn't care. She was on a roll.

"No? And what does Sweet William have to say about all this? Is he happy to have his mother weasel him out of doing his duty?"

"No, actually." Iris's voice was suddenly barely a whisper. "William seems to be quite excited about joining up, even though that means he'll have to leave his mother and father behind . . . and me."

All Iris's tight-lipped motherly condescension had vanished, and tears sparkled in her eyes.

"Oh, Iris, don't."

Iris wiped at her face with her sleeve.

"You just don't understand," she sniffed, "what it's like to be in love."

Lorna was stumped. She would have told Iris off, but her friend looked so sorrowful, Lorna just sighed and wrapped Iris into a hug.

"Oh, come on, silly, don't cry. The war could be over by then, and we'll get all our boys back, the sweet ones and the rough ones. Maybe William won't have to go at all." Lorna pulled out her handkerchief and handed it to Iris. "Anyway, I have something important to tell you, so please come for tea."

Iris managed a wan smile and sniffed.

As they walked toward Craigielaw, Lorna told Iris about the new arrival that morning, and gradually, Iris seemed to recover her humor. Within minutes, she was firmly agreeing with Lorna and was suitably appalled by the news. Hadn't they both always detested Germans? How could it be patriotic to let the enemy run amok on British soil, even if they were prisoners?

"I know that Dad and Nellie could do with more help"—Lorna picked up the rant where Iris left off—"especially since Old Lachie had to retire from the sheep before Christmas. But is there really no other option than dumping bloody Germans on us?"

"Apparently"—Iris sounded like she was spilling a secret, her voice dropping low—"the prisoner who was delivered to Esther's farm this morning was really old and fat, and Esther's dad was not happy. He said the chap would be worthless for any heavy work on the farm, which is what he was needed for. And Esther says their Land Army girl is useless and the size of a sparrow, not like your Nellie at all."

"Nellie's hardly enormous," said Lorna.

"No, but she's strong and she knows about engines and stuff."

"Yes, but she's still a woman. And apparently my dad would rather have a German on the farm than another woman, even a German who looks like *that*."

"Looks like what? Is your prisoner old and fat too?"

"Not exactly. . . ."

"Young and fat?"

"No. . . ."

"Well, is he young and handsome then?"

"Not exactly. . . ."

"He is, isn't he? You think he's handsome!"

"Oh stop!"

"You do, don't you? You fancy a German!" Iris cried.

"Iris, shhhh! I mean it, stop! He is young but . . . oh, it's awful. He's been . . . burned . . . his face . . . it must have been awful."

Lorna could picture him again: the tight angry, brilliant pink skin contrasting with eyes the color of snow-laden clouds, and the sneer that tweaked the corner of the disfiguring mask. Lorna wondered for the first time how bad his pain had been.

"Oh my goodness, no!" said Iris, looking more thrilled than horrified. "That's dreadful! Well, I suppose it's dreadful, isn't it? I mean, he is a German, so maybe he deserved it . . . not deserved it exactly, but . . . oh, you know what I mean."

"Iris! Just because someone's a German doesn't mean he deserves to be hurt so badly."

"But you hate Germans." Iris looked genuinely puzzled. "Aren't you pleased that this one's been hurt?"

"Well, yes . . . no . . . maybe . . . I mean, yes, but when you've got a real one standing right in front of you and the damage to his face is so terrible, well, it's . . . different. Somehow."

Lorna realized only then that her initial revulsion was passing on, allowing pity to creep in behind. She looked at Iris, expecting to see a reflection of her own discomfort, but Iris was smiling.

Iris leaned in close, her face eager.

"But you still haven't told me," she said in a loud whisper, "*would* your German have been handsome if he wasn't so . . . you know?"

"Iris!"

Three

Mrs. McMurdough had her coat on to leave when the girls walked into the kitchen. On the range behind her, a huge pot of stew simmered deliciously.

Lorna threw down her schoolbag and wrapped her arms around the housekeeper from behind. Taller by several inches now, Lorna kissed the old woman on the top of her head as she hugged her.

"Mrs. Mack," said Lorna, who had seldom heard the housekeeper called by her full name, "that smells wonderful."

Mrs. Mack had looked after Craigielaw since Lorna's mother died when Lorna was a toddler. She came in from the village every day to cook, clean, and care for the family. Now that the boys were away and Lorna was older, however, Mrs. Mack would leave when Lorna got home from school and go look after her own grandchildren while her daughter Sheena worked the late shift in the aircraft repair factory at Macmerry. Before she went, however, Mrs. Mack always had a meal ready for Lorna to serve up to her father and Nellie.

"And a good afternoon to you, too!" Mrs. Mack turned round and hugged Lorna back, but only for a moment. "But just look at my floor!"

Lorna stepped back. A trail of mud ran from the door to end at her filthy shoes.

"I did not spend half the morning on my poor old knees scrubbing, just for some young *besom* to drag mud across it. Out you go, and take those filthy shoes with you."

She gave Lorna a playful shove toward the door.

"Oh, and Iris is here, how lovely. Actually you've saved me a trip, dear. I've some cotton curtains that I want made into pinafores for my granddaughters." Mrs. Mack barely paused for breath. "I'd sew them myself, but my fingers aren't up to stitching anymore, and I know that you and your mum would do a lovely job on them. I saw the party frocks you did for Mrs. Gunn's twins. Very pretty. So shall I pop the material in to your mum on Sunday after church?"

"We'd love to help, of course," replied Iris, "but we won't be home after church on Sunday. The minister and Mrs. Urquhart have invited Mum, Dad, and me over to the Manse for Sunday dinner."

Mrs. Mack's eyebrows lifted slightly.

"Sunday dinner at the Manse with the minister? My, how grand!"

"Well, now that William and me, I mean William *and I*, are stepping out together . . ."

Mrs. Mack's eyebrows rose even more.

"Now, that's some news I hadn't heard about," she said, looking pointedly at Lorna.

"Well, it's only been a week or two, eleven days actually," continued Iris, "but we are very keen on each other. He's very good-looking, don't you think? Just like a young Tyrone Power, that's what we've always said."

Lorna vigorously shook her head behind Iris's back to make sure the housekeeper knew that she was not part of that "we," and Mrs. Mack suppressed a smile.

"Well, I don't get to the pictures very often these days, so I wouldn't know about that," Mrs. Mack said, "but I'm sure you're right."

"And he's very clever too, and very moral. So we're doing things the right way, and that's why our parents are meeting on Sunday."

"*Meeting* on Sunday?" Mrs. Mack burst out. "But your folks and the Urquharts have known one another for years. Decades even. Didn't Reverend Urquhart baptize you and Lorna and every other bairn born in the village these last twenty years?"

"But it's different now." Iris was pursing her mouth again. "They'll be meeting for the first time as the parents of a couple who are stepping out. Don't you see?"

Behind Iris, Lorna picked up an imaginary noose and mimicked hanging herself. She could see Mrs. Mack was struggling not to smile.

Suddenly, Iris spun around, catching Lorna with one hand in the air.

"What are you doing, Lorna?" she demanded.

"Sorry," Lorna choked out. "You know I was only kidding."

"You're just jealous because I have a young man now." Iris put her hands on her hips, like an angry old man in the cartoons, which amused Lorna even more. "And you're even more jealous because it's William."

Lorna and Mrs. Mack were both laughing now, even as Iris's voice rose with irritation.

"I always knew you secretly liked him. Well, bad luck, Lorna, he's mine now, and you can just die an old maid if that makes you happy."

Iris furiously buttoned up her coat.

"And if you ever want to escape off this farm like you say, Lorna Anderson, then perhaps you should just grow up a bit and find someone to marry who's as good and as clever and as driven as my William."

With that, Iris flounced out of the door.

"Iris!" called Lorna. "I'm really sorry. Come back! I was only teasing."

But Iris was gone. Lorna didn't go after her because Iris regularly flounced out after one disagreement or another, and they always made up at school the next day. Lorna rolled her eyes at Mrs. Mack, who shook her head.

"That wasn't very kind, you know," said the housekeeper,

"but my, it was funny."

"She's right, though," replied Lorna. "I probably will die an old maid, unless that German slaughters me in my bed first, just to put me out of my misery. Wait, do you even know about the German yet?"

"Aye, I've met the German, but what are you havering about?" said Mrs. Mack with a snort. "That young laddie hasn't enough gristle in his meat to choke a chicken, let alone to murder you. Did you not get a look at him? There's nothing to him. Hasn't had a square meal in months, judging by the speed he wolfed down the soup and dumplings I fed him at dinnertime."

"You gave him his dinner?" Lorna was startled.

"Of course I gave him his dinner." Mrs. Mack looked perplexed. "Why wouldn't I? The lad has to eat if he's expected to do a day's work. Or should I be giving him gruel like he was in the workhouse? And a hunk of stale bread every Friday if he's very lucky? Oh my goodness, but you're a hard one."

"I'm not hard, I just don't see why . . ."

Mrs. Mack was looking at her steadily, one eyebrow raised as if Lorna's words were simply proving her coldheartedness.

"So where is he now?" Lorna asked instead.

"They went over the back field after dinner," Mrs. Mack replied, turning back to stir the stew. "One of the heifers got herself hooked onto the fence. And our Nellie's getting the cows in for milking. She'll likely be in begging a cup of tea before you can say 'Where's the shortbread?'"

Sure enough, within minutes, Lorna heard the lowing of

the dairy cows as they shuffled toward the milking parlor, as they did morning and night.

Lorna went to the back door. Nellie was stamping along behind the cattle.

Like Nellie, dozens of Land Girls were working on farms around East Lothian, doing the farmwork left by men called up to fight. When she'd first arrived from London, aged eighteen, Nellie had never even seen a cow before, but soon it was like she had been born into farming. Not only was she now a trained tractor mechanic, more importantly, Nellie had beguiled the cows into their best milk production in years and was clearly happier in Aberlady than she had ever been in London.

Petite but buxom, Nellie was definitely the only Land Girl that Lorna had met who could wear the uniform of a thick green sweater and beige jodhpurs without looking like she was hiding a sack of potatoes up her shirt. And Nellie used her curves to great effect, by all accounts, in the pubs and dance halls on her nights off. She flirted unashamedly with local men and visiting servicemen alike and openly admitted that she was looking for someone who could offer her a better life after the war than she'd had at home in London before it.

When Nellie caught sight of Lorna through the kitchen window, she waddled over as fast as she could in rubber boots at least two sizes too big for her tiny feet.

"So what do you think?" Nellie said in a loud whisper.

"About what?"

"About the new chap, duckie. Didn't you see him?"

Lorna pretended not to understand.

"For Gawd's sake," said Nellie, "that new young lad, the German, with *the face*, you know. That poor boy. What a mess! I could scarcely look at the poor blighter."

Lorna couldn't think how to reply, but Nellie didn't seem to need her to.

"I don't know about you," Nellie continued, "but I'll be locking my bedroom door at night, I will, if they're going to let these Jerries roam around the place."

"They're not roaming around," said Lorna, unreasonably irritated even though she'd been thinking the same thing, "and he's not going to be here at night. He'll go back to the camp at night to be locked up again. At least, that's what they said."

"Fingers crossed they keep those gates locked tight then, eh?" Nellie said. "I've been quite happy up to now keeping as far away from German soldiers as I can get."

She wandered back toward the milking parlor, slapping the trailing cows on their rumps to speed them up.

"Good to know there's one kind of soldier you'd stay away from, Nellie," Lorna muttered to herself as she walked back to the kitchen.

The next morning, as Lorna cleared up the breakfast dishes, the dogs began barking at an approaching truck. Knowing it must be dropping off the prisoner from Gosford, Lorna rushed to put her coat on and grab her schoolbag. She needed another look.

The yard was murky as Lorna pulled the door shut behind her. The blackout curtains ensured no light escaped into the yard, and the early sun had not yet broken through the clouds that had rolled in overnight. As she put her gloves on, Lorna heard the cows stamping and Nellie cursing in the milking parlor.

The truck's tailgate slammed, and around the back of the truck came the German boy, an excited flurry of sheepdogs around his knees. He bent over and rubbed the dogs' necks.

Traitors! They didn't greet her like that anymore.

Even in this light, it was clear he was young for a soldier, barely older than some of the lads at school, so maybe eighteen? Nineteen at most. The knitted hat he wore over his shaved head was pulled lower on the left side, and his uniform was hidden now under some brown coveralls. Familiar brown coveralls, with an elbow patch and a torn pocket.

Lorna recognized them suddenly as Sandy's. Had the prisoner stolen them? No, that was silly, he wouldn't be wearing them around the farm if he had. Which meant that her dad, or perhaps Mrs. Mack, must have given them to him. What right did they have to give away her brother's belongings when he was gone? And to a German, no less.

As he walked toward the barn, he rubbed his hands together, his fingers fine-boned, almost delicate. Not the hands of a farmer, and certainly not hands that were used to the frigid air of Scotland in February. Lorna noticed he had no gloves, so at least Dad or Mrs. Mack hadn't given him a pair from the boys' bedrooms. The enemy didn't deserve to be warm, no matter what Mrs. Mack said, and no matter what injuries he'd suffered.

He stuffed his hands deep into his pockets and hunched his shoulders up to his ears. He looked . . . was forlorn the right word?

In spite of herself, Lorna suddenly felt almost sorry for him.

As the truck reversed, she stepped out of the shadows, her school shoes clicking on the cobblestones. The German saw her, and for a second or two, neither of them moved.

A frown creased the skin on the right side of his forehead, and as before, Lorna found herself mesmerized by the dreadful damage to his face.

Then embarrassment overcame fascination, and Lorna looked down at her shoes, still muddy from the day before. When she looked up, the frown had smoothed out, but the tug at the right side of his mouth was there again. That same sneer. Except, today, it did look more like he was trying to smile. Tentative, perhaps, but still, it lightened his face, filling out the gaunt flesh of his right cheek, though the left remained tight and static. He gave her a nod, and instinctively, Lorna nodded back, feeling suddenly shy.

Why should she feel shy, though? It was her farm, after all, and he was the stranger. She needed to be assertive.

"Good morning," she said, raising her voice as her father had done. "I. Am. LORNA. ANDERSON."

She drew out the sounds of her name, making every letter clear. She pointed her finger to her chest.

"Hello," the boy said, touching his own coveralled chest

with one long finger. "I. Am. PAUL. VOGEL."

He pronounced his words as clearly as she had, almost mimicking her. His English words were clipped and short.

"Hello," Lorna replied.

He bowed his little bow again.

"Em . . ." Realizing she wasn't sure what to say next, she hoped the poor light might cover the flush that was creeping up her neck.

The German stayed silent. Clearly he was waiting for her to speak. There was no sign of the smile now. But none of the frown either.

"Em . . . ," she repeated, glancing up at the lightening sky.

When she looked back at him again, his gaze was intent upon her and the smile was back, drawing Lorna's attention away from the burns. Its curve led her from his mouth up to his eyes, which sparkled.

Lorna suddenly felt furiously guilty about noticing that. Surely noticing an enemy's sparkle was tantamount to treason. She was betraying John Jo and Sandy and Gregor and all the others by even noticing such a sparkle, wasn't she?

And anyway, what right did this prisoner have to be smiling and sparkling at her?

At that moment, "Yoo-hoo!" rang across the yard. Mrs. Mack appeared through the gates to the lane, carrying as always her big carpetbag and waving her umbrella at them before heading toward the house.

Lorna straightened her shoulders and lifted her chin.

"I have to go to school now," she said slowly, pointing

imperiously in the direction of the village and then at her school tie. "To school."

The prisoner nodded.

"*Ja*," he said, "*zur Schule.*"

She nodded. "Yes, to shool, I mean, school."

He smiled again, or at least, that's what it looked like. "I hope that you have a very good day, Fräulein Anderson, and that your teachers are not too . . . strict?"

He spoke slowly and deliberately, seeming to taste each word, and his voice lifted at the end as if to question whether he had used the right word.

Lorna stared at him.

"You speak English!"

"Yes, a little."

"But why didn't you say so?"

"Because you did not ask. And I do not speak it well. But I will become better perhaps. Yes?"

"Yes, of course . . . em . . . I mean, no." Lorna swallowed and tried again. "I mean your English is very good, and I'm sure it will get better, while you're here, talking, with my dad. Though he speaks Scottish English, really, not English English."

Lorna knew she was babbling, so she stopped talking before she said anything else embarrassing. But then there was silence, and Lorna hated silences.

"So did you learn English at school?"

"No. My uncle is a farm . . . a farmer . . . in Germany. The wife of my uncle is—or was—an English lady, and I take my holidays on the farm with him when I was a schoolboy. So I give help to my uncle with the sheep and my aunt gives me, gave me, lessons to speak English."

Although he looked frustrated at having to correct his grammar, Lorna had no problem understanding him. Then something else struck her.

"So yesterday, when the sergeant who brought you here said you . . . called you . . ." She couldn't bring herself to repeat it. "That is, you understood him?"

The German shrugged.

"I have heard more . . . worse, I think," he said.

From somewhere came a sharp whistle. The dogs' ears pricked and they pelted toward the sound, vanishing around the corner of the barn.

"I think that your father calls to me also," said Paul. "*Auf Wiedersehen*, Fräulein Anderson. Good-bye."

He raised his hand in a wave, and without thinking, Lorna repeated the gesture.

Stop! He shouldn't be this friendly. She couldn't be this friendly. He was a German, after all.

"Wait!" she said. "I think you should know that people aren't happy that Germans are working on our farms."

Paul said nothing.

"I mean"—Lorna felt shaky under his intent gaze, but refused to be put off—"how could anyone here be happy about having a camp full of Nazis on our doorstep?"

Paul stiffened.

"Fräulein Anderson"—his voice was sharply polite—"I

am German, yes, but I am not a Nazi. There is a difference, and one day I hope you understand that."

His eyes were flint hard. With a sharp click, Paul brought the heels of his boots together. Then he spun on his toes and walked smartly away, leaving Lorna reeling.

As Lorna watched him go, Mrs. Mack came back out of the kitchen door, tying her apron strings around her waist. "So he'll not murder us in our beds in the name of the Fatherland, then?"

Lorna faced her, still rattled. "Did you know he speaks English?" she asked.

"Aye, I did notice that."

"But why didn't you tell me?"

"Because you never asked." Mrs. Mack was smiling at Lorna's confusion. "He seems a nice enough lad, though."

"But he speaks English," Lorna said, suddenly serious. "He might be a spy or something."

"Oh, I don't think we need fret now, do you?" Mrs. Mack replied, crossing her arms under her bosom. "And what do you think our John is out there doing, knitting sweaters? All these boys are just doing what their countries ask of them. But this lad's war is over now, and please God it will be over for us all very soon. What harm can he do stuck on this farm with us anyway? I trust him not to kill me in my bed, and I think you should too."

Mrs. Mack suddenly clapped her hands.

"But we've no time for chatter. You've a lesson to get to, and I've a midden of a kitchen to clean. So get off with you!"

Perhaps Mrs. Mack was right and Lorna was overreacting. Maybe.

And actually, the prisoner had seemed quite nice, and not particularly threatening. Well, at least until she'd called him a Nazi. Yes, he was quite nice really. For a German.

Four

For the next few days, Lorna barely saw the prisoner. The truck dropped him off in the morning, but he had vanished from the yard by the time she left for school. When she got back home, he was away with her father in one of the far fields until he was picked up again in the evening.

And that was fine. Lorna didn't want to see him anyway.

But even though she still felt queasy at the thought of having an enemy prisoner on the farm, she also found herself watching out for him, taking the longer route home, telling herself she was just enjoying the sunny and crisp winter weather. And she couldn't help feeling a little disappointed when she didn't see him.

But really, not seeing him was fine.

It was as if everyone else had forgotten he worked there.

Mrs. Mack was no longer around in the afternoons because of her grandchildren, and Nellie had little to talk about except the "cute" new American airman she was "dating"—two of the new American words that Nellie used constantly these days.

And conversations with her father were rare events. He would knock twice on her bedroom door in the morning to make sure she woke up, but was gone before Lorna got downstairs. In the evenings, he came into the house in time to eat his meal in silence as he read that morning's *Scotsman*. Then, with a cup of tea or sometimes a small glass of whisky, he sat in his chair by the fire and listened to the evening news bulletin on the BBC.

However, after almost a week of not talking about the German, Lorna realized that she did want to talk about him after all. She wanted to find out why her dad didn't seem in the slightest bit worried that he was there, and to ask if her dad knew how he had got the scars across his face. But how could she bring up the subject?

One evening after she'd cleared away the dishes, Lorna sat down with her dad to listen to the wireless. She tried to look casual by counting the rows in the woolen scarf she was knitting for the Red Cross collection as she waited for the news bulletin to be over.

For weeks now, the radio news had been full of the Allies' progress through Europe, chasing back the Germans from France, Belgium, and Holland. That evening's bulletin reported on more successful bombing raids by the British and

American air forces on German cities like Chemnitz, Dresden, and Magdeburg, as well as the destruction of a major bridge over the River Rhine at a town that sounded to Lorna like it was called Weasel.

As the news announcer moved on to more political news from London, Lorna decided she could ask her father now. But, as he so often did, her father had already dozed off in his chair and she didn't have the heart to wake him. Lorna wrapped the wool around her needles and tucked them away in her knitting bag. Quietly she took the glass from her father's hand and put it on the table beside him before she tiptoed upstairs.

As she brushed her hair in her bedroom, Lorna tried to put the German out of her mind, but the trouble was, he wouldn't go.

He'd even appeared in her dreams. The first time, his damaged face had reared up at her and she had run from it, screaming, waking herself as she did. Another night, she hadn't seen his face at all, but she still knew he was there, watching her. In one dream, she'd clearly seen his face as it would have been, or as it *might* have been, pale-skinned and clean—and handsome—and then he had been wearing a British sergeant's uniform like John Jo's.

And last night, he hadn't been wearing anything. . . .

Lorna shook her head, pretending to herself that she wanted to rid her mind of that image, and settled her head onto the pillow. Sleep took a while to come.

And it wasn't as if she were the only person obsessing

about the German. Iris seemed even more fascinated by him than Lorna.

Lately, if they walked down to the shops or to the beach after school, Lorna knew it would only be a minute or two before Iris brought him up.

The next day was no exception.

"So what's your German been doing?" Iris asked, as Lorna knew she would.

Lorna pulled her coat more tightly round her and tucked her chin into the loops of her scarf. They were walking along the edge of the beach, shadowing the winding Peffer Burn, which snaked its way through the mudflats and sandbanks near the village.

"I haven't seen him," she said, "and he's not *my* German."

This sent Iris into a lecture about why Lorna *should* be interested, and what if the prisoner sabotaged the farm, which was what William said was bound to happen. And William also said that . . .

Lorna wasn't really listening. Mrs. Mack had often said that Iris could talk the paint off a gatepost, so Lorna knew that as long as she nodded every so often, soon enough the "Threat from the German" lecture would wind down and the "Wonder of William Urquhart" lecture would begin.

Iris suddenly crouched down to retie her shoelace, without once pausing her flow of chatter. Lorna stopped too, and gazed out over Aberlady Bay.

It was a relatively calm day for February, but still freezing cold. The low sun was reflecting off the receding tide, making Lorna shield her eyes with her hand. The dunes of Gullane Point were bathed with golden light, and the exposed sands of Aberlady Bay were striped with ripples and dotted with wading birds, oystercatchers, and curlew, which darted around the huge concrete antitank blocks lining the shore. As an extra barrier to an invasion, an array of tree trunks had been sunk upright into the sand like the rib cage of some rotting dinosaur, but beyond them, Lorna could see fat-bellied seals lounging in what little sunshine was left, oblivious to the chill wind blowing across the water and the looming threat of the war.

"Come on, slow coach," Lorna moaned, "it's too bloody cold to hang around."

"Just give me a minute!"

While she waited, Lorna tugged off her gloves and picked up a pebble from the path, tossing it into the shallow burn with a satisfying splash and a light *plink*.

"Come *on*, Iris," she said, "Dad'll be wanting his tea."

Iris stood up, stamped her feet, and stuffed her hands deep in her pockets.

"Well?" she asked Lorna.

"Well, what?" Lorna replied.

"Oh, Lorna, sometimes I think you just never listen!" Iris scolded. "Which dress are you going to wear for the tea dance in Tranent on Saturday afternoon?"

"Tea dance?" Lorna was puzzled. "Saturday?"

"Yes!" Iris sounded like she was addressing a small child. "Dancing, on Saturday, with William and Craig?"

"William and *Craig*?"

"You must remember! When William asked me out that first time, he said we should all go to the next tea dance in Tranent, as a foursome. Me and William, you and Craig. Remember?"

Lorna realized she did remember, though clearly not in quite the same way as Iris did. When William had cornered Lorna after church that particular Sunday, he had indeed talked about going to the tea dance in Tranent. Lorna had been horrified by the invitation, but William had not appeared to notice. He just waited for her response. Then Iris had bounced up to them—Iris only ever bounced or flounced—demanding to know what they were talking about so secretly. Only at that point did William mention the idea of the two girls making up a foursome with him and his friend Craig.

At the time, Lorna had been under the unspeakable impression that William was asking *her* out, but Iris had grabbed his arm and excitedly assumed the invitation was for her. And maybe it had been. Either way, Lorna was so relieved, she had put the whole idea from her mind. But now . . . Craig Buchanan? Not a chance! Craig was so much worse than William. He was very good-looking, sure, but oh God, did he know it. And the way he treated girls was despicable. Lorna was sure that he and William had a bet that Craig could charm, kiss, and dump every girl in their class before graduation, and she'd long ago decided he damn well wasn't going to do it to her. Uggghh! Craig! So perhaps

William might not have been such a bad option after all.

"Well?" Iris repeated.

"I'm not sure I can go, actually." Lorna scrambled for an excuse. "It's getting close to the start of lambing, you know, so I doubt Dad would let me go."

"Well, don't tell him then," said Iris. "Just tell him you're going to be doing homework with me. He can't say no to that."

"I thought you were suddenly all moral these days, the influence of the church's favorite son on your soul, and all that," Lorna replied. "And now you are telling me to lie to my father?"

"Not lie exactly. Just not tell him the whole truth," said Iris. "That's not the same thing at all."

"Yes, it is, and you know it!" Lorna tried to sound light-hearted, but panic was setting in. "Honestly, Dad can't spare me."

"But you said yesterday that lambing won't start for another week or so. And anyway, he's got Nellie to help him, and the German."

"No, Iris, I really can't."

"It's Craig, isn't it?" Iris said. "You don't want to go out with Craig. But why? He's *gorgeous*."

Lorna pulled a face. "If you like that kind of thing, I suppose."

"Don't be like that, Lorna. Craig is actually very nice. And you're lucky he'll even bother, because I know he's been flirting with Esther Bell for ages."

"Craig and Esther? That's not an image I'll get out of my head anytime soon."

"But Craig is such a good friend to William that he says he will go with you even so," Iris pressed on, ignoring Lorna's snide comments.

"Well, that's flattering!"

"But you *have to*, Lorna!"

"Why do I *have to*, Iris?" snapped Lorna.

Iris suddenly smiled her most angelic smile and pulled Lorna into a tight hug.

"Because if you don't go too, I can't go," she said. "Mum wants you to act as chaperone to me and William."

"Iris!" Lorna was trapped, but only for a second. "Why don't you ask Esther Bell to go with you then, if she fancies Craig so much?"

"I don't want to go to the dance with *Esther Bell*!"

"You won't be going with *Esther Bell*." Lorna imitated Iris's dramatic tone. "You'll be going with *William Urquhart*. And *Craig Buchanan* will be going with *Esther Bell*. And everyone will be happy—especially Esther. When was the last time anyone asked her out?"

"That might work, I suppose," conceded Iris, "but I still wish you'd come with us."

"I told you. Lambing. My dad. And also the fact that I wouldn't touch the Adonis that is Craig Buchanan with a fifty-foot barge pole, even if I was paid to stab him to death with it!"

Lorna laughed, and soon Iris joined in, albeit sulkily.

Even though it wasn't yet five o'clock, the sun was already low and the temperature was dropping fast.

"We'd better get back while there's still some light," Lorna said, pulling her gloves from her pocket. "But let me skim one more stone first."

Lorna scanned the path around her feet, though it was getting harder to see now the sun had all but disappeared. There was a perfectly flat oval pebble a few inches from her shoe, and she picked it up with chilled fingertips, turning it to catch what light was left. It was the most beautiful blue-gray granite, with dark flecks that sparked even in the low light. It seemed a familiar color somehow. It reminded her of something, but of what, she wasn't sure.

Instead of tossing it into the burn, Lorna left the pebble in her palm as she wiggled her hands into her gloves.

"Never mind, I'm done," she said to Iris. "We need to get a move on anyway."

"You're not throwing that one?" Iris asked.

Already walking away, Lorna could feel the granite grow warmer against her palm, as it nestled between wool and skin.

"No, I think I'll keep this one."

Five

Dear John Jo,

Sorry it's taken me a few days to write to you again, but I hope you are doing well and that it's not as cold wherever you are as it is here.

Everything is fine. Mrs. Mack told me to send you her love and said that as soon as she's finished knitting this last sock, she'll get all of them wrapped up and sent to you in the hope that the parcel will reach you sometime before summer comes! If you are very lucky, you might get one of the fruitcakes she made the other day (not that there's much actual fruit in it, or sugar, but she still gets it to taste good all the same!).

Iris and I are knitting scarves for Red Cross—shall I send

you one of our marvelous creations? I'm not as good a knitter as Iris, you won't be surprised to hear, but you'll have to put up with one of mine since Iris has another neck to wrap hers around now. Yes, your greatest admirer is now madly in love with William Urquhart, of all people. (I know, disgusting!) She might have adored you her whole life, but now you're out and William is in. Bad luck!

Are there any pretty girls where you are? (Where is that? I wish you could tell me!) If anyone can find one, I'm sure you can!

Dad is fine, but it's almost lambing and there's always too much to do. The Ministry of Agriculture sent us a new farmhand to take over from Old Lachie. Dad says the new man isn't afraid of hard work and seems to know what he is doing, but ~~the only thing is~~

~~I know you won't like this, but~~

~~I can't tell you how angry I was when~~

Lorna put her pen down on the blotting paper. How could she tell her brother that a German was working at Craigielaw?

But did she have to? Surely Dad would have already told both John Jo and Sandy the news in one of the letters he wrote to each of them every Sunday. They were never long letters, and Lorna doubted that he ever told them how much he missed them and wished he had them home again like she did, but two letters were sitting on the table every Monday morning without fail, ready for Derek Milne, the mailman, to pick up.

She lifted her pen, but put it down again immediately.

She really wanted to be the one to tell her brothers about the prisoner, so they would know how angry she had been—how angry she still was—at the idea, so that they knew she was standing up for them, and so they would write back to her that they were angry about it as well. Then perhaps they would write to Dad and tell him he had to get rid of the German immediately.

But then again, perhaps they would feel reassured to know that their dad had a replacement for Lachie on the farm. And perhaps that also felt reassuring to Lorna. Perhaps the extra help would be . . . well, helpful.

So maybe she should say nothing. Yes, that was probably the best idea.

And anyway, how could she find the words to describe the way the burn had tightened the skin on that side of the prisoner's face, the way that she'd noticed that no beard grew through the scar tissue, but that the blond stubble that grew on the undamaged cheek was so fine as to be almost invisible. Or about the way his smile tugged at the pink scar and how it made his gray eyes sparkle . . .

Lorna jumped as Nellie banged open the door from the yard, shattering the evening's peace. She grabbed the unfinished letter and stuffed it into her pocket, as if she'd been caught writing something naughty.

But Nellie didn't even come in. She just called through the open door.

"Can't come in, love, muddy shoes, but is there any chance of another cup of tea? Your dad says the first ewe's about to drop, and it looks like she's going to need a bit of help. He says a cuppa would be spot on for us lot who could be up the rest of the night."

"Of course, I'll bring it over in a minute."

"Cheers, m'dears!" Nellie called back as she pulled the door closed.

Once the tea was made, Lorna placed the steaming mugs onto a tray and put on her coat and rubber boots. Outside, she balanced the tray on her hip, as she pulled the door closed carefully behind her to make sure no light escaped. The blackout restrictions they had lived with since the beginning of the war had been lifted across the country a few months earlier, except for those who lived in towns and villages on the coast like Aberlady, in case of an attack from air or sea.

Caddy and Canny were slumped outside the door. They both sat up as she made her way across the moonlit yard, tails wagging, but they made none of the fuss they had made over the German.

They were both traitors.

Inside the lambing shed, Lorna found her father kneeling by a ewe lying on the straw, rubbing her belly. This wasn't good. Sheep usually gave birth standing up, so this ewe must be exhausted by a difficult labor. Sure enough, every so often the animal would bleat pathetically.

Nellie was also kneeling, but at the tail end of the ewe. She looked disheveled but excited.

"Everything all right?" Lorna asked quietly as she laid the tea tray on the top of a wooden barrel just inside the door and rested a hand on Nellie's shoulder.

"Aye, it's her first time, but she's doing fine," Lorna's dad said, without looking up.

"Yes, I'm all right, really," said Nellie with a nervous smile.

"I was talking about the ewe," said Lorna's father with a sigh.

"Oh, right," said Nellie. "Sorry."

Her father palpated the ewe's distended belly again with gentle hands.

"Almost there," he said to Nellie. "Are you ready?"

At that moment, the ewe gave one agonizing bleat and a huge purple bag of semitransparent slop burst from her rear end. With a sickening squelch, the membrane burst. As the waters gushed out, Lorna could see the nose and front feet of the lamb for the first time. She waited for movement, but the lamb lay still on the damp straw.

"C'mon, girl!" Lorna's father urged Nellie. "Get a move on and get the lamb out of there. Use that towel to give it a rub. You need to get it breathing and then give it to its mother quick as you can."

But Nellie was still staring at the messy bundle that had almost landed in her lap, the color draining from her face.

"What are you doing," Lorna's father asked, "sitting there as if tomorrow would do? C'mon, girl, look lively!"

But still Nellie didn't move; her eyes were glued to the thing in front of her. Then she simply tipped over to one side in a dead faint.

"Oh, for crying out loud!" muttered Lorna's dad.

Lorna jumped to help. She pulled the towel from Nellie's inert fingers, leaving her where she was, and laid it across her own lap. Using the towel, she eased the sticky membrane off the lamb's nose and mouth. Then she rubbed its chest vigorously as if she were kneading life into a rag doll. The ewe lifted her head to see what was going on behind her and gave out another pitiful bleat. Lorna had done this many times before, but it didn't get any easier, and frustration prickled in her throat.

"Come on, come on," she implored the lamb. "You've got to breathe for me, wee man."

Suddenly one of the legs jerked, then another, and a tiny shudder rippled through the lamb's body. Lorna stopped rubbing and put her hand flat onto its chest. Yes! She could feel a fluttering; the lamb's heart was beating. Then a cough, a breath, and a wriggle, and suddenly Lorna was struggling to keep ahold of the lamb as it strained to get to its feet. Relief flooded through her and a tear escaped her lashes and dropped with a splash onto the lamb's sticky coat.

"Well done, lassie." Dad's voice was soft now. "Now, give him to his mother so he can get cleaned off and have a suckle. And then you can see to your other patient." He nodded toward Nellie, who was lying with her face on the straw, as if she were asleep. "Even if she can fix a tractor and milk a cow, it'll be a pain in the arse if she can't stay upright for a birthing."

Lorna waited for him to chuckle, but he never did. Looking up at her father's face, she saw only exhaustion. As he moved down to the next pen to check on the ewe in there, he muttered, "Something else I'll have to do myself."

"But I can help you, and we've got the German during the day," Lorna said, realizing again that his presence at Craigielaw was perhaps not so awful after all.

Once the lamb was suckling hard, safe in the care of its mother, Lorna went over to the windowsill, where there was a pile of freshly washed rags. She dipped one of them in a bucket of chilled water and returned to Nellie's side.

Squeezing the cold rag slightly, she wiped it across Nellie's face.

"Wake up, Nellie," she said. "It's all over and there's a cup of tea for you. Come on and look at the wee lamb."

Six

Lambing season was officially upon them. The next day, when Lorna got home from school, she headed over to the lambing shed in search of her father, but instead found the German prisoner. He was sitting on the straw with his back against the wall, watching as a ewe nudged her newborn lamb to its feet. From where Lorna stood by the door, she would never have known there was any damage to his face at all, and in that light and at that angle, she was reminded of her dream where she'd seen his face as it might have been. Handsome.

Remembering how upset he'd been the last time they'd talked, and suddenly embarrassed that he might catch her staring, Lorna backed out of the shed before he could even realize she was there.

Over the next few days, more than a dozen lambs were born with no danger to either lamb or ewe. But there were a couple that needed help with the birth, and both those ewes had pushed their lambs away, which meant they'd need to be fed by hand.

Mrs. Mack told Lorna that Paul had barely left the lambing shed each day. She was determined not to appear over-interested in him, but Lorna went to the lambing shed to offer help anyway. But Paul refused, saying he was fine. His manner was curt and efficient. Though Lorna knew she had said the wrong thing to him, she didn't feel she needed to give an actual apology. It wasn't like his feelings should matter to her or anything.

It was a relief just to know that the flock was well cared for during the daytime. The nights, however, were taking their toll on Lorna's father. Lorna hadn't seen him look so tired since he had been juggling days working on the farm with regular night patrols with the East Lothian Home Guard. Thankfully, those duties had ended before Christmas when the Home Guard had been stood down, but still, Lorna hated seeing her dad looking so weary.

One evening after tea, he announced that he'd written to the camp commander at Gosford, and Paul had been given permission to stay overnight at the farm, at least during the lambing season. Hearing this news, Nellie widened her eyes at Lorna in the mirror as she applied another layer of bright red lipstick in preparation for her evening off down in the village.

"So *now* shall we start locking our bedroom doors then, duckie?" she asked. "But then again, perhaps not!"

She gave Lorna a sly wink and danced out of the door before Lorna could respond.

Not that she knew *how* to respond. Would it make any difference at all to her if Paul was on the farm overnight? No, of course not, no difference at all. None.

The following morning, Lorna helped her father bring the old canvas camp bed down from the attic. They put it, with a pile of sheets and blankets, into the hayloft above the barn, where Paul would be sleeping until lambing was over.

It then fell to Lorna to take Paul's evening meals to him. That first night she found him sweeping the floor of one of the pens in the lambing shed with the big hard-bristled yard broom. He greeted Lorna politely, and she felt another pang of . . . not guilt exactly, but . . . well, she knew she ought to clear the air.

Lorna set the dishes down on the barrel by the door and watched Paul work. After a few seconds, he looked up.

"About what I said"—Lorna's throat caught on the words and she had to cough to clear it—"when you first arrived . . ."

Paul didn't reply, and she could read nothing in his face.

"I didn't mean to . . . at least, I didn't think . . ." Lorna couldn't find the right path at all. "I didn't mean to upset you."

"But you don't want me here, me or the other Germans."

"Well, no, I mean, yes, oh . . ."

Paul stood up straight and sighed.

"Fräulein Anderson, do you think that we like being here?"

It hadn't occurred to Lorna that these men might be as angry about being in Scotland as the people they met there. He must have seen the confusion on her face, and he softened. "But thank you for"—Paul seemed to be searching for the right English—"your words."

He went back to his sweeping.

Not sure what else to say or do, Lorna returned to the house. The conversation hadn't solved anything, but she was glad she'd said something.

Later, when she went back out to pick up his dishes, she found Paul sitting on the straw in one of the pens with his back against the wall, feeding a lamb with a bottle. Another lamb was curled up asleep beside him.

As Lorna pulled the door closed quickly behind her so no light escaped, he looked up at her, and this time he smiled.

"Forgive me, I cannot stand up," he said, lifting the lamb slightly as if to show he had his hands full. "But thank you for dinner. It was very delicious."

"Tea," Lorna corrected. "We have dinner at midday, in Scotland anyway, so we call this your tea."

"I will try to remember that, thank you."

As she cleared the plate, bowl, and empty milk bottle into her basket, Lorna became aware that Paul was still watching her.

"Sometimes," he said, "you make me think of Lilli."

Against her better judgment, Lorna asked, "Lilli?"

"My sister," he replied. "She will become sixteen in May, and she is not shy to say what she thinks. Like you, Fräulein."

Lorna wasn't sure how to react. It unnerved her to be compared to someone he loved. But she was also intrigued that he too had left a little sister at home, as her brothers had.

So would it hurt just to ask one question?

"Is Lilli your only sister?" she asked.

Now his expression did change, she could see that even in spite of the burns. But did he look pleased that she had responded? Or relieved? She wasn't sure.

"Yes, we are two," he replied, "with our father and mother. Or we were. Before. Now it is only Lilli and Mother and me."

"So your father . . . ?"

Paul looked down at his hands and picked at a dirty hangnail on his thumb, and Lorna wished she'd kept her mouth shut. He took a deep breath.

"My father was *ein Uhrmacher*, a clockmaker, before the war. In Dresden." He suddenly looked up at Lorna. "You know of Dresden, Fräulein Anderson?"

Lorna shook her head no, but then, perhaps she had heard something about Dresden quite recently. But where? At school? No, she didn't think so. Perhaps a news report on the BBC?

"Dresden is very beautiful, very old," Paul continued. "The River Elbe goes through the city, and there are many churches and art galleries. And parks, many parks. But you know, life in Germany has been difficult for some time, even before the war began. We had little to eat, and what food my mother could find was expensive to buy. And there was much to fear. But before that, I can remember a time when life was better. When my life was good."

He was smiling now. Lorna could see it in his eyes, as well as on his mouth. How could she ever have thought it was a sneer?

"When we were little children, our parents took us on a Sunday afternoon to the Zwinger museum sometimes. And after, if we were good, they took Lilli and me to a coffeehouse for chocolate cake. Lilli loves chocolate cake, but I know she has not had chocolate cake for a long time."

Lorna rested her hip against the pen gate. His tone was wistful. It must have been a long time since he'd last talked to anyone about his home and his family, she realized.

"In the summer, we all went to *ein Biergarten*, a beer garden, to hear the music, and our parents drank big glasses of beer, with lots of . . . *Schaum*."

Paul looked at Lorna questioningly and waved his fingers over the top of an imaginary beer glass held in his other hand.

"I am sorry, I do not know the word in English. The white on the top of the beer?" He mimed again. *"Schaum?"*

"Oh, um." Lorna was caught off guard. "Do you mean froth? Or foam?"

"Froth?" Paul repeated. "Beer with much *froth*, yes."

Lorna smiled back at him before she could stop herself.

"Of course, we were too young for beer with *froth*," he

continued, "so we ate *Bratwurst* instead."

"*Bratvoo . . . ?*" Lorna's attempt to repeat the word made Paul laugh. It was the first time she had heard it, a deep rumble in his throat, and it was unnervingly infectious.

"*Bratwurst*," Paul repeated. "German sausage. They are very delicious. I think you would like them as we did, Fräulein Anderson. But that was before the war, before my father went away."

He was quiet now, the laughter gone.

"Your father went away?" Lorna prompted.

"Yes. In 1939, he was called to the *Wehrmacht*, to the army. He left us on Christmas Eve. In April, he was already dead."

"Oh!" Lorna gasped. What could she say to that?

For a while, the silence was broken only by the soft suckling of the lamb in Paul's arms.

"After, life was hard for my mother, so when I became sixteen, I left school to work. A friend of my father said I would learn to be a clockmaker too."

"You were an apprentice?" offered Lorna.

"Apprentice?" Paul tried the word. "Is that a young man who learns when he works?"

Lorna nodded, and she could almost see Paul filing that new word into his mental dictionary as he had done earlier with *froth*.

"It was difficult work, very . . . small." Paul squeezed his fingers together as if to demonstrate. "But I liked it. For two years I learned about clocks and about watches, how to carve faces, grind cogs, cut jewels, and how to mend other makers' pieces. Sometimes I felt my father sitting at the table beside me, holding my hand as I worked.

"But then it was January of 1944, my eighteenth birthday, and I was taken away from my work and away from Dresden, and I too entered the army of the Third Reich."

As Paul lapsed into a thoughtful silence, stroking the lamb's neck with his thumb, Lorna realized that she wanted to hear more. She opened her mouth, only to close it again. And it felt strange, standing over him, so she sat down on a small wooden stool just inside the pen.

Paul looked up as she sat, and it seemed to bring him back from another place and time.

"You must miss your father," Lorna said simply. "I can't imagine what I would do if my dad . . ."

Paul was very still and Lorna regretted saying anything. But now that she had, she needed to keep going.

"And you must worry about your mother and sister too. I know I do. I mean I worry. About my brothers."

"Yes," he said quietly, "I miss my father and yes, I worry."

There was silence again, and Lorna determined that she would not break it this time with another silly . . .

"And *your* mother?" He was studying her now. "Do you miss her?"

Lorna's throat contracted. She hadn't expected this. "My mother died a long time ago."

"I know," he replied. What had Mrs. Mack told him? "But still you can miss her?"

Lorna shrugged. She didn't have any memories of her

own, only those borrowed from the stories her brothers told about their mother. How much could she think about missing her mother when her brothers were so far away and in such danger?

"I miss my brothers more," she replied.

Spoken on a breath held tight, her words were barely audible, even to herself.

Paul waited, but when she said no more, he prompted her again.

"And will you tell me of them? Have they been at the war for a long time?"

Could she tell him? *Should* she tell him? Wouldn't this be "careless talk"? But suddenly her desire, her need, to talk about them became overwhelming and she wanted desperately to talk about John Jo and Sandy, and how much she missed them. And who else was there who would listen?

"John Jo's the oldest of us, and has been away the longest," Lorna said, and the release of her breath came as a relief. "He could hardly wait to be part of it. He volunteered for service on the morning he turned eighteen, in 'forty-one. Of course, he'd tried to sign up the summer before, lying about his age, but by chance, the sergeant at the recruitment office had been at school with Dad. Can you believe it? So he knew John Jo wasn't old enough to join up. John Jo was so furious, we didn't dare go near him for days after."

Lorna found herself smiling at the memory, and Paul smiled too.

"John Jo was a ruffian." She noticed Paul frowning at

the word. "I mean, he was wild, always wrestling someone or something—a school friend, a dog, or Sandy. But he was fun—he *is* fun. When I was much littler, he would build forts in the woods for us to play in, or we'd run down to paddle in the sea."

She pointed in that direction, and Paul nodded.

"John Jo loves this farm so much. He's only ever wanted to be a farmer, like Dad, though he seems to be doing all right as a soldier. He writes sometimes, but he doesn't say very much, except to complain about the food and the weather."

"I think every soldier writes to home about those things. The food and the weather."

Lorna noticed then that when Paul smiled, and the raw skin was pulled even tighter across the cheekbone, it lost its pink color, becoming almost as white as the skin on his other cheek. It made the darker pink of his full, undamaged lips even more noticeable.

Lorna suddenly realized she was staring, at his burns and at his lips, instead of listening to what Paul had been saying.

"Sorry?" she stammered.

"I ask you about your other brother? Is it Sandy?"

"That's right. Alexander really. Mrs. Mack says he would have been called Alex, but he was Sandy soon as they saw that his hair was red like our mum's. He got Mum's blue eyes and freckles too."

"Freckles?" Paul asked.

"Oh, em, the brown dots, across your nose and face." Lorna prodded her face in explanation. "You know, *freckles*."

Paul nodded in understanding.

"Freckles," he repeated.

"Yes, Mum had freckles and blue eyes. And red hair. I don't really remember her because I was only three when she died, from the influenza. We have photographs of her, but you can't see that her hair was red."

Strangely, Lorna found it easy to talk about her mother, like this, in the abstraction of someone else's memory.

"But no red hair or *freckles* for you?" Paul asked.

"No, not for me, or for John Jo either. We are both true Andersons, like my dad—dark eyes, dark hair and dark souls, that's what my grandpa used to say."

"Dark souls?" Paul said, shaking his head doubtfully. "I do not think—"

"It's true," Lorna said, "Sandy's quite the opposite of John Jo and me. He's incredibly clever, and also kind and sweet. We're just selfish and bad-tempered. You just wait till you meet my brothers, then you'll see I'm right."

Something in Paul's expression made Lorna think about the words she'd just uttered. *Wait until you meet them . . .* Why would Paul ever meet them? John Jo and Sandy might not be back until the war was over, by which time the prisoners would be gone from Gosford. And then it struck her, how would either of her brothers feel if they found her cozily chatting with an enemy soldier like this? She knew *exactly* how they'd feel, and she knew what they'd do about it too.

Lorna suddenly felt panicked, as if there were army boots outside the door, and jumped to her feet. What had she been thinking, trusting this stranger, this enemy, with her precious memories?

"Sorry, I need to get back to the house," she said, grabbing Paul's dishes and dashing for the door.

Just as she pulled the door closed behind her, she heard Paul sigh and she hesitated. It was such a sad sound, from a boy far from home. They'd only been talking, but she'd been rude to him yet again. He didn't deserve that, but how could she make it right now?

"Good night," she said, trying to make her voice sound more friendly.

Just before she clicked the door into place, he replied.

"Gute Nacht, Fräulein. Schlafen Sie gut!"

Seven

Lorna stood at the scullery sink on Wednesday morning, washing the breakfast dishes and stacking them to drain in the wooden rack. As she worked, she gazed out the window. One of the cats sat on the wall, haughtily overseeing the activity of some sparrows pecking around nearby. Lorna was not on the lookout for the truck arriving, now that Paul was sleeping in the barn, but she was looking out all the same. Only to check that Paul was all right, of course, and that he didn't need any more blankets.

She was almost finished with her dishes when the side door of the barn opened. Paul came out looking tired and rumpled, yawning and stretching out his arms and his back, as if he had only just woken up. Perhaps he had. He'd been up most of every other night this week with the ewes, so he'd probably had very little sleep.

Lorna watched as he walked to the water pump over the horse trough and stripped his shirt over his head without unbuttoning it. He hung it on a lantern bracket on the wall, then lifted off his undershirt and hung that up too. Bending over, he pumped the handle up and down, muscles straining.

As the water flowed from the wide spout, Paul thrust his head and shoulders under the stream. Lorna knew for certain that the water must be icy, for the temperature outside was barely above freezing. Sure enough, as Paul stood upright again, his skin glistening in the soft morning light, a shiver ran through him.

Physically Paul had changed so much since he'd arrived a month ago, so skinny and gray-faced. Now his face had lost its skeletal look, the sharp edge of his jawline had softened, and his cheeks, even under the tight scarring, had become plump and full. His chest and shoulder muscles had filled out and were now rounded and smooth. His stomach was flat and strong, no longer concave with hunger.

Lorna had only seen a man with muscles as well defined as that once before, on a school trip to the National Gallery in Edinburgh, but it had been on the carved body of a marble statue, a Greek god with curly hair, playing a lute and wearing nothing but a large and serendipitously placed leaf. She and Iris had giggled for hours about his bare bottom and strapping thighs.

They had been much younger then, and Lorna was certainly not giggling now. She was barely even breathing.

Even his skin looked healthy and pink, almost rosy in reaction to the icy water. What might he look like once the summer sun had tanned his skin?

Summer.

Would this Greek god still be here by summer, washing at the pump in the warm sun? Or would the war be over by then and her brothers home?

Paul shook his head back and forth, sending water drops flying. His hair was growing out and was now sticking up in wet spikes.

He looked like Caddy when she'd been swimming in the Peffer Burn.

Almost as if Lorna had called her name, Caddy appeared at a run around the corner of the barn, her claws skidding on the wet cobbles. She bounded up to Paul and jumped to put her front paws onto the side of the water trough, attempting to get closer to him. Paul pulled on the handle again and a stream of water belched from the pump onto the dog's head. Caddy jumped back and then shook herself, just as Paul had done, sending water all over Paul. He laughed, and Caddy yelped in excitement, jumping up at him, and he rubbed vigorously at the wet patches in her fur.

Paul picked up a stick from under the trough. As he threw it, Lorna noticed there was another scar, this one under his left arm and around the side of his rib cage. Like the scars on his face, it was an angry pink against the white of his skin, but it didn't look like a burn. This one was a sharp gash, perhaps two inches wide, a deep groove, as if the flat of a knife had been dragged across a pat of butter.

Lorna was awoken from her daydream of Paul as a Greek god by the reality of his desperate scars. What pain must this boy have endured?

Just then, Nellie clumped down the stairs and into the kitchen. Lorna grabbed an already-clean plate from the draining rack and plunged it into the warm soapy water again.

"What you doing that for?" Nellie asked, sitting down at the kitchen table. "Isn't that Mrs. Mack's job?"

Nellie pulled heavy socks over her petite feet and up to her knees, first one pair and then another on top. She tied them with a cord over the hem of her breeches and folded them down again into a cuff.

"Just helping out," Lorna choked, glad that her back was to Nellie. "Heading off to school right now."

Lorna lifted her coat from the hook just as Mrs. Mack came bustling into the house. Before she closed the door, she glanced back out into the yard again.

"That young lad needs to put some more clothes on," Mrs. Mack said as she removed the first of the many layers of scarves, coats, and cardigans in which she had wrapped herself for the walk from the village. "I just told him he'll catch pneumonia bathing in that icy water. I feel like I'm catching a chill just looking at him!"

She looked up at Lorna. "Won't you be late, dear?"

"Going now," said Lorna, trying not to blush as she grabbed her bag and gave Mrs. Mack a quick hug. Her father banged his boots against the wall outside to loosen the mud and came through the door as Lorna made to leave.

"If it's not one thing, it's another," he said, unbuckling the leather strap of his old watch and laying it across his palm.

He studied the watch for a moment, shook it, and held it to his ear.

"What's wrong with Grandpa's watch?" Lorna asked. Even though her father had worn the watch ever since his father had died, she still thought of it as her grandpa's.

"After forty-odd years or more of keeping this farm on time, the damn thing has finally given up."

Dad carefully hung the gold buckle on a cup hook hammered into the wood of the kitchen dresser, leaving it dangling.

"I'll have to send it up to Christie's in Edinburgh to see if they can get it going again. In the meantime, I'll make do with my farmer's instinct, and my grumbling belly, to know when it's dinnertime."

He winked at Lorna.

"You mean the same farmer's instinct that can hear the sound of the pub opening at two o'clock every Saturday afternoon?" teased Lorna. "You and John Jo can hear the Gowff doors being unlocked all the way up here, can't you, Dad?"

Lorna's father laughed too, but then looked at the circlet of white skin contrasting with the deep tan of his wrist as if his watch was still there.

"And it's the *father's* instinct that knows that someone is going to be late for school again if she doesn't get a move on."

"I'm going, I'm going!"

After kissing her dad on the cheek, Lorna left the house, clicking the door shut behind her.

Across the yard, Paul was fully dressed now, but was still rubbing his hair with the towel as he walked back toward the barn. Suddenly, he changed course and walked over toward the drystane dyke that ran up to the gate, where he picked up two or three small items from the scrubby grass. He squinted at them and then, instead of tossing them down again, he put them into the pocket of his pants and headed into the barn.

Lorna was puzzled. What could he have found over there? Not nuts or berries at this time of year, and too small for sticks. Small stones, perhaps?

She imagined herself asking him about it. She found herself wanting to know more about him. And it was strange, the more they'd talked the evening before—and his English had improved in the month since he'd arrived—the less German he became. Or not less German, exactly, but more like any of the normal boys, the Scottish boys, she knew at school. Lorna didn't know what to make of that. He was not like she had expected the enemy to be at all. In fact, she was beginning to realize that he might not be so very different from her.

Eight

"Lorna, you are so unreliable," preached Mrs. Urquhart, the minister's wife, as she tied the ribbons of her starched white apron and proudly brushed some imagined fluff from the Red Cross insignia on the front.

Lorna could feel the other girls and the older village women watching her as they paused in their work filling the care packages in the church hall. It was Wednesday afternoon, and all the women in the village were at the weekly Red Cross meeting.

"I can't believe you left your scarves at home. And now there's no time to run back and get them," Mrs. Urquhart said. "So how many of our fine boys at the front will be left freezing cold because their care parcels are short of knitwear, I wonder?"

Lorna assumed the question was rhetorical, simply part of the telling off, so she didn't reply.

"Answer my question, please. How many scarves did you leave at home, Lorna?" Apparently not rhetorical. "You certainly were given enough wool last week for three or four."

"Em . . . just the one this week," replied Lorna.

"One?" Mrs. Urquhart sounded scandalized.

"Well, with the lambing, and school . . ."

Lorna wished she could stand up straight under the older woman's scrutiny, but really she wanted the ground to swallow her up. Why did Mrs. Urquhart have to do this in front of everyone?

"Please don't worry, Mrs. Urquhart," Iris interrupted, stepping forward with a pile of scarves. "I knitted six this week, so Lorna can share mine."

Lorna knew Iris was trying to help, in her own way, but did she not understand that by showing off for Mrs. Urquhart, she was just making things worse?

Mrs. Urquhart gave another dramatic sigh and laid a bony hand on Iris's arm.

"At least *you* won't be letting down those poor frozen soldiers, Iris dear."

Mrs. Urquhart seemed cheered enough to stop lecturing Lorna as she began inspecting Iris's scarves appreciatively. They *were* lovely, each one intricately patterned and tassled, as beautiful as every piece of knitting or sewing Iris produced.

"Oh, how clever you are," Mrs. Urquhart gushed, "and how thoughtful and caring. Thank you. You'll make *someone* a lovely wife one of these days."

Mrs. Urquhart gave a tight nasal laugh, and to Lorna's annoyance, Iris joined in.

"Now, everyone"—Mrs. Urquhart clapped her hands as she addressed the whole group—"Mr. John will be here any moment in his van, so can we get these boxes packed up and sealed? Immediately, please, so we still have time to practice our elbow bandages and slings."

"I hate that woman so much," whispered Lorna. "You'd think she was the bloody Queen of Aberlady, not just the minister's wife."

"I think you are being rather unfair," said Iris, without bothering to whisper.

"Shhhhh!" hissed Lorna. "She'll hear you."

Iris laid down the scarves and faced Lorna.

"Mrs. Urquhart has a lot of responsibility in the village as the wife of the minister, what with the church flowers, the Sunday school, and leading the Red Cross and the Girl Guides. She needs our support, Lorna, not your sniping."

Lorna rolled her eyes but said nothing more.

Iris put one scarf into each cardboard box on their table, tucking it carefully on top of the paperback novel, the packets of tea, the soap, and the Capstan cigarettes they had already packed inside.

"Anyway," Iris said after a moment, "you knew we were packing parcels today, so why didn't you bring your scarf? Did you even finish it?"

"Yes, I did finish it actually." Lorna was indignant. "But I was in a rush to get out the door this morning and left it in my knitting bag, that was all."

"Why were you late, anyway? You looked like you'd run all the way to school."

"Oh, you know, just chores and whatnot."

Lorna hoped Iris was busy enough not to notice the flush starting up her neck, because she could not possibly explain that morning's distraction of watching Paul from the kitchen window.

To move Iris's mind away from any further questions, Lorna asked one of her own.

"So do you and Prince Charming have more plans to go dancing with the delightful double act of Esther Bell and Craig Buchanan?" Lorna sniggered. "After all, the last outing was such a success."

Iris had moaned for days about how awful the evening in Tranent had been, with Esther being bitchy about everyone at school, including Lorna, and expecting Iris to join in, and Craig being . . . well, being Craig, so full of himself, he was chatting up other girls, even though he was there with Esther. Lorna was still so relieved she hadn't buckled under Iris's pressure to go with them.

"Stop it, Lorna." But Iris was giggling too. "You know I'd rather run through Aberlady naked on Easter Sunday than repeat that foursome. And it's all I can do to stop William suggesting we do it again this weekend. He didn't even notice there was anything wrong."

Lorna tucked her hands together in front of her chest and

did her best impression of their teacher, Mrs. Murray.

"And what can one learn from this experience, young Iris?" Lorna paused as if considering. "Perhaps that Craig Buchanan is an unbearable cad, Esther Bell is a complete cow, and William Urquhart really isn't worthy of your attention?"

Iris laughed as she slapped at Lorna's arm.

"I told you to stop it! Seriously, you can say all you like about Esther and Craig, but you know you must be nice about my William."

"That's right, I'd forgotten that Saint William is off-limits now."

"Lorna, *stop it*, please, I know you're just jealous!"

Though Iris was still laughing, a tightness in her voice told Lorna that she wasn't joking anymore, so Lorna backed off.

"That's it exactly, dear friend," Lorna said, allowing only a hint of sarcasm to creep in. "I'm jealous. Perhaps I need to find me a handsome, upright, and highly intelligent chap of my very own right now."

Iris jabbed Lorna harder, with her fist this time.

"Enough! Grab the string, would you? We need to get these tied up."

Lorna tossed Iris the ball of string, but before she closed the flaps on the nearest box, she let her fingers play in the soft wool of the scarf Iris had knitted so expertly. It would certainly keep some Allied soldier warm, whether he was at the front or in a prison camp. Perhaps it might bring him some comfort too, knowing it might have been knitted by a pretty girl back at home.

By the time the boxes were packed and sealed, and Lorna and Iris had practiced bandaging each other's elbows several times, it was well after six. Lorna had to hurry home to get the tea served up.

She was late getting Paul his evening meal, but he didn't seem to notice. When she opened the lambing shed door, he was sitting in his usual place against the wall. This time it was not a lamb in his hands, but a newspaper. He'd folded it in half and then in half again so it was more the size of a book, and he appeared to be studying it very closely, running a finger under each line as he read the tiny print. After a second or two, he cupped his hands in front of his mouth and blew warm air onto his fingers, then returned to his reading.

He was so engrossed that he didn't appear to have heard her come in. He opened the newspaper and tore out the page he had been reading. Then he tossed the paper back onto the stack of old *Scotsman*s that her father kept in that corner for fire lighters, leaving the torn page flat on his lap. Paul ran his finger along the lines again.

Lorna coughed and stepped forward.

Paul started at the sound but did not look up. Instead, he crumpled the page under his hand, as if he wanted to hide it.

"I brought your tea," Lorna said, puzzled, and trying not to be suspicious. "Sorry it's a bit late."

Without answering, Paul got to his feet and hurried toward the back of the shed, stuffing the paper into the pocket of his coveralls. As he went, head down, he swiped the sleeve of his sweater across his eyes and nose.

Was he crying?

Lorna hesitated. If he was crying, she doubted he would want her to stay, so she set the tray down on top of the barrel and walked back to the kitchen. What in the paper could have upset him so much? There were lots of stories these days about how far the Allies were pushing into countries that had been under German occupation, and even into Germany itself. Not easy reading for a German soldier, a German boy, so far from home.

By the time Lorna left the kitchen an hour or so later to get Paul's dishes, the evening air had grown colder again. As she buttoned her coat, she remembered the way that Paul had blown on his fingers to warm them while he read. She also remembered, with shame, how satisfied she had felt that first week to see him with no gloves at all, pleased to see this German suffering. Her stomach twisted at the memory.

She went back inside to where the single Red Cross scarf sat on her knitting bag. Lorna wound it round her hands, feeling again the warm comfort of the dark red wool. Did anyone deserve to be cold when there was an alternative sitting right here?

On an impulse, she tucked the scarf inside her coat and hurried up the stairs to John Jo's bedroom. But as she riffled through the drawers, she couldn't find a single pair of gloves. With a sigh, she gave up and went back downstairs and across the yard.

She didn't expect to see Paul, but he appeared from the storeroom at the back with a sack of feed when she entered the shed. He stopped, looking wary, perhaps wondering if she would mention what had happened earlier.

But she didn't want to embarrass him, so Lorna busied herself with tidying the empty dishes into the basket, and after a moment, Paul continued toward her.

"Thank you," he said.

"Glad you enjoyed it," she replied.

Lorna didn't pick the basket up, however. Instead, she took the maroon scarf from inside her coat where she had tucked it and held it out to him.

"I thought you might need this," she said. "I knitted it, so it's not very good, but it's warm."

"You knitted that for me?" Paul said quietly.

"No, no, for the Red Cross," said Lorna, "to be sent in the parcels for our prisoners of war. But then I saw you blowing on your hands, and I thought, well, you're a prisoner of war, so perhaps you need it as much as they do."

Paul laid the sack down beside the wall and took the scarf from her, losing his long fingers in it as she had done. Then he raised it to his face and pressed its soft wool against his undamaged cheek.

"Yes," he murmured, "it is very warm."

"I tried to get you some gloves, but I couldn't find any."

Lorna was starting to feel a little warm herself. "But I could try to knit you some, if I asked Iris to show me . . ."

Paul glanced to the windowsill as she spoke, and there lay the green woolen gloves she had been looking for.

"Oh! You have them. John Jo's gloves."

"Mrs. Mack gave them to me." He sounded apologetic. "I do not always remember to wear them. I hope you do not think it is wrong for me to have them."

Lorna felt flustered. "No, no, not at all. That's fine. Really."

Paul suddenly stepped forward with his hand outstretched. It took Lorna a moment to realize he wanted to shake her hand. Tentatively, she reached out to him, and as his fingers closed around hers, she looked up and their eyes met.

"Thank you for thinking of me, Fräulein Anderson"—Paul's voice was low—"and thank you for this gift."

At that moment, the kitchen door slammed and her father's footsteps sounded on the cobbled yard, so she withdrew her hand from Paul's and grabbed the basket.

At the door, she hesitated.

"My name is Lorna," she said over her shoulder.

For a heartbeat, she thought he hadn't heard her, but then he spoke.

"Good night, Lorna. I hope you sleep well."

Nine

"Will you come back to my house for tea?" Iris asked as they left the school the next day. "William has a Scout meeting this afternoon, and Mum is at my grannie's, so I have nothing better to do."

Lorna studied Iris's sweet smile and knew that her friend hadn't meant to sound rude.

"I'm flattered," she answered drily even so.

"Oh, you know what I mean." Iris nudged her arm. "So will you come?"

Lorna shook her head.

"Maybe another day? I've got things to get done while it's still light, but thanks."

In fact, Lorna couldn't face spending another hour or so with Iris as she prattled on about William, about school and

Red Cross, and oh, about William some more. Lorna wanted to clear her head. The night before, she had lain awake for a long time thinking about how upset Paul had looked over that piece of the newspaper. She shouldn't care if she saw him cry—she didn't really know him, after all, and it wasn't like he was her friend—but it had bothered her all the same.

Saying good-bye to Iris, Lorna decided to take the long way home through the woods. Though it would be a few weeks until the bluebells came into flower, she did love walking between the tranquil old trees. If she kept up a good pace, she wouldn't be back too late to get the tea on the table at the normal time.

The wind had got up during school, and it whipped Lorna's hair around her face as she walked. She pulled her scarf up over her head, tied it under her chin, and tucked the ends down inside her coat. Despite the wind, though, the sun felt warm on her face for the first time in months, and there was a mildness within the blustery air.

As she gave herself up to the rhythm of her feet on the path, Lorna allowed her mind to flit from Paul to Iris and William, to John Jo and Sandy, to Nellie and back to Paul again, and before she knew it, she was at the farthest end of Craigielaw's land, beside the beach beyond the woods.

She barely noticed when a large droplet of water hit the ground right in front of her. However, when the next four or five cold drops hit her face, and one sneaked into the narrow gap between her scarf and her neck, she paid more attention. Above the far shore of the Firth of Forth, a quilt of thick black rain clouds had darkened the bright sky, and its shadow was steadily creeping toward her over the water. And from the way the waves were dancing and bursting with white horses on their crests, Lorna could tell that the storm was coming fast.

Suddenly the clouds were illuminated from behind by a burst of lightning. Before she could count the seconds—*one alligator, two alligator*—a boom shook the air. Lorna almost lost her balance, as if the thunder itself had tried to push her over, so she ran, bent low, toward the edge of the woods.

With the rain's arrival, the last wash of daylight vanished and Lorna found herself in a soaking twilight. Sheets of water, woven stiff as canvas, swept her toward the trees as waves would wash a dinghy against a seawall. The lightning flashed and flashed again across the darkness, not waiting for the thundering fanfare to sound before crackling again.

By the time she reached the woods, she was drenched. The cold moisture seeped through her sodden coat, her tights were sopping inside her shoes. But the rain barely made it through the dense canopy of the old oaks, wych elms, and sycamores. Even though the thick branches were still mostly winter bare, with just the first pink buds coloring the brown bark, they still acted as soundproofing, deadening the ear-splitting noise of the storm.

Wet and miserable, Lorna threaded her way through the familiar woods in the direction of the farm, skirting the nettle beds until she found the well-worn path. She stuffed her scarf into her pocket, then shrugged out of her coat, the fabric soaked through so that even her sweater and shirt were already wet. Trying to keep her coat tucked under one arm, she wriggled her damp sweater off over her head, then squeezed the single braid that lay down her back until water trickled through her fingers.

"Bloody rain!" she said, shaking the excess water from her hand.

"I agree," said a voice behind her. "Bloody rain!"

Lorna spun around too quickly. Paul was sitting only ten yards away on the trunk of a tree that lay at a drunken angle to the ground.

Considering the deluge falling so near, he looked remarkably dry in his dark gray army sweater and the maroon scarf she had knitted. In contrast, Lorna knew she must look like a thoroughly drowned rat. Stray strands of hair were plastered to her face, and her white cotton shirt was sticking to her arms and shoulders.

Even though she knew—she hoped—that her wet shirt was not showing off anything more embarrassing than an unflattering undershirt, Lorna suddenly felt exposed under Paul's scrutiny and tried to pull her sweater back over her head. She only succeeded in dropping both her coat and scarf onto the ground, and anyway, she knew she'd never get the damp sweater back on with any dignity.

Then Paul was at her side, picking up her coat. Lorna started. Standing this close to her, he seemed far bigger than he had done when he was sitting at a distance in the lambing shed.

Paul squeezed the fabric of her coat with strong fingers.

"This is very wet," he said. "You will become sick if you put it on again."

"I'll be fine, it's just a bit of r-r-rain." Lorna shivered and tried to take her coat from him.

Paul held the coat just an inch or two beyond her grasp, then tossed it over the nearest branch. He then stripped off his own sweater before Lorna could protest and reached forward to put it over her head.

Lorna took a step away from him, feeling acute discomfort at this unexpected intimacy.

"No, really," she said. "I'm fine."

"But your coat is wet," Paul repeated, holding his sweater out toward her again.

The warm flush of blood rising in her cheeks stung under the biting chill of her skin.

"You really don't need to give me that," Lorna insisted. "You'll need it."

"But I do not shiver." Paul looked at her as if perplexed. "It is only a sweater. And you are very wet."

Lorna was shivering hard now, and his genuinely puzzled tone made her wonder if her pettiness was justified. It was only a sweater.

She took a tentative step toward him. He gently pulled the sweater over her head and down around her shoulders until she was swaddled in it to the hips, her arms stuck inside the warm body of the heavy sweater. When he moved even closer to reach behind her head to release her wet braid, Lorna did not resist.

Paul was less than an arm's length from her now, and Lorna let her eyes roam across the tight scarring of his face. Having given herself permission to look now, she realized that she was no longer as shocked by the damage as she once had been. The stretched skin, the puckering, appeared almost familiar.

Keeping close, Paul untied the scarf from his neck, looped it around Lorna's throat, and stepped back half a pace.

Lorna inhaled deeply, the shivers already subsiding. The wool was still warm and held a strong pleasant smell, of hay and sheep and mud and wood smoke. It was welcoming, comforting, and safe.

Paul was watching her carefully.

"Thank you," she said simply.

Paul smiled. "You are welcome," he said.

Leading her lightly by one dangling woolen arm, he guided her to the tree trunk on which he had been sitting.

"Perhaps we will sit here to wait for the rain to finish."

Lorna said nothing, but sat down on the lower end of the log.

Paul was about to sit down beside her but seemed to change his mind. Instead, he moved to sit on her other side, as if he deliberately wanted her on his right.

From this side, Lorna could see almost none of the damage to his face, and she regretted having stared so openly at it. Of course, he must be self-conscious. For a moment, she considered apologizing, but that would probably make matters worse. Instead, she tucked her mouth down behind the thick collar of the scarf, hugging herself within her warm cocoon, relishing the comfort she felt, both from the sweater and, she would admit, from Paul's presence.

Because in spite of herself, Lorna couldn't deny anymore that Paul was rather nice. And perhaps, if the war didn't exist, they might be sitting there simply as friends sheltering from the storm.

She allowed herself a quick glance sideways at him. He was looking out into the heavy rain.

"I did not know that your Scottish weather could be so . . ." He searched for the word. "So exciting. I have only seen a storm like this one time before, when I visited the great mountains of Bavaria. The thunder jumped from one mountain to the next."

"Like an echo?" asked Lorna.

She had never seen a mountain herself; a school trip to the Lammermuir Hills in the Scottish Borders was the highest she had ever been. She tried to imagine the Bavarian mountains.

"You call it *echo*?" Paul asked. "In German, we call it *Echo* also. And do you know what we call thunder and lightning?"

"I don't know any German at all," Lorna said, shaking her head. "You must think we're not very clever. You speak such good English and we speak no language other than our own."

He waved her comment aside.

"In Germany, we call thunder and lightning *Donner und Blitzen*."

"*Blitzen*?" repeated Lorna. "Like the Blitz?"

A shadow crossed Paul's face, and Lorna could have bitten her tongue. Why had she mentioned the German bombing raids on London, which had devastated the city and killed thousands of people? The war would never be far away, she knew, but did she have to remind him about it?

"I'm sorry, I didn't mean . . . I just thought it just sounded like the same word."

Lorna could feel her ears burning, but Paul only nodded.

"*Blitzkrieg* means 'lightning war,' so you are right," he said. "And do not apologize. I am not proud that my country has killed many of your people, though please remember, your country has killed many Germans too. But that is what war is about. We do not like it, but we must all live with it until it is ended."

There was an unmistakably bitter tone to his voice. Lorna wasn't sure how to respond, so they sat in silence for a few moments.

"What was it like for you in the war?" she asked finally.

Paul did not respond immediately.

"You don't have to tell me if you don't want to," she said. "My brothers never want to tell me anything either."

Paul took a deep breath and held it for several seconds before he spoke again.

"When the *Wehrmacht* called me to join, I tried to tell them I could not go because my mother and my sister needed me." Paul seemed to address his quiet words to the rain and the trees rather than to Lorna. "But the officer called me a

87

coward and asked if I knew what happened to cowards."

Lorna knew the answer to that as well.

"So I said good-bye to my mother and to Lilli and I went to the army."

Paul swallowed hard, and Lorna found her own throat tightening. She knew how it felt to say good-bye.

"When I had finished learning to be a soldier, they sent me to France. Not Paris. Paris was too good for us. Our captain told us that we were worth nothing, and therefore they were sending us to the most *gottverlassen* . . ."

He frowned.

"Is 'god-abandoned' an English word?"

"I think it would be 'godforsaken,'" offered Lorna.

"Yes, he said they would send us to the most *godforsaken* place on earth to keep us out of the way of far braver Germans who would win the war. So we sat on a beach in Normandy for three weeks . . ."

Normandy. The hairs on Lorna's neck rose. Could she guess what was coming?

". . . staring at the empty English Channel, and we began to believe him that we were worth nothing to the generals in Berlin. But Normandy was not godforsaken; it was very beautiful.

"There was little to do and the weather was hot, so we had picnics and we swam in the little river running down to the sea. But then a storm came down, so we went indoors to wait for the sun to shine again over the empty sea.

"But the next morning, the sea was not empty. It was full

of boats, and the sky was full of airplanes and parachutes, and the beach was full of soldiers."

"D-Day," Lorna whispered. D-Day, the day last June when the Allies had invaded the northern coast of France, pushing the German army back through Normandy to Paris, and onward to the low countries. Lorna was sure John Jo had been there, on D-Day—the Royal Scots certainly had been, she'd seen it in the newspaper, but he'd never told her anything of importance like that in his letters home.

Paul seemed not to have heard her. "I was in a *Blockhaus*, a machine gun post, looking over the beach. One of my friends was shooting on the gun, and it was so loud. . . . I tried to talk to the control room on the telephone, but it was dead."

Paul paused. He lowered his head and Lorna could not see his face.

"Then the *Blockhaus* was hit, by a shell or a grenade, and I was thrown behind a metal table. It gave me shelter from the explosion." Paul lifted his hand to cover the left side of his face, and Lorna could see his hand was trembling. "Or from most of it."

Lorna sat frozen, not daring to move, desperate not to break the moment. She couldn't bear to hear more, but she also couldn't bring herself to stop him.

"There was smoke, and I could not breathe. I knew I had to leave, but how? I could see nothing and I could hear nothing, but somehow I found a way out. There was so much pain, and I was bleeding very much from here."

Paul put his hand onto the side of his rib cage where Lorna

had seen the dark pink scar.

"I lay in the wet grass against the *Blockhaus* wall and I thought for sure I was in hell. The ground shook. I could not hear the bombs, but I could feel the air punch me as each one fell. And I remember feeling sad that I could not smell the sea anymore."

Paul's voice was barely audible, and Lorna had to lean in to him so she could hear. Although this meant she was pressing her shoulder against his arm, he seemed not to notice.

"After a long time, the bombs stopped and I tried to look, but my eyes did not work. There were men and trucks going past, I could feel them, but I could not see them. They did not come to help me, so perhaps they thought I was already dead. And the pain was so bad, I decided death would be best. So I lay there, and I waited to die.

"But I did not die. Instead I woke and an American soldier was talking to me, a medic. He knew I was still alive before I did. Is that not funny?"

He lifted his head and looked at her now.

Lorna squirmed until she had one arm into the sleeve of the sweater, and then she extracted her hand from inside the cuff and laid it on his arm.

"Were you hurt very badly?" she whispered. "I mean, apart from your . . ."

This time, she could not look at his face, could not study his injuries as she had done earlier. Now it upset her too much to think of the pain it had caused him, so instead she studied her own hand where it lay on the thin cotton of his shirt.

"I was lucky," he said quietly. "So many of my friends were not. In the hospital, they gave me operations to save the skin on my face, and they said that I might need more in the future, but still, I know I am lucky to be alive."

Paul put his hand into his pants pocket and brought out a handful of small pieces of metal and wire. From them, he picked up one of the larger fragments in his fingers. It was dark metal, about one inch square.

"The American doctor took this from here." He pointed to his rib cage. "From a grenade, I think. He was a very good doctor, but the hospital was only an old house, and he worked with the few tools he had. I was very sick for a long time, and often I wished I had died. But then I thought of Lilli and my mother waiting for me, and I made myself get better and stronger."

Lorna gingerly touched the tip of one finger to the piece of shrapnel, which could have, *should have*, killed him—it was a piece of an Allied grenade, thrown by an Allied soldier, just like her brother. Had John Jo been one of the men running up that particular Normandy beach alongside the Americans? The thought sickened her. But then again, Paul was not blameless either. Perhaps John Jo had faced the German gun firing from Paul's *Blockhaus* or one just like it on another beach. Had her brother watched as German bullets tore apart the men beside him?

Suddenly the doubts crept back in. She must not forget that this man was an enemy soldier, she must not forget he was German, that he had been trained to kill men like her brother and his friends. She forced herself to remember this, even though this new friendship was making it easier to forget thoughts like those.

Lorna came back to the moment and realized that Paul's palm was still outstretched, and it held other pieces of metal and wire. She remembered his strange behavior the day before. Were these the things she had seen him picking up in the yard?

"What's the rest of this?" she asked. "Why would you want it?"

Paul closed his fingers over the fragments and put them back into his pocket.

"It is nothing," he said. "I pick up little pieces of metal I find lying around. I like to keep them."

"For what?"

Paul turned his face toward Lorna, and though she was aware again of the scorched skin stretched over his left cheek, she was entirely distracted by his eyes as they held hers. How like the gray storm they were.

"The rain clouds . . . ," she said without meaning to.

Paul looked away from her and out through the trees. The unburdened clouds had lightened and were lifting away.

". . . have all gone," he finished, and stood up. "The rain is over, so will you let me walk you home?"

Ten

On the Tuesday after the rainstorm, Lorna returned home to find Mrs. Mack at the stove humming one of her busy-in-the-kitchen tunes. Lorna gave her a hug from behind.

"What are you still doing here?" Lorna asked. "You should be getting the bairns' tea, not ours."

"I'll be away in a minute or two. But Sheena's on a day off today, so there's no need for me to rush around for once. Now you're here, though, make yourself useful by filling the teapot while I get the eggs. Your dad and Nellie will be in soon."

Mrs. Mack disappeared through the scullery door with the egg basket almost the same time as Lorna's dad came in the other door from the yard.

"So what does a man have to do to get a cup of tea round

here?" he said, tossing his jacket over the back of a chair.

Once Lorna had poured the boiling water into the teapot, she lifted down three cups from the dresser. As she did, she noticed the little hook on which her father had hung his broken watch was empty.

"Did your watch get fixed already?" she asked.

"Oh, well remembered!" her dad said, and instinctively glanced at his empty wrist. "Where did you put it? Donald Hastie has business up in the Old Town on Thursday and says he'll drop it into Christie's the Jewelers for me."

"Me?" Lorna was confused. "I didn't put it anywhere. Maybe Mrs. Mack moved it to do the dusting. Why don't you ask her when she comes back in? Or maybe it was Nellie?"

Lorna's dad scowled. "Why on earth would Nellie have touched it?"

"I don't know why, but—" Lorna said as she poured out the first cup and handed it to him.

"Well, somebody's been having it. And nobody else has been in the house this last week except us four. So please ask Nellie about it if you see her before I do."

Nobody else has been in the house. . . .

"Because if I don't get that watch to Donald before Thursday, I'll be waiting weeks more to get it to the mender's."

Nobody else . . . except . . .

The floor dropped away from her. On Friday, the day after the storm, the day after he had wrapped her in the warmth of his sweater and they had talked for so long, Paul had been in the house.

Lorna had walked home along Coffin Lane as usual, and she'd seen Paul leave the barn. Dangling a large tin mug from one finger, he'd knocked once on the kitchen door before going in, even though he wasn't supposed to. After less than a minute, he'd come back out, and thinking about it now, Lorna remembered he'd been carrying something. Not the tin mug, too small, but something he'd slipped into his pocket before she could make out what exactly it was. And then he'd stooped to pick up something off the ground, which he'd also pocketed.

Lorna at the time had been so wrapped up thinking about the damage done by the shrapnel he carried around, she hadn't thought any more about it.

Until now.

What if it had been her grandfather's watch in Paul's hand? What if he had stolen it so he could sell it in the camp, or barter with it?

He might not need money to buy food or clothes. He had his uniform and Sandy's coveralls and the gloves and scarf. And it was clear from his developing muscles—Lorna pictured him again at the water pump—that he was being given enough good food to eat now. Who knew why he'd need the money, but her dad's precious watch had been sitting there for the taking.

Lorna struggled with the idea. The boy she'd talked to in the woods wouldn't have taken it, she was sure. He had been warm and kind. But was that enough? He was still a German. And while he might have told her of his home, his family, and his work, really, what did she actually know about Paul?

Her dad stirred milk into his tea. Should she tell him of her suspicions? She had no real evidence that Paul had taken the watch. Her dad needed Paul's help, and Lorna was glad he was here for that reason, if for no other. And Paul had been through so much already. But what else might he steal if she said nothing? And who else could have taken the watch anyway?

Lorna rubbed the heel of her hand across her forehead. Panic was building in her chest. She'd been so näive to be taken in by Paul, to have so easily forgotten where her real loyalties lay—with her father, with John Jo and Sandy, with her country.

She had to find out the truth. Leaving the teapot where it stood, she strode out into the yard just as Nellie and the cows were crossing it toward the milking parlor.

"Any chance of a cup of tea?" asked Nellie. "I'm parched."

"Where's Paul?"

"Paul?"

"Yes, Paul. Where is he?"

Nellie looked taken aback at Lorna's sharp tone but pointed toward the barn.

"Behind there, last I saw him. Is everything all right, love? You look like a bulldog chewing a wasp."

Lorna ignored Nellie and headed through the barn. Sure enough, Paul was on the other side, chopping wood.

His shirt was hanging on a nail, and he was wearing only his undershirt as he heaved the ax over his head. But Lorna's temper would not let her be distracted by that. Not for more than a second or two anyway.

Paul kicked pieces of split log to one side, and he must have caught sight of her as he did, because he smiled.

But Lorna was focused.

"So what other trinkets did you find lying around that you decided to keep?"

Lorna had not intended to accuse Paul of stealing so directly, but the words came out anyway.

Paul looked surprised. "I do not understand," he said, though she noticed that his hand went to his pocket, almost protectively. "Have I done something wrong? I did not think your father would mind if I cleared pieces of metal from the ground."

He pulled out a handful of the scraps to show again to Lorna. "These pieces of metal, they are worth no money, are they?"

"They might not be worth anything," she said, "but what about his watch? Did you help yourself to that little piece of metal too?"

For a moment, Paul didn't move, but Lorna knew she had hit the mark, because he dropped his chin down onto his chest. *Guilty.* Then he propped the ax against the wall and slowly walked into the barn. At the bottom of the ladder to the hayloft, he stopped. He didn't look back at her, but he was clearly expecting her to follow.

Lorna hesitated as Paul climbed up and disappeared through the hole at the top. Why was he leading her up to where he slept? How was this an answer to her question? Lorna knew her father would not be happy if she went up there with him, alone.

Paul's voice came back down to her. "Come, and I will show you."

Lorna put an uncertain foot onto the ladder but hesistated only a moment before she climbed.

The hayloft hadn't seen any hay for years. It had been used as a workshop for longer than Lorna could remember, though she and Sandy had also used it as their hideout when they were younger. It had barely changed since she was last up there, yet it was also not the same place at all. For a start, it was tidy, with tools hung up on nails, and cans of paint stacked carefully to one side.

The old camp bed was against the far wall, made up neatly with blankets and a pillow as if ready for a sergeant's inspection. On an upended crate sat a stack of three books, against which was propped a ragged photograph. It showed a woman sitting primly on a high-backed chair with a pretty young girl standing beside her, her blond hair in two tight braids. Was that Paul's mother and Lilli?

Paul was standing on the other side of the loft, leaning against the waist-high wooden bench on which her grandfather's hand tools had always been kept.

Now, however, on the bench lay a neat arrangement of other tools, many of them miniature versions of her grandfather's. There was a small hammer, numerous fine metal files, and two tiny screwdrivers with wooden handles. She nervously picked one up. It seemed to have been made by hand out of a thick nail and a piece of wood.

Paul was studying her as she approached the bench.

"Did you make these?" she asked. "But why?"

"I like working with your father on the farm," Paul replied. "I have work for my body, but I do not use my hands and my brain. I said I would clean your father's tools, so I oiled them, and sharpened them, and I enjoyed that also. But I miss working in fine detail. I miss working on things so delicate, so perfect, they can capture time."

"Clocks," said Lorna.

Paul nodded. "So when Mrs. Mack gave me your father's watch—"

"Mrs. Mack gave it to you?" Lorna was feeling queasy. "Why would Mrs. Mack have given it to you?"

He seemed surprised that she would ask that question.

"She knows I am a watchmaker, and she asked me to repair it. I thought she told Mr. Anderson. But it is clear she did not."

Paul lifted a small bundle from the shelf and laid it on the workbench.

"I should have told your father myself and asked his permission to touch it, but I will tell you it felt wonderful to have such a beautiful watch in my hands after months of guns and grenades, and spades and axes."

As he spoke, he opened the white linen bundle, and there lay the watch. Its gold and glass face glinted in the late afternoon sunshine that filtered through the dirty window of the loft. Paul wiped the corner of the fabric across the glass.

Lorna gingerly picked it up, as if it were a relic of immense value. It was heavy and trustworthy, and she could feel movement on her fingertips, slight and rhythmic. She lifted the watch to her ear and listened. Yes, there it was, the *tick tick tick* of the second hand.

"You—you fixed it?" she stuttered. "Here, in our hayloft? With these little tools?"

"And with things like these," he said, putting his hand into his pants pocket. When he took it out again, he let all the small pieces of metal and wire pour from his hand onto the bench.

"Paul, that's amazing."

Lorna was feeling very uncomfortable now. Why hadn't she waited to talk to Mrs. Mack before racing off to accuse Paul?

"Once I took the watch apart," Paul explained, "it was not difficult to clean it and put it back together again. As I said, it is a very fine watch, and your father is right to value it."

"It was my grandfather's," Lorna said.

"Yes, but did you know that it is German?" he asked.

How had her grandfather come by a German watch? He had never even left Scotland, as far as she knew.

"It was made around 1900, I think," Paul explained, "by the Glashütte company—one of my country's finest watchmakers."

"So will you come to give it back to Dad now?" Lorna asked, placing the watch carefully back on the linen. "He will be very grateful, I know. He'll want to say thank you."

She wrapped up the watch again and held it out to Paul, but he didn't take it.

"He does not owe me his thanks. I enjoyed the work. I am just sorry that I did something to make you angry. I do not want to be sent away from Aberlady."

Something wistful in his tone made Lorna look up at him.

"Really? I'd be away from Aberlady like a shot, if I could. I mean, haven't you even once thought about escaping?"

Probably not a question she should ask a German prisoner.

"I would only think about escaping," said Paul, a smile tweaking the corner of his mouth, "if I could fill my bag first with dozens of Mrs. Mack's tattie scones."

He laughed, and Lorna joined in.

"Tattie scones?" she said. "You are sounding like a real Scotsman now. You'll be one of us before you know it."

"Maybe." Paul looked thoughtful. "But no, I think I will always be German. But I know I would also be happy if I never left Aberlady. It is very beautiful here."

Paul's gray eyes held hers fast, as they had done that very first day.

"Very beautiful."

"So it turns out your watch wasn't stolen, after all, Dad," Lorna burst out as she went back into the house with Paul. "It's a funny story, but—"

"—the lad here was fixing it. Aye, I know. Mrs. Mack told me."

"Oh, when—?"

"When she came back with the eggs, just after you tore off with a face like a bulldog chewing—"

"A bulldog chewing a wasp, yes, I heard that already. But look, Paul's done a lovely job."

Lorna waved Paul forward. He placed the white bundle carefully on the table and stepped back respectfully.

Lorna's dad studied Paul for a second or two, then drew the watch from its linen swaddling. He ran his thumb over the gleaming glass, then lifted it to his ear. As he listened, Lorna noticed that he looked up at the two photographs sitting in tarnished silver frames high on the mantelpiece, next to the certificate of thanks that His Majesty King George had signed and sent to every member of the Home Guard.

One was a picture of Lorna's mother, taken on her wedding day, but Lorna's dad seemed to be focusing on the other. It was a picture of her grandfather standing proudly with his four sons—her father; her uncle Harry, who was now the police officer in Port Seton; and her dad's two older brothers, Billy and Frank, who had gone off to fight in the Great War not long after the photograph was taken. Neither had come back.

Her father seemed lost in the photograph, but after a moment, he looked back at the watch, and carefully placed it on his wrist. He said something as he fitted the brown leather strap exactly onto the white circlet of skin, but it was too quiet for her to hear the words.

As he secured the small gold buckle, Lorna's dad looked

up at Paul and nodded once. Paul nodded back. Nothing more.

"They'll be delivering the wire to repair the fence over yonder in the morning." Suddenly Lorna's dad was all business. "So we'll get a start on that straight after breakfast."

He turned to Lorna.

"I've to run over to Luffness in a wee bit, but I'll be back by seven for my tea and the news."

Lorna's father stalked past her and turned on the water in the scullery sink to wash his teacup. She was stunned. He hadn't even said thank you to Paul. But was she one to talk? She hadn't yet apologized for accusing Paul of being a thief either, had she?

"Paul"—she dropped her voice as she turned to him— "I'm sorry, you know, that I—"

Before she could say any more, the kitchen door was thrown open and Nellie rushed in, muddy boots and all, panting and holding her waist on one side.

"You ain't never going to believe the news!" she gasped. "I didn't believe it myself, excepting I got it from the very best source."

She gasped again and rubbed the sleeve of her sweater across her forehead, adding a wide smudge of dirt to the sheen of perspiration.

"What news, Nellie?" Lorna asked, hardly daring to guess. Was the war over? Would John Jo and Sandy be coming home? "Come on, tell us!"

The old water pipes clunked and rattled as her father

slammed off the faucet. In the resulting silence, Nellie drew an enormous breath and let it burst out again.

"They're throwing a dance!" she crowed. "The Yanks! At the air base! On Saturday! *This* Saturday! I just met my friend Doris cycling down the road there, and she told me. Isn't that something? A real-life American dance!"

A disgusted grunt came from the scullery, and Lorna guessed that her father too had been hoping to hear that piece of news that would bring their boys home. Two seconds later, the back door slammed shut and he crunched away over the gravel.

Nellie was hopping around the kitchen, trying to pull one of her boots off while still standing up. After a couple more hops, she collapsed into a chair, pushing off one boot with the toe of the other. She was giggling like all her Christmases had come at once.

Even in her disappointment that the news was not more important, Lorna was finding Nellie's delight infectious, and she glanced up at Paul to see if he too was caught up in Nellie's enthusiasm. She found no smile, however, no emotion at all. It was as if the Paul she knew had stepped behind a mask.

For her part, Nellie did not seem to have noticed Paul was even in the room. With a huff, she finally kicked off her other boot and spun to face Lorna, grasping the back of her chair.

"There's going to be a band, and drinks," she trilled happily, "and food, and dancing. Well, obviously there'll be dancing, it is a dance after all. And guess what?"

She leaned toward Lorna significantly.

"What?" Lorna shrugged, though her pulse was quickening.

"Guess!"

"Nellie, just tell me."

"Since it's an American Air Force dance, there's going to be lots of American pilots needing partners to dance with," said Nellie hungrily, "and lots of navigators and mechanics, I shouldn't wonder. So guess what *that* means?"

"Nellie!"

"It means that we're invited! You and me!" She winked provocatively at Lorna. "What d'you say? You game?"

"Really? Me go to a dance with you?"

"Just call me your fairy godmother, duckie."

Lorna couldn't suppress her smile any longer, but then something struck her as not quite right. "Hold on, how can we already be invited? You've only just heard it's happening."

"All right, Miss Fussyknickers, I can *make sure* we get invited when I see my Charming Charlie later tonight in the pub. Yes? You up for it?"

"Oh, Nellie, yes please!"

Nellie jumped out of her chair and whirled Lorna around, giggling.

Even through Nellie's squeals, Lorna heard the kitchen door click shut. By the time she looked round, Paul was gone.

Eleven

"I'm telling you, duckie, it'll be crawling with *gorgeous* blokes, all desperate to dance with a beautiful girl."

Nellie was still talking about the dance at teatime. Lorna put two plates of rabbit stew and dumplings onto the table, suddenly hoping the food might distract Nellie, for a while at least.

Ever since the US Air Force's arrival last December at the East Fortune Airfield, Nellie had been raving about *gorgeous* American airmen. Nellie and her Land Army pals had tracked the Americans down to a couple of pubs in Haddington and North Berwick and had been regulars there ever since. For a while, Nellie had talked about different airmen each time, but recently only one name was on Nellie's lips.

"My Charming Charlie will work it all out," Nellie said,

stabbing a plump suet dumpling onto her fork and waving it at Lorna. "He's got a dozen *gorgeous* pals who'd be perfect for you, and by all accounts, they've been having a rotten time of it this last week or two, so they'll be looking for some fun."

She stuffed the whole dumpling into her mouth, chewing it quickly.

"In fact, Charlie told me about a certain gentleman friend of his just the other day. Except when he says it, his American accent makes it sound like 'gennel-man'—isn't that cute? Cute—that's another of his funny words, you know, he has lots of them. Cute, and swell, and soda pop."

Lorna smiled at all these Hollywood words, but below her bubbling anticipation, something else was stirring.

Had Paul left so suddenly because she hadn't apologized? She had tried to say sorry before Nellie interrupted, but then she'd got so caught up in the invitation, she hadn't finished. Then he'd stalked out, though only after she had said yes to the dance invitation. But why should that upset him?

She hadn't got the chance to talk to him when she had taken his tea over. She'd shouted that she'd brought his meal, but he'd called from the back that she should just leave it on top of the barrel.

Even as she'd left the tray in its usual place, she'd still been tempted to go check he wasn't sulking.

Sulking? Why would he have been sulking?

It wasn't like Paul could go to the dance with them, so why was she even thinking about Paul just now? She should be concentrating on Saturday's dance, not worrying about him.

"This dance is going to be so exciting," Lorna said as she sat down beside Nellie at the table, determined to make herself believe it. "Thank you again for including me. Dad'll be back soon, so I can ask him if I can go."

Nellie raised one perfectly plucked eyebrow. "You need to ask your dad?"

"No, no, of course not." Lorna fought to keep her voice from rising, suddenly embarrassed in front of Nellie who went anywhere anytime she pleased. "Of course I don't need to ask his *permission*. I just need to check that he can spare me that night. From the farm, I mean. Because we're so busy."

Nellie nodded as if she understood, but she was also pressing her lips tightly together as if she were fighting a smile.

At that moment, Lorna's dad kicked his boots against the wall outside, and Lorna leaped up to get his plate from the oven.

"Perfect timing," said Nellie. "You can ask him now, I mean, check he can spare you. Unless you'd like me to."

"No, Nellie, I'll do it," Lorna whispered as her dad opened the kitchen door. "I'll just give him his tea first."

But her dad looked so tired and anxious when he came in that Lorna decided to bide a while before asking him about it. She set his plate on the table next to his newspaper and sat back down to finish her own meal. Perhaps she'd ask him after he'd listened to the news.

"Now, Mr. Anderson, about this dance on Saturday,"

Nellie blurted out before Lorna's dad had even picked up his fork. "You don't mind if I whisk young Lorna away with me, do you?"

Nellie! Lorna wanted to clap a hand over that unstoppable mouth.

"You know, for an evening of very-well-chaperoned entertainment."

"And which one of you will need chaperoning, I wonder," Lorna's dad muttered without looking up. Nellie gave a hoot of laughter.

"Mr. A., you are funny sometimes."

But Lorna's dad wasn't laughing, and neither was Lorna. She was silently cursing Nellie.

After an eternity, he looked at Lorna.

"So, lassie, are you wanting to go to this dance too?"

Not a straight no. That was good.

"Yes, please, Dad." She glanced at Nellie, who was smirking again. "At least, if you can spare me for the evening."

After a few heartbeats, he nodded.

"Well, if you've found some blokes willing to dance with a couple of giggling jennies like you two, it seems a shame to waste the invitation."

Nellie clapped her hands gleefully.

"But you girls must mind three things." He looked at each of them in turn. "You must stick together. You'll be back by midnight. And you'll be sober. Yes, even you, Nellie Clarke. Do you understand?"

Nellie opened her mouth to protest.

"You live under my roof and you will be responsible for my daughter on Saturday, so you will follow my rules. Do you understand?"

Nellie gave an unconvincingly meek nod.

"And," he continued, "you will both be up in time to do the Sunday milking."

"Yes, of course," agreed Lorna quickly, but Nellie's only response was a quiet groan.

"And there's no clothing coupons to spare for a new dress and whatnot, Lorna. And you'll not go borrowing anything from this one." He jerked his thumb at Nellie. "I'll not have you looking like a dog's dinner as well."

Yet again, Nellie opened her mouth to protest, but Lorna flashed her a warning glance, and she stayed silent.

"Thanks, Dad," said Lorna, "and I promise I'll do just as you say."

"Aye, well, mind you do." He looked back to his plate. "Now, for the love of God, will you two let me eat my tea in peace."

The next morning, Mrs. Mack was just as excited as the girls about the dance. The whole of Aberlady, she told Lorna, was gossiping about it.

"So what'll you wear?" she asked Lorna.

Lorna had been wondering that same thing. The truth was nothing she already owned would be suitable. Even her best dress for church made her look like a schoolgirl. There was nothing that might suggest she was a mature woman of the world, and she couldn't even borrow something from Iris or Nellie. Iris's wardrobe was pretty much as boring as her own, and Nellie had half Lorna's height and twice her bust. And with there being no clothing coupons left to buy something new, she was starting to despair.

"Oh, I'll find something," she said with a shrug.

Mrs. Mack contemplated Lorna, running her eyes up and down.

"I've got to pop into the village later on, so let me see what I can do," she said with a wink. "You can't go to your first real dance in your school uniform or church clothes, so come home extra quick this afternoon, and bring Iris with you."

Mrs. Mack refused to say any more, so after school Lorna grabbed Iris—virtually out of William Urquhart's arms—and dragged her back to Craigielaw.

Iris pumped Lorna for information on the dance as they walked.

"Will you get to dance with an actual pilot?"

"Not sure. The problem is," Lorna said, "Nellie is so pretty and so, well, womanly, any pilot will be very disappointed to end up with me."

Lorna looked down at her chest meaningfully.

"I'm not exactly endowed with Nellie's 'assets,' am I?" She and Iris both giggled. "Compared to Nellie's Bavarian mountains, mine are barely even Lammermuir Hills!"

A picture of Paul striding up a Bavarian mountain formed in her mind. If a man like Paul had already seen the majestic slopes of German mountains, would he ever be interested in exploring small Scottish hills?

A bubble of laughter caught in her throat, choking her at the idea of Paul or any other man *exploring* her very own decidedly unimpressive Lammermuirs.

"What's so funny?" Iris slapped her on the back. "I don't understand."

Lorna shook her head as she coughed.

"Sorry, I'm fine." She wiped at her eyes. "Something went down the wrong way."

"Sometimes, Lorna"—Iris shook her head—"I wonder about you, I really do."

When they clattered into the Craigielaw kitchen, Mrs. Mack shouted for them to come up to Lorna's bedroom. On top of the quilted comforter lay a beautiful peacock-blue dress, and both girls oohed over it, fingering the fine fabric.

"This dress belongs to my Sheena," said Mrs. Mack. "She wore it as her going-away outfit after her wedding. It's not really the latest style, and it'll be a little big for you, but if we can pin it on you now, Iris and her mother will take it in for you in time for the dance."

"B-but I can't take Sheena's—" stammered Lorna.

"Yes, dear, you can. Now pop it on, so we can see what needs to be done."

Lorna looked at Iris. "But do you really think you could—"

"It'll be easy. You know Mum's a genius at alterations, and I'm not so bad at them either, even if I say so myself."

Letting herself be persuaded, Lorna quickly stripped off her school uniform and put on the blue dress before looking in the wardrobe mirror. The dress was a simply shaped satin shift, with a wide curve at the neck. Over the top was a layer of floating organza, which caught the light as it moved, appearing sometimes blue, sometimes green.

Behind Lorna, Mrs. Mack seemed to be struggling with the tiny buttons at the back until Iris stepped forward and took over. Once it was done, she and Mrs. Mack also studied Lorna's reflection in the mirror.

"I think, if we just"—Iris pinched up the fabric on Lorna's shoulders—"add in shoulder pads, like this, and lift the hemline higher . . ."

Moving one of her hands down, Iris pulled the bottom of the dress up to just below Lorna's knees, then looked to Mrs. Mack for approval.

"Not too high," the housekeeper said.

"And what about the neckline? A bit lower, I think," Iris said.

"Aye, but not *too* low."

It was like they were discussing a dress on a mannequin, though Lorna didn't mind. The dress was so beautiful, and the alterations were bound to make her stand out. For this dance, she wanted to look like . . . well, *not* like herself. Not so much, at least.

Iris was drawing a new imaginary neckline with her finger a couple of inches farther down Lorna's chest. Even though it would be more revealing than anything Lorna had ever worn before, it was nowhere near as low as Nellie or any other older woman would wear. Feeling a flush of bravery, Lorna took hold of Iris's finger and used it to trace a much more daring line low across her chest.

"Yes, much lower," she said, winking at Iris. With her other hand, she lifted the hem up so she could see her knees. "And much higher."

Iris was laughing now. "And tighter?" she asked, grasping the back of the dress until it fitted snugly, accentuating the smooth line of Lorna's waist.

Lorna grinned and nodded.

"And with your hair up in a swanky Victory roll," Iris said, using her fingers to loop Lorna's long hair into a messy twist at the back of her head, "I think we'll have a winner."

Lorna looked at herself again in the mirror. She looked different, older. With the alterations in place and her hair set properly, she might really look the way a girl, no, a woman, going to a big dance should look. "But is Sheena sure?" Lorna asked. "It'll mean she can't wear it again."

Mrs. Mack chuckled at Lorna's reflection. "Don't you worry. Sheena has had the three bairns since she wore this, and she's glad you'll have the enjoyment of it. She said it would bring out the beauty of your skin, and she was right."

The old housekeeper suddenly pulled a handkerchief from her apron pocket.

"You don't remember, but your mother had the same skin, like peaches and cream. You've not got her freckles, and of course, her eyes were blue. . . . Cornflower blue, your father used to tell everyone who would listen. . . ."

Mrs. Mack touched the hankie to her eyes and sniffed.

"Och, listen to me, havering on like this. Now, Iris, take that wee box there so we can get this dress pinned."

Iris lifted a tortoiseshell pin box from the bed and set it onto Lorna's upturned palm. With a few pins held deftly between her lips, she pulled the fabric into tiny tucks around Lorna's waist and hips, pinning as she went. Then she set a scooping line of pins to mark the new, and much lower, neckline.

Lorna suddenly felt a twinge of sadness. The pin box had belonged to her mother. Lorna didn't think of her often but wondered now how it might feel if the hands working so deftly now to pin the dress had been her mother's.

"Oh, Iris," said Mrs. Mack, peering over Lorna's shoulder as Iris worked, "that will look simply lovely. She'll be the belle of the ball."

"Lorna, you will," Iris whispered from behind Lorna's other shoulder, meeting Lorna's eyes in the mirror. "No pilot could be disappointed in you."

"Disappointed? In our Lorna?" Mrs. Mack looked indignant. "Now why would any man be disappointed in Lorna? Or in you, for that matter, Iris? You two girls have grown into a couple of real stunners. You'll have no problem finding yourselves some handsome men to marry, I'm sure of that."

"Of course, I've already found my handsome man, Mrs. Mack," simpered Iris. "And I know we're going to be very happy together."

Lorna pulled a face, but Mrs. Mack studied Iris in the mirror.

"You're still young, so no need to settle down yet."

"No, no, this is definitely the real thing, I know it." Iris sounded entirely convinced. "Although . . ."

"Although?" Lorna prompted.

Iris looked embarrassed.

"Well, it might have been fun to dance with a real American, just once."

"Maybe it's not too late," Lorna said brightly. "Perhaps Charming Charlie could find another friend so you could come to the dance with us."

"What a wonderful idea!" agreed Mrs. Mack. "Nellie will be in the parlor shortly if you want to ask her."

"Lorna, do you think she could?" said Iris, but then she frowned. "No, that wouldn't be right. William wouldn't be keen on me going to a dance without him."

She grasped Lorna's arm.

"Maybe William could come as well."

Lorna exchanged a glance of disbelief with Mrs. Mack in the mirror.

"I'm not sure . . . ," Lorna said.

Downstairs, someone rapped hard on the kitchen door.

"I'll go! That'll be William," Iris said excitedly. "He's here to walk me safely home."

Lorna and Mrs. Mack exchanged another glance.

"Quick, Lorna," said Iris, oblivious to their astonishment, "get changed so William's not kept waiting, and then we can all go and talk to Nellie."

Lorna was happy to keep William Urquhart waiting, so

she took her time changing; then she went downstairs, leaving Mrs. Mack folding the blue dress into a wide white box. By the time Lorna got to the kitchen, Iris had clearly told William about her idea for Nellie to get them into the dance.

"Won't that be wonderful?" she said, gazing up at him.

William patted Iris's shoulder. "Certainly not," he said with unconcealed disdain. "It would be entirely inappropriate."

Iris's face crumpled, and she started chewing on her bottom lip.

"How is it 'inappropriate'?" Lorna glared at William, though he didn't seem to notice.

"Inappropriate for someone of my standing in the parish, as the minister's son, to be seen *consorting* with Americans. *Standing* is something you will have to think about in future, Iris."

"Oh yes, of course. You're right," Iris said immediately.

Lorna stared at Iris. Why was she agreeing with him?

"And in future," said William, "before making such suggestions, ask yourself, in these circumstances, what would Mother do?"

Lorna looked at Iris, hoping to find derision, but all her friend did was nod as if she understood exactly what William meant.

Well, even if Iris couldn't find her internal well of sarcasm, Lorna could.

"I think Iris's mother would tell her to have a jolly nice time."

William's sneer was withering. "Not *Iris's* mother. *My* mother."

"And why would *your mother* say that going to the American dance would be a problem for Iris's *standing in the parish*?"

"It's not something you would find easy to understand." William lifted Iris's hand into his own. "But fortunately, Iris gets it completely."

Lorna wanted Iris to smack his hand away. She couldn't believe her friend was putting up with this.

"Iris, how can you . . . ?"

"Ever since these Americans came to East Lothian," William continued, "they've been arrogant and unbearable, throwing money around and treating us Scots as if we're second-class citizens. I swear they all think they're John Wayne."

"Iris, you can't agree with him," Lorna said, but Iris wasn't listening. William was patting her hand rhythmically as if he were calming a petulant child.

And Iris was letting him.

"Come, come, Iris," said William with oily reassurance. "Don't snivel over a silly dance. We'll have a grand time on Saturday evening playing bridge with my parents, and perhaps we'll even teach you canasta. Lorna can go off to the dance with all those John Waynes, and good luck to her, because I, for one, would like to spend no more time in the company of an American than I would in the company of a German, thank you very much."

At that moment, there was another, softer knock, and Paul stepped into the kitchen carrying his empty mug. He stiffened as he saw other people were there. For just a split second, his eyes met Lorna's, then William's, and he gave one of his polite nods.

"Good afternoon," said Paul.

"Good God!" said William.

Without any discernible movement, Lorna saw Paul withdraw behind his protective mask.

"Good God!" said William a second time. "What the hell happened to him?"

Bile rose in Lorna's throat. "An American grenade *happened to him*!" she spat.

Iris yelped. The sound was muffled by her hand pressed over her mouth, but it seemed to help William regain his bluster.

"Didn't I tell you? Bloody Americans, leaving us to pick up the pieces of their dirty work." William was on his soapbox again. "I mean, could the Yanks not even do their job properly and spare us all such a sight? I can hardly bear to look at him!"

Lorna had to stop William talking, so she spun to face him. But Iris beat her to it.

"William, please," Iris said, laying a hand on his arm. "There's no need to be—"

At last, Iris was standing up to him.

"What nonsense!" William pulled his arm away, and to Lorna's dismay, Iris simply stepped back into silence.

Was Iris going to just accept such a dismissal? "Iris!" she cried. "Don't let him talk—"

"It's not like the chap can understand me," William carried on, with a jerk of his thumb toward Paul.

"Actually—" Lorna wanted to tell him Paul spoke very good English, but Paul was still standing quietly, no expression, no eye contact, the way he had with the sergeant the day she'd met him. Lorna realized this was Paul's protection against arrogant buffoons, so she let her words die.

"And Iris," William had already continued, "from now on, you should only visit this farm with my personal protection. Who knows what these Jerries are capable of?"

"Oh, William, really?" peeped Iris, apologetic and simpering, as if trying to make up for having ever questioned his authority. "But what about Lorna?"

"You don't need to worry about—" began Lorna, but William still wasn't listening.

"My father has tried to make farmers like Mr. Anderson see how unwise they were to accept these prisoners, but to no avail."

William was sounding more self-satisfied with every word. He looked like he was giving a sermon, mimicking his father spouting from the pulpit.

"Of course, if that is Mr. Anderson's choice, I can't be expected also to protect Lorna or his other staff."

"I'm quite sure his *other staff*," Mrs. Mack said, from the doorway, "will need no such protection, thank you very much." She had just descended the stairs, holding the wide white dress box, and she did not look happy. Like a great gray battleship, formidable and threatening, she crossed the kitchen. "Now, Iris, here's the dress for you to take to your mother. Carry it carefully, please."

Lorna helped Iris into her coat, and Mrs. Mack handed her the dress box. As Iris and William readied to go, Lorna turned to Paul. But he had left the house without another word.

Again.

Twelve

"Ladies and gentlemen, from the Hammersmith Palais in London, I give you Johnny Tredegar and his Big Band."

Nellie's gramophone, which Lorna had set carefully on a tarpaulin on the barn floor, crackled and spat.

The recorded audience clapped politely as the gravel-voiced announcer continued.

"And first, the fox-trot . . ."

The band played the opening bars of Glenn Miller's "Moonlight Serenade," and Lorna tried to forget that she was wearing her oldest dress, and that her hair was stuck fast to her head in a dozen or more pin curls in the hope that tonight she would be able to tame it into something more glamorous than its usual single braid. Instead, she was already at tonight's dance with a tall, handsome man standing in front of her, one hand resting on his shoulder and the other holding his hand. She closed her eyes and rocked forward onto the balls of her feet, setting off into the steps and turns that she and Nellie had been practicing all week—*back and back and side and close, and* . . .

Lorna knew most of the dances—the waltz, the quickstep, the fox-trot—but she was glad to have had the chance of a refresher from an accomplished dancer like Nellie. Of course, with Nellie being so short, and also dancing as the man, the pair of them had ended up tripping over each other's feet several times, collapsing in heaps of giggles on the barn floor.

Practicing alone now, Lorna was able to move without fear of tripping over Nellie, and she looked forward to being led around a real dance floor by a real man—and hopefully a man taller than Nellie. It felt so elegant, so Fred Astaire and Ginger Rogers, as if she were actually in the Hammersmith Palais. As the music swelled, Lorna stepped and spun, her breath shortening with the burst of exercise, and she realized that keeping her eyes shut might have been a mistake. The ballroom seemed to be whirling faster than she was, so as the band played its final repeat of the melody, Lorna opened her eyes to regain her balance, though she continued to turn and turn.

It took her a few spins to get accustomed to the light, to remember that she was in the Craigielaw barn, and to notice that she wasn't alone. Someone was standing silhouetted against the bright spring sunshine streaming in through the barn door. She stopped spinning and stood, dizzy, seeking out the features of the face, shadowed against the light.

Then she knew who it was. Paul. Standing, simply watching her dance.

Lorna tried to get her breath under control and lifted her hand to the scarf covering her hair to make sure the pin curls hidden under it weren't unraveling. Not that a colorful scarf would make much of a difference to how Paul must see her, more Aberlady wifey than Hollywood starlet.

Yet she couldn't work out what he was thinking, the shadow over his face made his expression indecipherable, though she was relieved that he wasn't laughing at her. But he wasn't smiling either.

The music on the gramophone finished, and the announcer spoke again.

"Ladies and gentlemen, please take your partners for the waltz."

The band struck up the familiar tune of "The Blue Danube Waltz," and Paul's eyes flickered toward the gramophone for a second as he recognized it too. Then he stepped toward her.

"Möchten Sie tanzen, Fräulein?" Paul held out his hand, palm up. "Would you like to dance?"

Lorna's left hand automatically reached for his, and he laid it gently onto his shoulder. Then Paul placed his own hand against the small of her back and drew her toward him. He took hold of a strand of Lorna's hair that had escaped the scarf and gently tucked it behind her ear. As he did so, his fingertips grazed the skin at the nape of her neck. Lorna hoped that he didn't feel the shiver that ran through her at his touch.

Then Paul took her other hand and they danced.

As the lilting *one-two-three, two-two-three* rhythm of "The Blue Danube" filled the room, Paul led Lorna around the barn in a sweeping waltz, both lifted slightly on their toes, their eyes locked on each other.

This wasn't like any dance she had ever known, certainly nothing like the dance lessons at primary school, where the girls had been tortured by the gripping fingers, sweaty palms, and tripping feet of boys like William and Craig. It wasn't even like the genteel tea dances in Tranent and Haddington when she and Iris danced together, taking the lead in turns.

This was something else entirely.

As they moved, Paul pulled her closer until their chests were almost touching. Her cardigan was open at the front, and she could hear the rustling of her cotton dress as it brushed against the rough wool of his sweater. This was the closest Lorna had ever been to Paul. His injured face was only inches from her own, but she only saw his eyes, silver gray and sparkling. Her heart was pounding, but whether this was from the exertion or from the thrill of his hands holding her body so close to his own, she wasn't sure. And at that moment, she really didn't care.

The band played its last few bars, but still they kept dancing until there was nothing but a crackling silence from the gramophone.

Paul slowed Lorna to no more than a gentle sway, and she

allowed herself to relax against him, laying her cheek onto his shoulder. As Lorna absorbed his warmth, Paul let his hand trail down the length of her spine. Their feet scarcely moved, a mere echo of the waltz, but Lorna could still feel the rhythm of the dance between them.

Eventually, they came to a gentle stop. Paul didn't release her or remove his hand from her back, but Lorna lifted her head so she could look up into his face again.

Paul bent toward her then, and she thought for one heart-stopping moment that he would kiss her. In anticipation of his touch on her lips, she offered her mouth to his, but Paul simply laid his smooth right cheek close to hers. It was close enough for his light stubble to brush her skin, for his breath to whisper warm on her ear.

"'An der schönen blauen Donau,'" he said. "'On the Beautiful Blue Danube.' One day, Lorna, I will dance this waltz with you again."

Paul pressed his cheek more firmly against hers, and perhaps his lips brushed her skin, she couldn't tell. Then he walked away.

Lorna couldn't move, couldn't think, she could do nothing but gaze at the space where Paul had been. Her whole body was frozen to the spot, yet every nerve hummed with longing for him to hold her again. Nothing existed beyond the barn, beyond the waltz, beyond Paul's arms.

"Ooh, are you dancing?"

Iris was walking toward her. William was there too, just

inside the door, looking incongruous against the backdrop of feed sacks and hay. Iris was carrying the wide white dress box.

"But dancing on your own? Oh, you poor thing." Iris sounded sympathetic.

William was staring toward the far door, and Lorna hoped against hope that he hadn't been standing there long enough to see Paul go through it. Or longer. She couldn't imagine how awful he'd be if he knew she'd been dancing with the German prisoner.

"Don't worry, though," said Iris, "you won't be dancing alone for much longer. You'll soon have all those handsome American airmen to sweep you off your feet. You lucky thing!"

"Iris!" William's voice held a clear warning.

"I only meant—"

William gave Lorna a supercilious sneer.

"Lorna wouldn't dare risk her own reputation, or her father's, by letting an American, or any other foreigner, 'sweep her off her feet,' as you so blithely put it."

Lorna stared back at William. He must have seen them, or he had just guessed. Had her shortness of breath given her away, or her flushed face? Either way, it wasn't good. She tried to keep down her rising sense of unease by adopting a nonchalant air.

"I was just practicing so I don't make a fool of myself tonight."

"Indeed." William gestured to Iris. "Well, here's the dress. We must be on our way. Mother is expecting us for tea at four o'clock."

"Yes, of course." Iris stepped forward and held out the dress box to Lorna. "I hope you like what we've done with it. Mummy said the material is so fine, it was like trying to sew the sea mist. But all the tucks have been done just like I pinned it, and the new neckline is just gorgeous. I really think it'll be perfect. I wish I could stay to see you in it, but William and I are expected . . . well, you heard."

Iris gave Lorna an apologetic half smile, and Lorna felt a twinge of annoyance that her friend was letting this arrogant so-and-so dictate where she went and when.

"We need to go, Iris." William's voice was firm. "So why don't you take the box into the house? We don't want Lorna's precious dress to get dirty, do we, not before her big night?"

Lorna caught the sarcasm in his tone, even if Iris didn't appear to.

"No, of course we don't," said Iris. "I'll pop it into the kitchen right now."

At the barn door, she turned. "And while I'm gone, don't you two start dancing behind my back or anything."

Iris trotted in the direction of the house, carefully holding the box, and Lorna self-conciously fingered the scarf round her hair. Almost immediately, William was in front of her. He grasped her round the waist and pulled her toward him, leaving barely any more room between them than Paul had done. But this was not the same.

"Just like old times," said William, with a tight grimace masquerading as a smile.

And Lorna was suddenly back in the Aberlady kirkyard again, aged eleven, being kissed for the first time. It had been a kiss too dry and stiff to be much more than a peck, an embarrassment, an aberration, but it had been her first kiss all the same. It was a kiss that Lorna had never told anyone else about, not even Iris—especially not Iris—because the kiss had been from William Urquhart. But Lorna had never forgotten it, and right now it seemed that William hadn't forgotten it either.

"What—?" Lorna rocked back on her heels to try to put some space between them.

"You need to be more careful, Lorna." William's voice was raspy, too close to her ear. "Even your father has his standards. And if you want a man you can dance with, you only need ask."

Lorna looked up at him, horrified.

"So don't you throw yourself into the arms of just anyone."

His voice had dropped even lower, almost to a croak, as he stressed his last words.

Lorna couldn't work out if he was talking about the American airmen or about Paul. Either way, she didn't care. It was none of William's business.

"Don't tell me what to do!" Lorna tried to move past him, but William stood firm in front of her. "I said, get lost!"

Lorna shoved her hands against his chest, hard enough to make him stagger back a step or two, just as Iris walked back into the barn.

"Gosh, Lorna, all this dancing has made your cheeks terribly pink," Iris said. "You should borrow some face powder from Nellie, just so you look beautiful in your dress tonight. I mean, I know you'll look beautiful, but you know how much you blush, and . . ."

Iris only then seemed to notice that Lorna hadn't responded. She looked from Lorna to William and back again.

"Everything all right?" she asked.

"Of course," William said. "Why on earth wouldn't it be? Can we go?"

He tucked his hand under Iris's elbow and guided her out into the yard.

"Cheerio, Lorna." Iris waved over her shoulder. "Have a lovely time tonight. I can't wait to hear all about it."

William too turned back. "Remember what I said, won't you? You only have to ask."

Lorna tried not to throw up as she got ready for the dance that evening, but nerves were fluttering in her stomach. Mrs. Mack had arranged for a neighbor to have the grandchildren so she could help Lorna, and Lorna was grateful to have her there, and not only because of all the tiny buttons up the back of the dress.

Iris's chic redesign had been sewn to perfection, and as

Lorna had dropped the dress over her head, it slid over her white slip as if it were made of silk. As Mrs. Mack finished the buttons and smoothed the dress down at the sides, Lorna regarded herself in the mirror. The dress hugged her waist before flowing out to her knees, and the adjustment that Iris had made on the neck—a deep heart-shaped curve—made the dress look even more stylish and grown-up.

Lorna had spent half an hour carefully removing all the pins from her hair, letting the tight little curls fall in loose waves around her neck, then gently brushing out her hair with the silver-backed hairbrush her parents had given her when she was a baby. The soft bristles found gold and red highlights that usually lay hidden in her boring brown hair, but didn't ruin the waves in it either. Several times during the week, Lorna had watched Nellie twist and pin her hair high above her forehead and roll it at the back, before she had felt confident enough to try it herself. Amazingly, today she had managed to get it right on only the third attempt, sweeping her hair across her forehead and pinning it into a roll above her left ear, then securing the rest into a neat roll all around the back.

As Iris had suggested, Lorna gratefully accepted Nellie's offer of some face powder, though she said a very firm no to the rouge. Lorna knew exactly why her cheeks had been so pink that afternoon when Iris had mentioned it—remembering those moments with Paul, and trying to forget those with William, brought an immediate flush to her cheeks again—and she didn't want to risk adding color when she knew she blushed so easily.

Lorna asked Mrs. Mack to pass her the tube of pink lipstick, the only one Lorna owned, from the nightstand drawer and then went back to the mirror. But she hesitated before putting any on. She didn't want to give her dad an excuse to spoil her evening by telling her to "wash that muck off your face." Then again, what he didn't know wouldn't hurt him, so she decided to get Nellie to help her put it on properly on the way to the bus stop and hope she didn't end up looking like a clown. In the meantime, she put just a smudge of pink onto her lips, then rubbed it until there was almost no sign.

The only thing to spoil the view now were her shoes. There had been no point in asking her dad for new ones, since there was no time to find them, and no spare clothing coupons available anyway. So she was wearing her plain black school shoes, though she had polished them until they shone. Wishing she had feet as tiny as Nellie's so she could borrow a pair of high heels, Lorna pushed herself up onto her tiptoes and turned around in front of the mirror, peering over her shoulder at the back view.

There was a light tap at the door.

"That'll be your daddy," whispered Mrs. Mack. "I think he has something for you."

Sure enough, Lorna's father was standing in the hallway with a small blue box in his hand.

Mrs. Mack stood to one side.

"Come away in," she said kindly, "and I'll leave you to it."

"No, no, Edna," he replied, stepping into the room, "please stay."

He looked at Lorna for a long time before he smiled and took a deep breath.

"Lorna Jane, I was thinking it was about time you have this."

He held the little box out toward her and gently opened up the lid so she could see.

Inside curled a fine silver chain, and lying on it was a miniature silver butterfly, its wings inset with mother-of-pearl, which flashed blue and green as the box moved in his hand.

"It belonged to your mother. I bought it for her birthday."

With trembling fingers, Lorna lifted the butterfly into her hand, letting the chain dangle. From somewhere deep in her memory, she remembered this butterfly lying against a pale, warm throat.

"I remember this necklace. I remember her wearing it."

Lorna looked up at her father and found that his eyes were as misted as her own.

"You used to love it back then," he said, "always tugging at it as she carried you about. Eventually she put it away in case you broke it. She said she'd save it for special occasions like Christmas or her birthday. But . . ."

He sighed and closed his eyes but said nothing more.

Lorna looked to Mrs. Mack for more explanation. The housekeeper had pulled her lacy handkerchief from her pocket and was dabbing at her nose.

"But then . . ." Mrs. Mack glanced at Lorna's father. "But then, there were no more birthdays, and our lovely girl was given only one more Christmas before the good

Lord came to take her to a better place."

Her father stiffened, but after a moment he opened his dark eyes, so like Lorna's own, and cleared his throat.

"But now you have a special occasion yourself, and I think she'd . . . she'd be pleased to know you were wearing it."

Lorna held the necklace out toward her father.

"Would you help me put it on, Dad?" she whispered.

"No, no, not with my fat fingers, no. This needs a woman's touch, I think."

He stepped back out into the hallway. "But I'll be downstairs when you're ready."

He looked at Lorna for a moment more, and then, with a gentle double pat on the door frame, he disappeared down the hall.

"Here, let me," said Mrs. Mack as she took the necklace from Lorna's fingers and stepped behind her.

Mrs. Mack placed the butterfly delicately at Lorna's throat and Lorna tilted her head forward as Mrs. Mack clipped the tiny clasp on the chain at the back of her neck.

"It could have been made for that dress, my dear," Mrs. Mack said, looking at Lorna's reflection. "You look so beautiful."

They went down to the kitchen a few minutes later to wait for Nellie, who was still crashing around in her room, singing loudly as she got ready. Lorna's father stood up from his chair and nodded thoughtfully as he looked Lorna up and down.

"You look bonny, very bonny indeed. Your brothers will be sorry they missed seeing you like this."

Behind Lorna, Mrs. Mack chuckled.

"They might not have let her out of the house if they had been here."

Lorna's father nodded.

"Aye, you might be right, Edna. You might be right."

Then he walked over to his seat by the fire and switched on the wireless. Before he opened his paper, however, he pulled a handkerchief from his pocket and blew his nose.

Mrs. Mack bustled about the kitchen, gathering her bags and coat. "I'm popping over to get the young lad's tea dishes before I head home, but don't you two leave before I get back."

"Let me go, Mrs. Mack," offered Lorna. "I'll get them."

"But your dress, and your nice clean shoes . . ."

"I'll be careful, don't worry. It'll only take a minute or two."

The notion that she wanted Paul to see her in her dress had come to Lorna as she'd stood in front of the mirror, and she'd initially dismissed it. Paul wasn't her dance partner tonight, he wasn't even coming, so why should it matter what he'd say when he saw her?

But it did matter, she really wanted him to see her, so before Mrs. Mack could argue again, Lorna opened the door to the yard, only to stop short.

Paul was standing there, one hand raised to knock, the other cradling two empty plates. He looked as startled as Lorna felt, but then he smiled.

"You are still here," he said quietly.

"Yes, still here." Lorna's mouth had inexplicably dried, and she had to clear her throat to speak. "Nellie's not ready yet."

"But you are . . . ," Paul began, though his eyes no longer held Lorna's. They took in her dress and her shoes, before coming to rest on the butterfly at her throat.

Lorna realized that she wasn't breathing, waiting desperately for his reaction, wanting him to smile, to say something nice. To say anything.

After minutes that were probably only seconds, Paul looked again at Lorna's face. She suddenly wished she had put on the pink lipstick properly, and instinctively licked her bottom lip to feel if any of the smudge she'd applied upstairs was still there.

"I think your American will be a very lucky man," Paul said.

Before Lorna could point out that there was no such person as *her* American, Nellie burst into the kitchen, singing "Rose-Marie" at the top of her lungs, and clip-clopped over to Lorna on her ridiculously high heels.

"Come on then, duckie! I've got my dancing shoes on, so let's go find us some gorgeous Yanks!"

Thirteen

The driver looked like he was going to have a heart attack when he saw Nellie tottering up to the bus stop, waving at him to wait. Nellie's dress was lush and red, wide-shouldered, low-cut, and figure-hugging, and it proudly pushed up her "assets" into an even more impressive cleavage than they formed naturally. Not the kind of outfit normally found on a number 126 bus to North Berwick, even on a Saturday night.

The dress ended just below the knee, but it clung to her thighs so tightly that Lorna had to hoist Nellie up onto the bottom step of the bus, causing loud giggles from Nellie—and more strangely, from the bus driver—and loud tutting from the two old ladies sitting in the front seat. Nellie could barely make it down the aisle in her red patent heels. How on earth would she dance in them?

As they sat, Lorna caught sight of Nellie's legs, which looked unusually tanned and smooth. Where had Nellie got nylon stockings? No one could buy nylons in stores at the moment, even with clothing coupons. Perhaps having an American boyfriend offered more than the obvious benefits.

Once the bus set off, Nellie instructed Lorna to apply not one, but three coats of the bright pink lipstick. Working quickly between jolts and sways as the bus hit bumps in the road and wound around corners, Lorna used the mirror in Nellie's powder compact to get the lipstick on perfectly. Nellie chatted to the bus conductress for most of the journey to East Fortune, about how she'd achieved her hairdo, gesticulating wildly as she described curling her hair into such tight waves at the back, while sweeping it up at the front into two dramatic rolls high above her forehead.

"You look just like Betty Grable, hen," cooed the conductress.

As Lorna sat listening and watching them chat, she couldn't help but wish she looked even half as beautiful as Nellie. Even with the powder and lipstick, her own face felt plain and bare, while Nellie's cheeks were rouged pink, and black mascara coated her eyelashes until they seemed inches long. And of course, there was the red lipstick.

At home, Lorna had felt radiant, as if she were the most beautiful girl in all Scotland. Then Nellie had appeared, looking stunning, sexy, and grown-up, and suddenly Lorna was only a plain bread roll sitting on a plate with a fondant fancy.

Lorna wished that Paul had not seen them side by side. He had seemed to like how Lorna looked, but then he'd seen Nellie . . . how could he think of Lorna with beautiful Nellie there?

Walking into the dance at East Fortune air base drove Paul from Lorna's mind. As she let Nellie pull her by the hand from the black-curtained hallway into the brightly lit aircraft hangar, Lorna felt as if she was being pushed back out again by the noise.

The huge room was decorated with sparkling drapes, and there was an enormous American flag down one wall. Below it, on a stepped stage, was a band bigger than Lorna could ever have imagined. Rows and rows of men, splendid in their dark blue uniforms with buttons shining, were playing "Little Brown Jug," a tune Lorna knew from the wireless. In front stood the bandleader, slender and lithe, bouncing on the balls of his feet, waving a fine white baton.

Lorna was mesmerized. How on earth would she ever be able to describe all this to Iris? This was certainly nothing like the tea dances or the village ceilidh band.

Nellie was on her tiptoes, looking for someone across the crowd. Lorna doubted they would ever find anyone. There must have been close to four hundred people in the hangar. Couples flowed around the enormous dance floor, and there were so many men, all in uniform, standing in groups against a long bar, laughing uproariously and slapping one another on the back.

There were women too, dressed to the nines, with powdered faces and dark red lipstick like Nellie. Many of them were also in uniform, yet they still managed to look unbearably elegant, and straight out of Hollywood.

Despite the crowds, Lorna found her spirits rising, buoyed by the glitter and the noise. She drew herself up on her toes, moving her hips until the soft silkiness of her dress brushed against her thighs. She lifted her chin until the pins holding her hair pressed against her neck and she squeezed her lips together searching for the reassuring oiliness that meant her pink lipstick was still in place. But even without moving, Lorna could feel the slight pressure at her throat of her mother's silver butterfly, and the warm touch of Paul's hand on the small of her back, and his breath on her cheek. . . .

"There they are!" cried Nellie, tugging Lorna's hand and waving frantically in the direction of the bar.

Lorna let Nellie pull her along in the direction of four airmen, all standing holding glasses and cigarettes. Their dress uniforms were pristine and their hair slicked back. They were all very handsome, but what struck Lorna most was that they were much older, even than Nellie, in their late twenties at least.

Before they reached the men, Nellie spun to face Lorna.

"The redhead is mine," she said, "and the dark brooding one is yours. And don't forget, I told them you're the same age as me."

Nellie gave Lorna a quick and brilliant smile, and dragged her to stand in front of the men.

The same age as Nellie? How could anyone look at Lorna and think that she was twenty? She wasn't even eighteen yet, and even with her dress, lipstick, and hair, compared to Nellie, Lorna was sure she still looked like a little girl.

Nellie looked stunning and she knew it, and the men did actually look stunned. However, all four seemed to be staring, Lorna noted with distaste, at Nellie's cleavage rather than her face as she bounced around in front of them.

"Hello, darling." Nellie gave the red-haired man a kiss full on the mouth, leaving behind a smudge of rich red lipstick, all without letting go of Lorna's wrist.

Did she think Lorna was going to run away?

Lorna realized that such an idea, right then, seemed quite appealing.

Too late.

"Gentlemen, may I present my very good friend, Miss Lorna Anderson."

The men grudgingly looked up from Nellie's chest to Lorna, and she was glad that their gaze actually met her eyes.

"Lorna, this is my fella, Charles," Nellie said, running her flat hand possessively down the front of the redhead's jacket. "Or Charming Charlie, as I always call him."

"It's very nice to meet you, Miss Anderson," Charles said, "but most folks call me Chuck." He smiled at her, his freckled skin flushing pink.

Nellie shifted Lorna to face the next man. He was darker

than Chuck and even taller.

"Lorna," Nellie twittered, "this very handsome gentleman is Eddie, and he's your partner for tonight."

"Actually, it's Ed," said the man, "not Eddie."

"Ed, Eddie, either way." Nellie shrugged.

"It's just Ed," he repeated.

"And isn't *Just Ed* divine?" Nellie said in a stage whisper to Lorna. "Like Rhett Butler from *Gone with the Wind*."

Nellie was right: Ed might have stepped straight out of the screen at the Palace Picture House. His shoulders were wide, his face tanned, chiseled, and handsome, and his deep-brown eyes regarded Lorna with an unnerving intensity.

Ed proffered a hand, and to Lorna's embarrassment, Nellie lifted Lorna's hand into his. Her hand looked delicate and pale against his tanned and strong fingers. But his hand was warm and rather damp. Not like Paul's.

"As I recall it"—Ed's voice was deep and his accent strong—"Rhett Butler was from South Carolina, whereas I'm from Georgia. But I suppose we are both good Southern gentlemen."

Beside Lorna, Nellie gave a squeak, and Lorna almost giggled. His American accent did make it sound like "gennel-men."

"And if you would care to be my Scarlett O'Hara this evening," Ed continued, breaking out a dazzlingly white smile, "then I'm sure we'll have a mighty fine time."

Ed bent and lifted her hand to his mouth, and Lorna's blush burned even hotter. His lips left a warm glow on her fingers, and Lorna wasn't sure what do next, but since Ed didn't immediately let her hand go, she left it in his. It felt strange, but exciting, and it made concentrating on Nellie's next introduction hard—had she said his name was Brian? He raised his glass to Lorna in greeting, but the fourth man, younger than the others and introduced as Pete, was already looking over Lorna's shoulder and didn't even bother to acknowledge her.

She found Ed studying her. Though his eyes didn't leave hers, they somehow also roamed over her body, and her skin prickled.

"Can I get you ladies something to drink?" Chuck said, slipping his arm around Nellie's shoulders. "I'm afraid that this here's a dry bar, no alcohol allowed, so it's a choice between lemonade and iced tea."

Tea with ice? That was strange. Lorna was used to drinking her tea hot enough to burn her tongue.

"Though perhaps we can help out you ladies with some cocktails of our own." Chuck patted his pocket and gave a throaty laugh as he winked at Lorna and then headed for the bar.

Lorna didn't know what he meant, but his easy manner had made her warm to Chuck already. She could see why Nellie liked him so much; he looked as if he would be fun to spend time with. She wasn't so sure about Ed, though. He made her feel very young and rather wanting. But still, this was her first dance, and she would enjoy it.

And for a while she did. Chuck came back quickly with

their drinks, and he whispered something to Nellie, who whispered something back. He glanced quickly at Lorna and whispered again. Nellie shook her head. The two of them casually turned their backs to Lorna, glasses in hand. After a moment or two, Chuck slipped a silver hip flask into his pants pocket before raising his glass to Nellie.

"Cheers!" he cried, and knocked back the whole glass of lemonade in two gulps.

"Bottoms up!" cried Nellie, and she gulped down her drink too. Lorna glared at Nellie, but she didn't seem to notice.

Unlike Chuck, Ed didn't bother to hide his hip flask. He held it over Lorna's glass, hesitating before pouring, and Lorna noticed that the flask quivered as if Ed was struggling to keep his hand steady. Lorna was torn for a moment. Would he think her childish if she refused the alcohol? But no, she wasn't used to drinking, so accepting his offer could only lead to trouble. She covered her glass protectively. Ed shrugged and splashed some of the clear liquid from the flask into his own lemonade. He then raised his glass toward Lorna.

"Here's to my good fortune in having the most beautiful young lady in the room to dance with."

Lorna was flattered by his gallantry, even if it was plainly not true, so she lifted her glass to his. Then she sipped the lemonade self-consciously and surveyed the packed dance floor, trying to unflush her pink face simply by force of will. What could she say that this handsome man would find both interesting and charming?

"So," she tried, with casual airiness, "do you fly the planes?"

"No, ma'am, I'm a navigator. Pete over there's our pilot, new, just arrived a day or two ago from the training camp."

He nodded toward a group of men nearby, but Lorna couldn't quite remember which one was Pete, even though she knew she'd been introduced to him only minutes before.

Ed continued to regard her but said nothing further, not even when Chuck brought Lorna a second glass of lemonade. Chuck might have winked at Ed, but then again, it might just have been a trick of the flashing mirror ball above them.

Feeling painfully awkward, Lorna studied the pink smudge on the rim of her glass before sipping the lemonade again as she cast around for something more to say.

"And, em, what sort of planes do you fly, I mean, do you . . . em . . . navigate . . . in?" Her nerves were firmly in control of her mouth now. "I saw them outside, but I'm afraid I don't know your planes very well. My brother and I used to study all the British planes when we were younger, but . . . I mean, I could see that they were bombers, but I didn't recognize what they were."

She knew she was chattering, but she couldn't work out how to shut herself up. Ed must be sick of her already.

But he continued to smile indulgently.

"Flying Fortresses. We all fly in those Boeing B-17 Flying Fortresses."

He indicated all the men in their vicinity with a circle of his cigarette, but then there was another silence.

"Gosh," said Lorna. "That's very, em . . . And have you always flown in the same plane?"

Lorna immediately knew she'd said something wrong, because Ed's smile hardened into a tight, thin line.

"We sure as heck tried to," he said, and dragged at his cigarette. "Until we found a gaping hole where our tail used to be."

Lorna swallowed hard. What had Nellie said the other evening? Something about these airmen having had a tough week?

"So we had to beg old Uncle Sam for a new one. And a new rear gunner. And a new pilot."

Ed raised his empty glass toward Pete, though if Pete saw, he ignored it.

Lorna was mortified at her crass mistake. To cover her embarrassment, she lifted her glass, but it was empty now too. Ed studied the glowing tip of his cigarette, but after a moment he lifted up his head and shook it, almost as if he were shaking raindrops from his hair. Then he gave Lorna a wide smile that was only slightly less convincing than his earlier one.

"So, Miss Lorna . . ." Instead of finishing the thought, Ed pulled at his cigarette and blew the smoke out the side of his mouth.

To Lorna's relief, Nellie appeared at her side, snatching Lorna's empty glass from her hand and handing it to a passing waiter.

"Come on, you two," Nellie giggled, gathering up Lorna with one arm and Ed with the other. "Are we here to dance, or what?"

As soon as they reached the dance floor, Nellie and Chuck flew off into the swirling crowd.

Lorna looked up into Ed's handsome face, feeling like she should apologize, but before she could say anything, Ed held out his hand to her again.

"Miss Lorna, may I have this dance?"

Perhaps to dance would be the best apology.

So she laid her hand lightly in Ed's, and he put his other hand on her waist. As they moved off into the throng, Ed pulled her close to him, shifting organza to stiff serge, and Lorna had little choice but to follow.

Ed was a very good dancer, light on his feet for such a big man, and Lorna really began to enjoy herself. When the dance allowed, they made small talk about their homes. Ed had been brought up on a cotton farm and told her his uncle grew peaches. Lorna laughed, replying that cotton and peaches seemed so much more exotic than the carrots and turnips they grew at Craigielaw.

Every so often Ed went to the bar and brought more delicious lemonade—another wonderful thing that Iris was missing—and Lorna drank hers down quickly and they danced some more.

"This doesn't taste much like lemonade, you know," she said to Ed after her fourth glass, and she leaned against him as she spoke. She was getting tired.

He gave her another matinee-idol smile and laid his hand low in that same familiar place in the small of Lorna's back, pulling her toward him until their hips touched, and Lorna found she didn't even mind. Then Ed bent to whisper a secret in her ear.

"That's because it's *American* lemonade."

That was strange. She hadn't noticed the American lemonade tasting any different from any other lemonade at the beginning of the evening, but then they were off dancing again.

When the bandleader announced that there would be a short break, everyone groaned in disappointment. Chuck and Ed brought over more drinks, along with two slices of rich and luscious chocolate cake for Nellie and Lorna, the first real chocolate cake that Lorna had tasted in years.

"Chocolate cake?" she asked Ed through a mouthful. "Does the American Air Force not understand rationing?"

"You forget, Miss Lorna, that we're Americans, which means that we always like to get what we want."

Ed dragged the tip of his little finger across the top of her cake. Without looking away from her, he licked the thick brown icing from his finger. Lorna was revolted, and for a split second she contemplated throwing the cake away, but then again, Ed was just being playful, wasn't he? And when might she get chocolate cake again?

As Lorna finished her last mouthful, Nellie demanded that they swap partners for the next dance.

Chuck wasn't as capable a dancer as his friend, but they managed without too many bumps. Lorna wondered again how Nellie could dance with him so effortlessly in those high heels. It was hard enough in Lorna's flat pumps.

As the fox-trot ended, Lorna bobbed Chuck an unsteady curtsy. Chuck giggled, sounding not unlike Nellie, and gave her a low, sweeping bow. Then Ed handed Nellie to Chuck and came to stand behind Lorna, wrapping his warm arms around her as they waited to hear what the next dance would be.

"Miss Lorna," Ed murmured against Lorna's hair, "you are not like any of Nellie's other friends that I've met. You're quite different, and far more enticing."

Lorna felt wonderfully happy and light-headed and let her head rest back against Ed's shoulder. With all the dancing and the music, and Ed's charming attentiveness, her anxieties seemed to have vanished. She barely noticed anymore the bitter smell of sweat and tobacco that she'd noticed during her first quickstep with Ed, all those dances ago.

The bandleader tapped his microphone, just like on the gramophone record.

"Ladies and gentlemen, please take your partners for 'The Blue Danube Waltz.'"

As the opening bars rose, Lorna's heart gave a jolt. All of a sudden she was back in the barn with Paul, his long cool fingers entwined with hers and his sweet breath on her cheek.

But this wasn't Paul sliding a heavy arm around her, pulling her against the rough, moist fabric of his uniform.

Lorna's stomach lurched, sickly chocolate in the back of her throat, the image of Ed's slick pink tongue licking his iced finger clean. She tried to take a step back, but Ed spun her into a waltz turn, and again she had no choice but to follow.

Lorna's head swam, and she pushed herself away from him. Suddenly Ed was absolutely enormous, horribly sweaty, and, as he pressed his stubbly cheek against hers, very, very threatening.

"I must go to the ladies', I'm sorry."

Lorna's hand flew to her mouth, and she ran for the door.

Dodging around people dancing or chatting, Lorna threw herself into the darkened hallway, then into the bright ladies' room. She dashed to the sink and clung to its cool porcelain. Then she turned on the faucet with shaking fingers and let the cold water run over her wrists.

She looked into the cracked mirror above the sink. A sheen of perspiration covered her flushed face, but even as she watched, the color drained. She was going to throw up. Running into one of the cubicles, she vomited into the toilet bowl, retching once, twice, before slumping to her knees on the cool tiled floor.

Resting her spinning head against the partition, Lorna burst into tears.

Fourteen

It took Lorna fifteen minutes to regain her sense of balance, to wash her face and hands, and to sponge the few staining spots off her dress. Several women offered their help, but Lorna was so embarrassed that she refused. She'd be fine, thank you.

Her reflection in the mirror looked ghastly, gray skin and red eyes. The lipstick had smudged and stained her chin pink. The blue-and-silver butterfly at her throat was the only thing sparkling about her now. She rinsed her mouth out again and again to get rid of the vile, sweet taste of the American lemonade and chocolate vomit. How could something so delicious going down taste so dreadful coming back up?

Lorna needed to go home. Retrieving her coat from the cloakroom, she went to find Nellie. Ed was waiting in the darkened hallway, a shadowed figure lit at random moments by the light escaping through the swing doors every time someone came and went. He was leaning casually against the wall, his hands in his pockets and a cigarette dangling from his mouth, its orange tip glowing in the gloom.

She gave him as strong a smile as she could muster.

"I'm so sorry," she said, "but I need to find Nellie and go home. I've had a lovely evening, though."

She took a gulp of air, not sure if she was lying or not, for she had been enjoying herself. So why did she feel so guilty and so unwell?

Ed didn't move.

"I think Miss Nellie left already," he drawled, without removing the cigarette from his mouth. "But why don't you c'mon with me and have another of those delicious lemonades, and we can talk some more?"

He patted the pants pocket from which he had taken his hip flask earlier in the evening and winked.

Oh God! Had he been putting spirits into her lemonade? Why hadn't she realized?

Lorna was horrified. The only alcohol she'd ever had before had been a sip of her dad's beer, but the taste was quite foul, so she'd never asked for it again. She had no idea it could taste so sweet.

Someone pushed through the doors, and Lorna tried to spot Nellie or Chuck, but she couldn't see either of them.

Was Ed right? Had Nellie gone home already, forgetting she was with Lorna?

Then Lorna's head swam again. Nellie hadn't gone home, had she? She had gone off with Chuck, leaving Lorna alone. Or rather, not alone. Worse. She had left Lorna with Ed, whose predatory gaze now roved all over Lorna's body.

"Don't you worry, Miss Lorna," he drawled—no, he slurred—as he dropped his cigarette to the floor and ground it out with his heel. "Why don't you and me find somewhere more comfortable to carry on this fine evening?"

Ed pushed himself off the wall and came to stand right beside her, swaying slightly. Licking spit off his dark red lips, he looked as if he wanted to eat her.

Lorna gave an involuntary shudder.

"No, no, I'm fine, really," she said, stepping back from Ed's smirking face. "Thank you for a very nice evening, it was lovely meeting—"

Ed lunged toward her, his mouth searching for hers. He caught hold of the soft skin at the top of her arm and tugged her toward him. It felt like the flesh would tear off the bone, and Lorna instinctively pulled back. Ed went with her, pushing his body hard into hers instead, shoving her up against the wall and forcing his leg between her knees. A sharp pain stabbed between Lorna's shoulders, and she gasped.

Ed groaned.

"Oh, yeah, you want this too."

Had he thought she was gasping with pleasure? Lorna's guts roiled, and she knew she would vomit again from the stench of his breath and the pain in her back.

As she slid along the wall to get away from the cause of

the pain, the electric light in the hallway suddenly came on. She realized fleetingly that she must have been stabbed by the light switch, which stuck out from the wall by half an inch or more. In the sudden glare, she could see Ed's face, flushed and sweaty and leering as he pinned her with his body, trapping her arm behind her back with his weight. His hand wrapped around the back of her neck, and his mouth finally found hers. Lorna wrenched her head sideways, feeling a slicing pain across her throat just as she felt his lips sucking at her chin and cheek.

She tried to cry out, but her voice betrayed her. Another sickening groan of pleasure rumbled in Ed's chest.

His free hand pulled her skirt up her thigh. His fingers scraped her skin as he fought to lift her skirt even higher. The fine material tore under his force, and anger surged inside Lorna.

This could not happen! He was not going to destroy her beautiful dress!

Lorna's fury burst. Enough! She'd grown up with two older brothers. She knew how to fight dirty.

She managed to free one hand and drove one fist hard onto Ed's nose. His head shot back and, as he overbalanced, Lorna brought up a swift knee into his groin, pushing against his chest with the flat of her hand as she did so, sending him sprawling back with a grunt. So much for the matinee idol.

Lorna grabbed her coat from where it had fallen, tore the blackout curtains aside, and threw open the door to the outside.

The light spilled out onto the darkened drill square as she tripped over the threshold and fell to her knees in the gravel.

"Hey! Get the damn light off!"

The voice of a patrolling guard was close by, but Lorna didn't make any effort to close the door behind her. She scrambled shakily to her feet, ignoring the stinging of her knees, and ran sobbing from the nightmare behind her.

No footsteps followed her, only the muffled band music coming from the hangar, so she slowed to a walk and concentrated on her breathing. The frigid night air was clearing her befuddled brain, and she gratefully gulped lungful after lungful. The shaking was now shivering, and she took a moment to put her coat on.

The top half of her body felt warmer immediately, but not her legs, and Lorna realized that her skirt was hoisted up around her hips. As she desperately tugged it back down, something dropped onto her shoe and landed with a tinkle on the gravel in front of her. She bent to pick it up and realized, as it caught the moonlight, that it was her silver butterfly. Lorna touched her throat gingerly with her fingertips, following the raw gash where the silver chain had sliced the skin, then snapped, when Ed had grabbed her. With a sob, she thrust the butterfly and broken chain into her coat pocket and headed for where she thought the gatehouse should be.

The moon was shimmering low in the sky, lighting the Flying Fortresses lined up in ranks as if ready for her inspection. Thankfully the hangar was close to the entrance of the air base, and she soon found the guard post at the front gate.

Lorna wiped the tears from her face with her coat collar, pulling it high around her chin. The soldier on duty shone his flashlight at her face, then touched his cap.

"G'night, miss. Sure you'll be all right to get home?"

"Yes, fine, thanks," Lorna lied, and walked briskly past him.

Once she was out of his sight, Lorna hesitated, trying to work out the best way back to Aberlady. She kicked herself for not asking Nellie for the exact time of the night buses that ran from the base to Haddington, where she could change to a bus that took her to Craigielaw. Well, she would have to walk in that direction and hope that if a bus came past, the driver would stop for her.

She wished she had her flashlight, but she hadn't thought she'd need it at a dance. So, alone, and with no light but the moon's silver dust, Lorna set off in the hope of home. Her tears had stopped, but the pain and shame still tore at her insides and questions whirled around her mind. What time was it? How long would it take to get home? Dad would be furious if she got back late, and worse, if she came home without Nellie. And there it was, the biggest question of all. Where was Nellie?

As Lorna walked, for the first time glad to have on her comfortable school shoes, she thrust her hands into her pockets. The delicate wings of the butterfly grew warm as she fingered them gently, but then her fingers found something else, something smooth and cool. She brushed it with her fingers, trying to work out what it could be.

She pulled the thing out of her pocket and laid it in the palm of her hand. It was the pebble she'd picked up by the shore, and in the bright silver moonlight, it looked even more gray than blue. The exact color of a certain pair of eyes, she realized with a jolt. She found the thought strangely comforting, as if someone was looking out for her in the dark of that night after all.

When she eventually arrived at the main street of Haddington, Lorna was relieved both to see one of the old green buses waiting at the stop, and to find her return bus ticket in her other pocket. The bus took forever to get to Aberlady, but the driver was kind enough to drop her right at the end of the lane to Craigielaw, so her last bit of the walk home wasn't too long on aching feet.

She paused outside the kitchen door, wiping her eyes one last time and trying to summon the courage to face her father, Nellie-less as she was.

There was a flicker of movement in the barn's upstairs window. She waited a while longer but saw nothing more. It must have just been the reflection of a high cloud floating across the moon. Suddenly sadness overcame her. How could such a perfect evening go so badly wrong?

Lorna cracked open the kitchen door, and slipping off her shoes, she crept inside. The fire had burned down to almost nothing, and her father was asleep in his chair. His head lolled, a heavy book balanced precariously on his knee.

According to the mantel clock, she hadn't missed her

curfew. It was only just approaching midnight. The relief of knowing she wouldn't have to deal with a telling off from her father about being late almost made her start crying again.

Lorna hung her coat on its hook and picked up her shoes. They were scratched and muddy, so she would have to wash them off before breakfast to save tricky questions about her journey home. Quietly, she poured herself a glass of water and walked behind her father's chair. She lightly kissed the top of his head.

"Dad, I'm back," she said softly.

Her father stirred slightly, and then jerked awake as if shocked to find that he had been asleep at all. He sat up and shook his head to clear the fog of sleep.

Before he could turn around, Lorna gave him a pat on the shoulder.

"It's been a big night, Dad," she said. "I'm off to my bed now. See you in the morning."

Lorna fled through the door and up the stairs.

"Did you have a good time?" he called just as she closed her bedroom door.

Lorna couldn't bring herself to reply.

Fifteen

The next morning, Lorna had risen early so that she and Nellie could do the milking as they'd promised, only to find that Nellie's bed had not been slept in and her father had already gone out to do it after all.

So now she sat at the kitchen table, playing with her porridge instead. At first the comfort of the warm and creamy oats had made her feel better, but after two mouthfuls she'd realized she wouldn't be able to keep much more down, so she'd given up. Her head was splitting, but she knew that it was neither a hangover, nor lack of sleep, making her feel so unbearably wretched.

Lorna was still staring into her bowl when the door creaked open. Nellie slunk in, high heels dangling from her hand. She was still wearing her red dress, but it was creased and crumpled. Her hair was all over the place and her makeup, so pristine the night before, was now smudged into dark rings halfway down her cheeks. She looked like she had barely slept. And she probably hadn't.

Nellie carefully closed the door with a soft click, and it was only as she tiptoed toward the stairs that she spotted Lorna and straightened up, flashing a self-satisfied grin.

"Morning, duckie. What's for breakfast then?"

She walked over and peered into the pot on the stove.

"Ooh, porridge, yum! I could eat a bloody horse!"

Noticing Lorna's glare, Nellie looked sheepish, like a child caught stealing cake from the pantry.

"Sorr-eeeee! But I knew you'd get home fine, clever girl that you are."

Nellie set her shoes down. Lifting the porridge ladle toward a bowl, she glanced down at her clothes.

"Oops! Now that would let the cat out of the bag, wouldn't it? Back in a tick!"

A few minutes later, Nellie had changed into floaty pink pajamas and a thick cardigan, her hair pulled up with a silk scarf. She cut a wide slice of bread, smeared it with two days' rations worth of butter, and bit into it with relish. As she chewed, she filled her bowl with porridge and poured herself a cup of tea, all the while humming, and waggling her backside to her own musical accompaniment.

Lorna was speechless. Nellie was acting as though nothing were wrong, as though last night had been the most wonderful evening. As Nellie continued to eat and hum and dance, it became clear that, for Nellie, it had been.

"Oh my poor feet." Nellie sat and propped her feet onto another chair. "I love those shoes for dancing, but my word, they're no good for walking. Not that I had to walk far. Charlie nabbed one of them Jeeps—you know, the ones with no top—and drove me all the way home."

She took another enormous bite.

"Well, not straight home, of course. We did take, em . . . a little detour."

This set her giggling. Was Nellie still drunk?

After a while, Nellie gave a big sigh.

"Oh, he's just lovely, my Charming Charlie," she said. "And what a dancer! Swept me off my toes all evening, he did."

She laughed throatily and gave Lorna a long, loaded wink with a black-ringed eye.

"And not just dancing either!"

The innuendo made Lorna feel queasy again, and she contemplated smacking Nellie in that very eye to shut her up, but it was taking all her energy to keep her stomach in place.

Nellie scratched her hair, finding something stuck in the tangled mop. She extracted a short piece of straw, almost as golden as her hair, and hooted again.

"Oops! No feather pillows on our detour last night!"

Nellie continued to chuckle as she ate, oblivious to the fact that Lorna had contributed nothing to the conversation so far. Eventually she looked up.

"So, what about you, luvvie? Did you have fun? Wasn't

your Eddie simply luscious?" She pressed forward conspiratorially. "Did you get your first kiss then?"

Suddenly all the fury and shame erupted inside Lorna's skull. She crashed back her chair and stood glaring at Nellie.

"No, no, and NO!"

Then she ran, out the door, across the yard, and down toward the beach. Her stockings snagged on the grazes on her knees, tugging at the torn skin. She ached all over.

Lorna wanted to run and run, down to the water, into the Forth. She'd take her chance with the barbed wire and mines. But before Lorna reached the sand, she slipped on a tuft of damp grass and collapsed onto a sandy hillock. Once down, she couldn't bring herself to get up again, but buried her face in the grass and wept, the furious fire inside her chilling to loathsome despair.

How long she lay there, she wasn't sure, but soon she heard footsteps, soft thuds on the muddy path, and long grass brushing against moving legs.

Instinctively, Lorna sat up, tugging at the high neck of her sweater to make sure the fine red cut around her throat remained hidden. Then she dug into her skirt pocket and pulled out a wrinkled white handkerchief. She wiped her tears and runny nose so she didn't have to explain them to her father. She had been lucky the night before, and she knew she wouldn't evade his questions again if he found her in this state. Looking up, however, she saw that it wasn't her father. It was Paul.

He was ten yards away, leaning slightly on a shepherd's

crook she recognized as her grandfather's. The red cherry-wood staff, topped with the curving ram's-horn handle, had been cleaned and polished after years of dusty neglect.

Paul seemed to be waiting for her to speak. His face was inscrutable, but the expectant silence revived Lorna's anxiety.

Could she tell him that she had had a good evening? Would he spot the lie, or did he already know it had been a nightmare? How? Anyway, she didn't owe him an explanation, did she? It wasn't like they were even friends. Not really.

And what was he doing standing there in silence? She didn't need his scorn or his sympathy, whichever he was about to offer, and she certainly didn't need his judgment.

"Go away!" she muttered. Hugging her legs to her chest, she laid her forehead on her knees. "Please leave me alone!"

She heard no movement.

Oh, bloody hell.

"Please, go away!"

Instead, she heard Paul come closer, and from the corner of her eye, she saw him crouch down a yard or so away, balancing himself with the crook.

"Let me help," he said simply. "You look sad. Or perhaps you are just tired. It was a late night, yes?"

"How do you know how late I was?" she spat into her knees.

"I waited to know you were home," he said, "to know you were safe."

"Safe," Lorna muttered. "Yes, I got home . . . *safe*."

"But you were alone. Fräulein Nellie was not with you,

and that worried me. I think your father was also not happy?"

"Dad doesn't know. He was asleep when I got in. And you'd better not tell him, or . . ."

Lorna looked up at Paul then, ready to challenge him. But he seemed so concerned, so kind, so blond, so slim—so not like Ed—that Lorna wanted to throw herself at him. He might not have the brash self-confidence and matinee-idol looks that Ed had, nor the swarthy tan and the rugged jawline, but at that moment, Paul was so much more beautiful. Even the scars on his face were comforting in their familiarity. Lorna realized that all she wanted was for Paul's arms to be around her, and for his long fingers to wind through her hair, to caress her aching head. She wanted to lay her face against his chest and to breathe him in, knowing he wouldn't smell of sweat or gin or tobacco, but of wood and hay, of compassion and of home.

But she was too ashamed to move.

"Please don't tell him," she said.

Paul nodded slightly.

"I will say nothing. But please remember, Fräulein Nellie is not like you. She is more bold and less sensible. Yes?"

How much had he guessed?

"Will we walk back now?" Paul asked quietly.

He helped her to stand, holding her as she found her balance. And then, he did not let go.

He was right. Lorna did feel very sad and very tired. She fell against him and he wrapped his arms around her in a comforting embrace, and Lorna let the night before ebb away.

He took a breath as if he were about to say something but then remained silent. Resting against his soft sweater, Lorna knew that there was one thing about the evening before that she would share with him.

"Paul?" she murmured.

"Hmmm?" His reply was more a rumble under her cheek than a sound.

"I wouldn't dance the waltz with him."

Paul didn't reply, but his arms tightened around her, and finally she could breathe again.

The next day, Mrs. Mack arrived early in the morning, eager for details of the dance, and at the school dinner break, Iris virtually pinned Lorna against the wall with questions. Lorna tried to be enthusiastic about the glamorous people, the decorations, the dancing bandleader, and the delicious lemonade—at least, the first glass of it—and the chocolate cake. She sidestepped all their questions about her partner, trying to erase Ed with mysterious smiles and half nods. Even if Iris didn't seem to notice Lorna's evasion, Mrs. Mack clearly knew something wasn't right. But being Mrs. Mack, she didn't press too hard. Lorna just hoped that she wouldn't find the blue dress stuffed in the drawer where she'd left it, at least until Lorna had had time to stitch the ragged tear.

As for Nellie, when Lorna had left for school, Nellie had been dancing across the yard behind the herd, singing loudly and lightly tapping the beat on the rumps of the nearest cows with her stick. Still infuriatingly happy.

But Paul? That was more difficult. Lorna was embarrassed by the comfort she had found in his arms. In those moments, it hadn't mattered to her who he was—her father's farmhand, a German prisoner, the enemy, a friend—all she knew was that he understood and he cared that she was hurting.

The night before, she'd dreamed of being smothered and mauled, not by another person, but by something she couldn't see but that she desperately feared. She'd lain awake trying to calm her heart until, unbidden, her imagination had flown her up into the hayloft, into the comfort of Paul's arms.

And in school today, just as Paul's fingers were caressing Lorna's neck, and his body was swaying with hers in time to "The Blue Danube Waltz," Iris had elbowed her hard, tapping on the geometry test paper sitting in front of them.

"Shhhh!" Iris had hissed. "Stop humming!"

Even so, Lorna felt unsettled about seeing Paul in person. What if he expected something more from her? Worse, what if he acted like nothing had happened at all? Knowing she could not avoid seeing him, she decided to get it over and done with.

After school, she went directly to the lambing shed. She found Paul with the older orphaned lambs. He looked up and smiled as she walked in.

"This little girl," he said, "is almost ready to go out with the others. *Nicht wahr, mein kleines Lamm?*"

He rubbed the coat of the nearest lamb.

"About yesterday . . . ," Lorna said.

Paul stood up and put his hands into his pockets.

"Yes," he said, "about yesterday."

Lorna noticed that the frown lines on his forehead were deep enough to pucker the tight, shiny skin, and she realized how little she consciously thought about the damage to his face anymore. He was now simply Paul.

"I wanted to say I'm sorry . . . ," said Lorna.

"I must give you an apology," said Paul, at exactly the same moment.

Lorna was caught by surprise. Why was Paul apologizing? She was the one who had made a fool of herself, not him.

"It was not right for me to dance with you," Paul said. "And it was not right for me to . . . at the beach."

How could he say that their dance, their "Blue Danube Waltz" in the barn, was not right? Or the way he had comforted her? How could that not have been right? And yet, wasn't that why she was apologizing too, because she knew they'd stepped over some invisible line?

"No, no, please don't apologize," she stammered. "It was right, I mean, you were right, I mean . . . I mean, yesterday was all my fault. I was upset, and sad, and you were just being kind. I should be saying thank you."

"But I should not have danced with—"

"I liked our dance."

"I liked our dance also, but it should not happen again." Paul studied her before speaking again. "Before the British allowed us to do farmwork, they gave us a paper to . . ."

Paul mimicked holding a pen and writing, looking at Lorna for the right word.

"To sign?"

"To *sign*, thank you," Paul said. "They gave us a paper to *sign*. My English was good enough to know that we promised that we would not become friendly with the Scottish people on the farms."

"Not become friendly?"

"Not make friends," Paul corrected himself as if Lorna hadn't understood his English, "with the Scottish people we will work for."

He smiled at Lorna sheepishly. "I think I broke my promise, Lorna, because I think I am now friends with you."

His smile broadened, and Lorna felt the first flush under her collar. What was Nellie's favorite American word again? Cute?

Paul's smile faded, and he was looking at her intently.

"Am I right, Lorna? Are we friends now, you and me?"

"Yes." Lorna's voice came out as a hoarse croak. "Yes. We are friends, you and me."

And suddenly the pressure lifted. They were friends, and knowing that made Lorna happy.

Within the week, spring was showing winter the door. Drowsy snowdrops huddled just out of the frost's reach, and the promise of the early blossoms stained pink the tips of the bare trees. She and Paul chatted when they saw each other, and she helped him with the lambs when her other chores allowed, but he did not try to touch her again, nor she him. And that was fine. They were just friends, after all.

But then the camp commander wrote to withdraw the overnight leave for prisoners, now that the lambing was all but over, and a truck duly arrived from Gosford one evening to take Paul back to camp. As she watched him toss his kit bag into the truck, Lorna had a moment of panic that Paul would no longer be sleeping in the Craigielaw hayloft. How could her nighttime imagination find Paul if he was sleeping in a place she'd never seen, under armed guard, where he was the enemy, a prisoner, where he was not simply Paul?

Lorna had gladly let the evening of the dance fade into a story told to her by someone else, had let the grazes on her knees heal and the nightmares recede. But she kept a firm hold on those perfect stolen moments when she'd danced with Paul in the barn, and when he'd comforted her at the beach. She realized she'd been wrong to agree with Paul that they were just friends. Watching him leave that night, she knew she wanted to be more than that.

He had said he would not dance with her a second time, but now, as the truck rumbled away, she wished desperately that he would. She wanted, more than anything, to have Paul touch her again.

Sixteen

On the Wednesday before Easter, Lorna and Iris were leaving school, and Lorna was trying not to be annoyed at Iris for deliberately hanging back, waiting for William. She paused just outside the school gate, so Iris could catch up with her.

"So you've no hug for your big brother then, Lorna Jane?"

Lorna spun round at the sound of the gloriously familiar voice. John Jo was standing only yards away. His army greatcoat was hanging open, his Glengarry cap was pushed to the back of his head, and there was a stained canvas kit bag at his feet. Lorna ran and threw herself into his arms, pushing her hands inside his coat to hug him. John Jo wrapped his arms around her, enveloping her in his warmth.

"John!" she cried. "John Jo, you're actually here?"

"No, lass. I'm just a figment of your deranged imagination." John Jo laughed. "And it's not April Fools' Day until Sunday."

Lorna looked up into John Jo's handsome face, blinking away tears.

He had changed in the year since he'd last come home on leave. He looked fit and tanned, but somehow much older. The skin was loose around his jaw, and his brown eyes were underlined with dark gray smudges, but still, Lorna was glad to see that they hadn't lost their sparkle.

"But how come they gave you leave just now?"

"Oh, you know, for special people like me—"

"John! I'm serious. We didn't expect you home anytime soon."

"It came as a surprise to us too. The lads and me had to escort a VIP cargo back to London, and they gave us a few days off for good behavior."

John Jo bent and kissed Lorna's head, and she caught a whiff of beer on his breath and pulled back, feigning incredulity.

"You've been to the pub already. You have been away from Aberlady more than a year and the first place you go is the Gowff?"

John Jo opened his arms wide, as if that would prove his innocence.

"Well, I had to find something to do for an hour until the school released you from its evil clutches, didn't I? So yes, I dropped in at the Gowff for a quick one."

John Jo belched, then smiled as Lorna waved her hand in front of her face in disgust.

"And it was the best pint, or three, that I've had in a very long time!"

John Jo glanced behind Lorna and his smile broadened even further.

"Now, who do we have here? I didn't realize they'd evacuated Hollywood while I've been away and brought all the starlets to Aberlady."

Iris choked back a giggle, flushing as red as Lorna had ever seen her. It was no secret that Iris had been besotted by John Jo since they were tiny—as Lorna had been with Gregor Murray—when she would follow him around like a puppy. Her adoration had never wavered, even when Lorna had told her she'd seen John Jo and Lizzy Crichton kissing behind the laurel bushes in the kirkyard one summer. All through those years, John Jo and his pals had gone to great lengths to escape their devotees' attentions, but now he seemed to find it quite flattering and highly amusing.

"Hello, John. How nice to see you," said Iris, speaking slow and low, enunciating each word clearly. Lorna could tell that she was trying to sound sophisticated, as if she were Ingrid Bergman in *Casablanca*, but the end result was more strangled than sultry.

John Jo stepped forward and whisked his cap off his head with a flourish. Then he took Iris's hand and kissed it before replying.

"I am all the better for seeing you, my dear."

Iris looked like she was about to explode with delight.

"Iris? Iris!"

From behind them, William appeared. Iris tried to pull her hand from John Jo's grip, but he held on to it firmly, giving her no escape.

"Look, William, Lorna's brother is home." Iris's sultry purr was now a panicked squeak. "Isn't that . . . wonderful?"

A frown creased William's high forehead.

"Yes, it's always gratifying to see our lads home from the front." William sounded like his father. He even offered a handshake to John Jo, who ignored it completely.

"Now, Iris." William sounded shaky, his nervousness beginning to show. "I think it's time to be getting home. Your mother will be expecting you."

Iris tried to extract her hand again, but John Jo wasn't giving it up.

"I think the young lady can decide for herself when she goes home, don't you?" John Jo said, with undisguised contempt.

As if to prove his point, he winked lasciviously at Iris and kissed her hand again.

Lorna was tempted to laugh as Iris seemed to both melt with pleasure and freeze in horror. But at the same time, Lorna wanted to tell John Jo to stop, to let Iris go if she wanted him to.

William stepped forward and put his hand on Iris's other arm as if to pull her away.

"I don't think that Iris . . ."

William's voice was not as strong as Lorna suspected he'd like it to be, and he was shorter than her brother by a good couple of inches; slighter too. And John Jo was a man now, and a soldier, and William was still only a schoolboy, for all his posturing. William Urquhart did not measure up to John Anderson in any way. And he knew it.

"You don't think that Iris, *what*?" John Jo's voice was suddenly hard and aggressive. "Who the hell are you, anyway?"

The two men—or rather, the man and the boy—continued to grip Iris as if she were a disputed toy train, each challenging the other to dare to hold on. Iris stood between them, glancing from one to the other.

Lorna could see that Iris was getting anxious, and indeed she could feel her own breath shortening as if it were her own hand held against her will.

"John Jo," she said quietly, "please let Iris go. And William, just step back."

William held John Jo's glare longer than Lorna had expected. After all, William had just been one of the young runts when John Jo, Gregor, and their gang had the run of the village. Ultimately, William wasn't up to it, though, and he let his hand fall from Iris's arm.

It was as if the sun had come out from behind a rain cloud. John Jo burst out laughing, raucous and loud, and let Iris's hand drop. Then he launched himself at William, clapping him on the back and shaking his hand fervently. William flinched at the strength of the handshake.

"Good lad, good lad." John Jo playfully punched William

in the chest. "I was kidding you, wasn't I? Just having a joke! You make sure you're doing the right thing with this lovely young lady. She's a pearl, you know, a diamond."

John Jo grabbed Iris's hand again, but this time he pressed it into William's hand and held it there, almost as if he were the minister marrying them.

"You look after her now, Little Willie," John Jo said earnestly, and William flinched again, "because you'll answer to me if you don't."

John Jo gave William and Iris another broad smile, patted their heads, and ushered them on their way with calls of "Bless you both."

As Iris let William walk her away, she looked back to Lorna in total confusion.

All Lorna could do was shrug. Iris must remember how much John Jo always loved to tease the younger kids. This time, however, Lorna couldn't help but think it didn't feel the same.

But whatever it was about, her John Jo was home, and she would not think about William Urquhart a second longer.

John Jo lifted his kit bag from the ground, and it clanked.

"What on earth have you got in there?"

"Just a bottle or two for the old man and me. You wouldn't have me come home empty-handed, would you?"

John Jo slung the kit bag over his shoulder, grabbed Lorna under the other arm, and they set off toward Craigielaw.

"How long are you staying? Can you stay until my birthday?"

John Jo shook his head.

"Sorry, Patch," he said, using the nickname he'd given to her as a newborn when he'd told his mother he'd rather they'd given him a puppy than a sister. "I'll have to be away by Sunday lunchtime."

Although she was disappointed, it didn't lessen Lorna's excitement that he was here.

"So we'll have to celebrate your birthday tonight instead," John Jo said, giving the bottles in his bag an extra tuneless shake. "Now, tell me what you've been up to."

At the corner, as they turned onto the High Street, something made Lorna turn back to look at the school. Mrs. Murray stood on the sidewalk, her hand to her throat, staring after them.

When she saw Lorna looking at her, Mrs. Murray lifted her hand to wave, and Lorna remembered about Gregor.

"Was Gregor with you on the escort to London?" she asked John Jo.

"Aye, he was. Why?"

He glanced back to see what Lorna was looking at and lifted his own hand to wave, but he kept on walking.

"You mean, did Gregor come home too?" he asked.

"Well, did he?"

"No, Patch," John Jo said with a sigh. "As far as I know, Gregor stayed on in London with the other lads. He'll not be coming home. Not this time."

"Poor Mrs. Murray, she'll be so disappointed," Lorna said.

"Didn't you fancy spending your leave in the bright lights of London?"

"And miss seeing my wee sister? Not a chance!" John Jo took her hand and squeezed it gently. "Lead me home, Patch, lead me home."

Lorna tucked herself under her brother's arm again. It was as though someone had just put a wad of paper under the wobbly leg of her stool. With John Jo home, she finally felt stable.

By the time their father strode into the kitchen, the kettle was whistling on the range and Lorna was shrieking at the story of the night John Jo had left his billet in the dark to have a pee, wearing only his underwear, and had then lost his way back. He'd ended up sleeping in a complete stranger's sleeping bag, someone who wasn't at all pleased to find John Jo there when he returned from sentry duty in the middle of the night.

Her dad stood by the door, looking at his son and daughter. He was trying to look stern, but Lorna could see his eyes were twinkling with delight. "Keep the noise down, you two hooligans. You'll wake the neighbors."

Then the two men came together, clapping each other in a tight embrace. Lorna's dad stood back and held his son at arm's length, looking him over with pride.

"So the Royal Scots have had enough of you, have they?"

John Jo stood up to attention with a stamp of his boots.

He brought his right hand up to his forehead in salute.

"'First of foot, right of the line . . . ,'" he began the regimental motto at the top of his voice, as if on a parade ground.

"'. . . and the pride of the British Army!'" Lorna's father bellowed back to his son, returning the salute.

"Talk about waking the neighbors," Lorna said as she poured boiling water onto the tea leaves in the pot.

"Don't you dare!" cried John Jo. "I've had enough army tea to last a lifetime. Let's have the good stuff!"

With that, he picked up his kit bag and clanked it onto the kitchen table. Within moments, he had retrieved a dozen brown bottles, which he lined up along the center of the table.

"Now that's what I call a homecoming!" John Jo declared, flipping the lid off one of the bottles with a pocketknife and offering it to his father.

Lorna's dad shook his head.

"No, lad, a cup of tea will do me fine just now, but a beer with the mince an' tatties sounds like a rare treat."

John Jo lifted the bottle in the air to toast his father before placing it to his lips and glugging down half the bottle in one swallow. He then burped loudly and threw himself down into a chair with a laugh.

Lorna filled her father's favorite mug with the strong tea and added some milk, the way he liked it. Having set it on the table beside him, she busied herself with the dishes that Mrs. Mack had left prepared for them, all the while listening to her father and brother talk. She hadn't seen her father this animated in months.

If only Sandy would come home too, then everything would be truly wonderful again.

It was only as she put the bread basket onto the table that she realized that the tea she had made for her father was still sitting there, untouched. The cream in the milk had floated to the surface as it had cooled and was forming a pale scum across the rich brown liquid.

She looked at her father. Like John Jo, he had a beer bottle in his hand, and two more empties were on flagstones at their feet.

So much for him having just one beer with his tea.

At the table, Lorna was content to let the two men discuss the farm and the village and the war, feeling no need to say much herself; she just reveled in the return of her brother and enjoyed the unconcealed happiness on her father's face.

Nellie came in from the yard a few minutes later. She gave John Jo an unusually brief and disinterested hello. Then she excused herself and disappeared up to her room, saying she wasn't hungry and wouldn't need any tea.

What was up with Nellie? When she'd met John Jo the year before, she'd been all smiles and giggles, the same flirtatious manner she used with every man she met under seventy—make that eighty. So what was wrong with her tonight?

John Jo was looking at the door through which Nellie had just gone, and he gave a long, low whistle.

"Now that is one pint-pot packed full of woman!" he said. "I wouldn't mind sharing my billet with that one!"

"John Joseph, mind yourself, now!" said Lorna's father, though a smile played on his mouth. "I don't need anyone meddling with my farmhands. It's all I can do to get them to do their work, without distractions from my own children."

Although the comment was addressed to John Jo, their father glanced at Lorna as he finished. He was obviously talking about Nellie, but could he be including Paul in that comment too? What had her dad noticed?

To cover her embarrassment, Lorna turned the subject back to Nellie.

"Anyway, Nellie's already taken. She's been seeing one of those American airmen over at East Fortune for weeks now."

"Bloody Yanks!" John Jo groaned. "They're everywhere. London's swarming with them, flashing money around and acting like it's their God-given right to take all the prettiest girls."

He lifted another bottle.

"You know what they say about the Yanks, Lorna, don't you?"

Lorna shook her head.

"That they're overpaid, oversexed, and over here!"

He threw his head back in a guffaw, and Lorna's father joined in the laughter. An image flashed into her mind of Ed's wet mouth forcing its way onto her own, and she shuddered.

"Talking of farmhands, how is Old Lachie these days?" John Jo asked his father. "Still on his feet and breathing?

That's one of your farmhands I won't be tempted to meddle with."

Lorna waited for her father to reply, but he was studying the mince and mashed potatoes on his plate instead. Hadn't he told her brother yet that Old Lachie had retired months ago? After a moment or two, her father glanced at Lorna and then answered John Jo's question slowly and deliberately.

"Aye, Lachie's doing fine, lad, but he took quite a tumble out in the Glebe field before Christmas and hurt his hip. The doctor told him to retire. He still drops by to say hello, though I'm surprised you didn't see him in the Gowff earlier on, since he mostly lives in there now."

Her dad chuckled, but then looked sideways at John Jo.

"So who's minding the sheep then, Dad?" asked John Jo. "Don't tell me you're trying to do it all yourself with nobody but the little crumpet upstairs."

"No, no," Lorna's father replied. "The ministry sent us someone—"

"Another delicious Land Girl?" John Jo looked in the direction Nellie had disappeared. "Oho, you old goat! Two for the price of one, eh?"

Her father's face darkened.

"No," he said sharply. "Not another lassie. The ministry sent us a young lad from Gosford Camp."

Lorna could see her father was nervous about revealing that there was a German soldier working on the farm. She could understand why—hadn't she been upset by the idea herself at first?—but she'd never known her father to kow-tow to anyone else's opinion before. How badly did he expect John Jo to react?

"Gosford Camp?" John Jo said. "Didn't I hear they'd thrown the army out and locked up a bunch of Germans in there?"

"Aye, that's right," Lorna's father said. "But none of the prisoners are dangerous, so they've put them out to the farms to work for their keep. We've got one of them comes here every day . . . a young lad . . . name of Paul Bogel."

"Vogel," Lorna corrected him before she could stop herself.

Her dad flashed her a look, and she could have bitten her tongue. She waited, like her father, for her brother to explode with fury at the idea of a German on his farm.

To Lorna's astonishment, John Jo's head went back again in another belly laugh, then he bent forward, slapping his hand on the table. Lorna and her father looked at each other in reserved surprise.

"Well, if that doesn't beat it all," John Jo said. "Here's me, sent away to fight the evil Hun for years on end, only to find him sneaking into my own home by the back door! That's just rich!" He continued to laugh, but Lorna couldn't join him. He was being loud and boisterous, perhaps, but John Jo was lacking one thing—humor. There was a rawness she didn't recognize, a brittle tone she didn't like. Beside Lorna, her father sat straight-faced and silent, leaving his son to enjoy his big joke alone.

Lorna served Mrs. Mack's stewed apples for dessert. Within two mouthfuls, the tension had relaxed, and John Jo's stories—truly funny this time—had lightened the mood again. The three of them spent the rest of the evening reminiscing and teasing as if nothing about a German prisoner had been said.

Her father retired to bed only a little later than usual. Lorna tidied up the kitchen and lined up ten empty bottles by the back door so she could take them back to the little window behind the Gowff and get the threepence return on each of them. When Lorna suggested John Jo should go to bed too, he waved her away with his bottle.

"I'm fine, Patch, I'll just sit here a few minutes more. On you go."

So Lorna left him sitting in their father's chair, staring into the fire, eyelids drooping, and went upstairs to bed.

It was wonderful to have John Jo home again, but she'd seen a hard edge to him today she'd never seen before, a hint of hidden menace that unnerved her. Lorna couldn't help feeling this visit might not be all that she'd hoped it would be.

Seventeen

On Thursday after breakfast, John Jo told Lorna that he and their father would be going to Dunbar in the afternoon to see the feed merchant. Lorna had a feeling they would also visit a few of the farms and pubs where John Jo was best known. Though part of her wished she could go too, and spend more time with her brother, she was also pleased to know they would be away from the farm till teatime at least.

Over the last week, after she'd come home from school and finished her chores, she'd spent an hour or so helping Paul with his work in the vegetable garden or the lambing shed, until she had to go to serve up the tea, and Lorna enjoyed this brief time together.

That afternoon, she headed out with a bowl of kitchen scraps to feed to the chickens and was delighted to find Paul at the chicken run, filling a hole under the wire netting where a fox had been digging. Caddy, the young collie, sniffed busily around. When she heard Lorna approach, she dashed over with a quick bark and gave Lorna's shoes, skirt, and the bowl of scraps a cursory sniff before returning to the more interesting smells near Paul.

"Once upon a time, Caddy-girl," said Lorna, "you and I were inseparable. Look at you now, you fickle *besom*."

Paul looked up from where he was crouched and smirked, nodding at the china bowl in her hands.

"My tea is ready early tonight, yes?"

Lorna regarded the chopped mess of potato and carrot peelings, apple cores, and goodness knew what else and grimaced.

"I think there may be something tastier still to come, but if you're hungry now . . ."

She moved toward Paul, holding the bowl at an angle as if to pour the scraps over his head, but she swerved away at the last second, opening the catch on the gate instead.

"*Das wagst du nicht,*" said Paul, sitting back onto his heels and shaking his head. Was there a wicked glimmer in his eye?

"I beg your pardon?" Lorna giggled. "You called me a *what*?"

"I said, 'You wouldn't dare.'"

"Oh, wouldn't I?"

Lorna picked up a handful of the slimy scraps and made to throw it at Paul. He laughed and put up an arm to protect himself, but instead, Lorna just tossed the scraps into the run toward the chickens, which all came over bustling and pecking as if they hadn't been fed in a week.

"I told you that you would not dare," singsonged Paul, as Lorna emptied out the remainder of the peelings, and then shut the gate and slid the wide wooden catch back into place.

"Ha! Don't count on it. I'll get you next time." Lorna loved seeing Paul relaxed and having fun, almost as if they shared a normal life.

"Can I help you?" she offered.

"Not right now," said Paul, "but in a minute, yes, if you have time."

"Of course. I'd be happy to."

If only he knew how happy.

Lorna walked over and set the bowl on top of the bomb shelter that her dad and John Jo had built between the chicken run and the barn back in 1939. They'd joked as they worked that this was an Anderson Shelter not only because it had been introduced by the government minister, Sir John Anderson, but also because it was quite literally, the Andersons' shelter. It was a corrugated iron arch sunk several feet into the ground, with soil piled along its sides to deaden the impact of any bombs falling nearby. In the early years of the war, Lorna and the others had run regularly from the house when they heard the air-raid sirens, tugging on boots and coats over their pajamas as they jumped down the four steps into the shelter. But there hadn't been an air raid for almost two years, and even if the siren sounded now, Lorna doubted they'd run to the shelter. It was flooded knee-deep with rainwater last time she looked.

The day was mild, so Lorna took off her cardigan and folded it onto the corrugated iron surface before hoisting herself up on top to sit. And to watch Paul.

Caddy suddenly set off toward the woods with her nose to the ground, only to sprint back again. After doing this three times, the dog settled near Paul, resting but not relaxed, prepared to tackle any intruder if she needed to.

Lorna smiled wryly. The puppy had fallen for Paul as hard as Lorna had. Poor little thing.

Paul stamped on the earth he'd packed into the hole, then unfurled a roll of chicken wire, kneeling on it to flatten it out.

"Would you pass the cutters to me, please?" he asked, pointing to a pile of tools nearby.

As Lorna jumped down, her foot caught in the tufty grass, and though she managed to get her hands up to break her fall, she hit the dirt hard.

"Oh God," she croaked, as the gravel bit into her hands and knees.

Paul was at her side, quickly followed by Caddy, who gave a sharp bark of concern. Lorna tried to catch her breath and calm her racing heart as she sat and clutched at her knees, trying to push the pain back in.

She hadn't bothered with stockings that morning because it was so mild. So when she lifted her hands, her palms came away covered in blood and grit.

Were her hands bleeding, or her knees, or both?

On closer inspection, her hands had got off lightly. On

her knees, however, the fall had torn open the soft pink scar tissue left by her fall after the dance. Putting her hands back over the grazes, she swallowed hard against the tears.

Paul lifted one of her hands to study the damage. He pushed Caddy's inquisitive nose away and brushed the tiny pieces of grit from her palms with delicate fingers.

"Ooh, that is looking very hurtful . . . very sore," he corrected himself, then reached out a hand and steadied her leg while he studied the damage. "We must wash out the dirt quickly."

Before Lorna could stop him, Paul stood up and stripped off his shirt, leaving him in his once-white undershirt. He doused the tail of the shirt in water from his canteen and gently dabbed at the graze on her right knee, dripping water onto it as he did so.

Lorna gasped slightly at the sting, and Caddy barked again.

"Oh, be quiet, you silly dog!" she muttered.

Paul smiled as he pushed the dog away.

"She only wants to help," he said.

As he continued to wipe grit away with the wet shirt, Lorna let herself be distracted from the pain by the taut muscle of Paul's bicep moving only inches away. Her pulse was still racing, but now for a very different reason.

Lorna could smell him, that clean earthy farm scent, and she dropped her face closer into the curve of his neck, savoring the scent of him. She wanted to run her hands over his smooth, bare skin and to pull his pale pink, soft, and inviting lips onto hers. But she knew she shouldn't.

Lorna let out a long sigh.

Paul must have heard her or perhaps he felt her breath on his skin, because he lifted his head and his gray eyes met hers.

"I hurt you?" he barely whispered.

Lorna shook her head very slightly. Even when they had danced, she hadn't been this close to him, so close to the damaged skin on his face. Again she wondered what pain Paul had suffered.

She lifted her hand until her fingertips were barely a touch away from his damaged cheek. "Does it still hurt?"

He gave her a rueful smile.

"The skin does not hurt anymore," Paul said softly. "But my lost face, my vain-ness—my *vanity*—may never recover."

He smiled with self-mockery.

"I'm serious," said Lorna.

"I know. If it is cold, or if it gets hit, then yes, it hurts. I think I will never be a boxer."

Paul smiled again, and Lorna lost all sense of will. She wanted to wrap herself in his arms and feel his lips hard against her own.

Beside them, Caddy barked, but Lorna ignored her, desperate to stay locked in Paul's gaze. But when she heard a low growl in the dog's chest and a crunch of boot on gravel, she looked over his shoulder at what Caddy had already seen.

Lorna almost fell backward.

John Jo was standing not six yards away from them, arms crossed, legs apart, a brick wall of muscled fury.

"Get your filthy hands off my sister!" he roared.

Lorna scrambled to her feet. "John Jo, what are you doing back so early? Where's Dad?"

She could feel the embarrassment of being caught so close to Paul flooding her face, but John Jo couldn't have seen her flush because he wasn't looking at her. His dark eyes were narrowed at Paul.

Paul stood up and took a step away from Lorna.

Caddy, still growling, moved to Paul's side. Unlike her mother, Caddy was too young to know who this big man was. John Jo hadn't been back to Craigielaw since she was born, and she clearly didn't trust him.

Lorna instinctively moved toward John Jo, putting herself directly between him and Paul. Did she trust her brother as little as the dog did?

Paul, however, stepped out from behind her and walked toward John Jo, right arm outstretched, offering a hand to shake.

"Hello, I am Paul Vogel. I am pleased to meet you."

John Jo glanced down at Paul's proffered hand but didn't take it.

"Christ! I heard you were ugly—"

"John!" Lorna was horrified.

"Get into the house, Lorna!" John Jo bellowed.

"John Jo, stop this, please." Lorna again stepped between the two men, close enough to her brother to catch the reek of the pub on his uniform—stale beer and cigarette smoke. "Paul was just helping me. I hurt myself—"

"Into the house, NOW!"

Caddy barked another sharp warning, but John Jo paid no attention. He just stood, swaying slightly, muscles locked so tight he looked like he might explode.

Lorna was scared. She had seen John Jo drunk before, but never this angry, his face red and contorted, almost unrecognizable, his fists balled at his sides.

"John, stop it! Please. You've got it all wrong! And where's Dad?"

The dog barked again.

"Caddy! Here!" Paul patted the side of his leg, and though she went to stand beside him, Caddy was focused on the intruder.

"Lorna fell." Paul's voice was calm but firm. "I cleaned the wound. That is all. If you allow her to—"

John Jo lunged forward, right into Paul's face. His bulky, dark frame cast an ominous shadow over Paul, so pale and blond.

"Don't you *dare* tell me what to do, on my own farm, in my own home!"

Spit flew from John Jo's mouth, spattering his chin. For a moment he reminded Lorna of a rabid dog, slavering and vicious.

"You are here to work," he snarled at Paul, "not to back-chat me and NOT to put your filthy Hun hands on my sister. So get on with that damn fence, and if I see you within half a mile of her again, I will tear the other half of your ugly face off."

John Jo lifted his fist as if to strike Paul, but Paul didn't flinch. He raised a hand, his palm open in a conciliatory gesture. For what seemed like a year, the two men stood facing each other, carved from the same granite as the barn wall behind them.

With a final growl of contempt, John Jo grabbed Lorna by the arm, exactly where another man's bruises had so recently faded, and pulled her away.

Now it was Paul who looked angry.

"Let Lorna go," he said firmly, following them. "She did nothing wrong. Let her go."

Without releasing Lorna's arm, John Jo thrust the flat of his other hand into Paul's chest and shoved him backward, sending Paul sprawling. A grunt of air was forced from Paul's lungs, and then there was a sickening crack as his head hit the ground.

"Paul!" Lorna cried, struggling to free herself, but John Jo dragged her back toward the house. Her embarrassment and fear vanished, replaced by a hot flare of anger.

"What are you doing? You've hurt him! John Jo, for God's sake, let me go!"

The dog was now crouched beside Paul, barking furiously and teeth bared, ready to attack at his first signal.

As John Jo dragged her to the corner of the house, Lorna watched as Paul pushed himself up onto his knees unsteadily and pressed his hand to his head, wincing.

Lorna swung at her brother with her free hand, trying to push him away, but his grip was like steel. The stench of beer and tobacco threw her back to Ed and the dark hallway and to the sickening, petrifying fear.

But Lorna wasn't scared now, she was bloody furious.

"Stop!" she shrieked. "You pig! You are a stinking bloody mucking pig, John Anderson. Now LET. ME. GO!"

As John Jo threw open the kitchen door, Caddy came tearing across the yard after them, snarling and yapping. Pushing Lorna inside, John Jo aimed a kick at the dog. It glanced off her flank, but still sent her sliding over the cobbles.

The dog yelped as John Jo slammed the kitchen door behind them and locked it. She couldn't believe that he had just kicked the dog, that he would kick any dog. John Jo loved dogs, he always had. He'd wept for days when Bess—her father's old sheepdog and Caddy's great-grandmother—had died after being hit by a car in the lane. The John Jo she knew would never have deliberately hurt any dog, any animal.

So who was this man in front of her now? She didn't even know.

"You beast!" she yelled. "She's only a puppy, for God's sake. You didn't need to kick her! Dad'll kill you for that."

"Well, Dad's not here, and that bitch is a working dog, not a pet. No dog should turn on her master to protect an outsider."

"You're not her master. She doesn't even know you."

"Aye, well, she'll know me soon enough. When I'm back, these dogs will learn to work damn hard or they will feel my boot. And the same goes for every other *traitor* on this farm."

The two of them stood glaring at each other, as they had

done on so many occasions as children, but this fight was something else entirely.

"Traitor?" she spat. "You are calling me a *traitor*? Are you really that drunk?"

John Jo hissed through his teeth, "I have not spent the last four years sitting in mudholes, getting my arse shot at by Jerry, to come back here and find my little sister getting felt up by one of those bastards."

"Getting felt up? What are you talking about?" she screeched, her throat grating raw. "For goodness' sake, Paul was wiping blood off my knee because I fell. He wasn't groping me."

"Yeah?" John Jo shouted back. "Well, only because I stopped him. And I am telling you right now, if I ever see that dirty filthy Hun anywhere near you, or if I catch him even *looking* at you, I will rip his head off. Do you hear me?"

"How dare you!"

"And as for you, have you lost your bloody mind, or your eyesight? I don't know how you can even bear to look at him. It's just disgusting!"

Lorna was shocked by the manic hatred distorting the face of her much-missed brother.

"He is not disgusting, he is *burned*," she screamed. "His face was *burned* in an explosion caused by Allied soldiers just like you. And it doesn't matter if he looks that way, because inside he is a nicer and kinder man than you could ever be."

"So you do fancy him. My God! It's *you* who's the freak, not him. You get your kicks from letting some Hun bastard stick his filthy hand up your skirt!"

"You are such a hypocrite, as well as a dirty pig!" Lorna screamed. "You seemed happy enough to stick *your* filthy hand up Lizzy Crichton's skirt, and your tongue in her mouth, didn't you?"

John Jo's furious face registered the shock she had hoped for.

"Yes, I saw you, all over each other. *That* was disgusting! But of course, that was just fine, because Lizzy was the love of your life, wasn't she?"

Lorna's fury was so intense, she didn't even hesitate before she delivered the deathblow.

"Or she was, right up until she dumped you for that short-arsed Welsh sailor!"

John Jo recoiled as if she'd slapped him.

"Or was it for the American soldier? Or the Polish pilot? She certainly had them all, from what I heard."

"You little bitch!" he spat, but Lorna hadn't finished.

"And for your information, Mr. High and Bloody Mighty, Paul was not feeling me up. Paul has never even touched me."

The lie registered in Lorna's mind, but she hoped it didn't show on her face.

"And even if he had, and even if I wanted him to, it would be *none of your damn business*! Don't you dare come in here, John Joseph Anderson, shouting the odds at me. You have no right. No right at all! So go on, piss off back to your bloody mudholes and let Jerry shoot the arse off you some more."

Lorna's throat was agonizingly hoarse now, and she had to

fight to get any volume at all.

"And if you never come back? Well, I DON'T CARE!"

Lorna pushed past her brother, but he stepped in her way. She tried to move toward the scullery, but again, he blocked her. Suddenly feeling tears coming and determined he would not see them, Lorna turned and crashed up the stairs to her bedroom. Slamming the door behind her, she sat down hard on the bed, the iron springs of the mattress screaming under the sudden weight.

She took off her shoes, throwing one hard at the wall, then the other. Lying down, flat on her face, she pulled the pillow over her head and screamed the worst swearwords she could muster into her mattress.

She thought she heard banging on the kitchen door and pulled the pillow off, listening for the knocks to come again, but there was nothing. A short while later, however, the kitchen door slammed again and the percussive ring of army boots stamping away from the house echoed around the farmyard.

"Just piss off then, you git!" she tried to shout, but her throat could barely croak the words.

Then the tears finally came, and the guilt flooded through her.

How could she have said such a terrible thing to John Jo? Of course she cared about what happened to him. But then again, he had no right to treat her like that. She and Paul hadn't been doing anything wrong.

Not yet, anyway.

And what about Paul? Was he okay? Was his head badly hurt? Would he ever want to talk to her again? How could John Jo have said those awful things about Paul's face? How could he? She had to find Paul and apologize, to see if he was okay. But how could she face him?

At that moment, she heard the roar of the army truck in the farmyard.

Parp! Parp!

The driver was clearly keen to be off.

Parp! Parp!

She jumped to her window and looked down into the yard just as Paul climbed onboard and slammed the tailboard. Then the truck roared off up the lane.

Paul was gone and she had missed her chance to say sorry. Lorna lay down on her bed and wept herself to sleep.

Eighteen

When Lorna woke up, it was dark, though pale moonlight filtered through the window. The bedside clock read almost midnight. She felt wrung out, though calmer, as if a more rational voice had soothed her misery as she slept. Yes, she would have to face Paul when he returned to the farm in the morning, but first she needed to talk to John Jo. He would be leaving again the day after tomorrow, and she couldn't let him leave without apologizing.

She had to make him realize, though, that she would be eighteen in less than two weeks, an adult, and he would have no right to interfere again.

Lorna padded into the upstairs hallway. The door of John Jo's room was ajar and the room dark, so she went down to the kitchen, but it was empty as well. The dinner dishes had been washed and stacked to dry, and the house was completely quiet, but the kitchen lamp was still on. John Jo's big army boots were not beside the others by the door.

He couldn't still be down at the pub, because last orders would have been called a couple of hours ago. All the same, she slipped her bare feet into her shoes and walked down to the gate.

It was a cold, clear night, and the moon was full—what they called a "bomber's moon"—so the road was well lit, but empty. Panic rose inside Lorna. She ran back to the house and up the stairs, pushing the door of John Jo's bedroom fully open. The room had been stripped. Not one piece of John Jo's uniform remained, no kit bag, no dirty socks and undershirts tossed in the corner, and no pile of freshly ironed laundry stacked by Mrs. Mack on the chair.

John Jo had gone, back to his unit and the war, and Lorna was the one who had driven him away. She went to her room. How would she tell her father? How could she admit what had happened, what she'd said that made him leave? Without bothering to change into a nightdress, Lorna lay down, staring at the moonlight on the wall until wretched sleep eventually came again.

Lorna woke to raised voices. Thinking John Jo had come back, she ran to the window and looked out.

It wasn't John Jo. It was her father shouting at two of the cows, which had wandered away from the milking line and were headed for the vegetable garden. Nellie, who should have been supervising them, was bent double over a tin bucket, her body jerking as she vomited into it.

Lorna hurried downstairs, stuffing her feet into her shoes and grabbing her coat as she went. By the time Lorna reached her, Nellie was leaning heavily against the wall, her face gray and shining with sweat. She was shivering, so Lorna wrapped her coat around Nellie's shoulders.

"Are you feeling poorly, Nellie? Because you look awful," Lorna said. "What have you eaten recently?"

Nellie shook her head.

"I've hardly eaten anything for days." Her voice was pathetic. "I've been feeling so sick."

Nellie glanced down at the tin bucket and heaved again.

"I think you should go back to bed right now," Lorna said, rubbing Nellie's back.

"No, no, really, I'll be fine," Nellie said, wiping the sleeve of Lorna's coat across her forehead. "I've the milking to do."

Lorna looked pleadingly at her father, who was herding the stray cows into the parlor with the others.

"Dad, will you tell Nellie to go back to bed? I'll help her upstairs and come and do the milking instead."

"I'll not have you late for school," he grumped.

"But it's Good Friday." With all yesterday's drama, Lorna had forgotten that herself until now. "No school today, so I've loads of time. And remember, church doesn't start until ten, not that you'll be coming with me, of course."

Lorna's father tutted loudly.

"Fine! We'll let Princess Nellie off this once, but you'll not do it alone. Away up and get your brother out of his bed now so he can help. You might have to fire off a shotgun to wake him, though. He was back so late from the pub, I gave up waiting and went to my bed."

It took a moment for Lorna to realize that Dad didn't know John Jo had gone. Goose bumps rose on her arms. Her father would hate her if he knew why. And he would be right to.

She couldn't tell him the truth.

"But Dad, did John Jo not tell you?" Her throat was rough as she spoke. "A message came saying he was needed back immediately, an emergency."

Lorna busied herself doing up the buttons on the coat around Nellie so she didn't have to look at her dad.

"He got the bus back up to Edinburgh at teatime, but he must have missed you." Lorna could only imagine the disappointment that must be crossing her father's face. "Where did you go anyway, after you dropped him off? John Jo didn't tell me."

When her dad didn't answer, Lorna put her arm around Nellie and guided her toward the house.

"I'll be back in a minute," she said over her shoulder. Still her father didn't reply.

Once Nellie was settled with a cup of tea, Lorna headed back outside. She picked up the bucket Nellie had thrown up in, rinsed it out, and left it to be disinfected at the end of milking. Having washed her hands, Lorna fetched a couple of clean buckets from the shelf and got on with the job.

It felt good to concentrate on something. She didn't mind doing the milking now that it was warmer—she had been glad to escape it through the bitter dark mornings of winter. There was a welcoming stink to the milking parlor, one of the familiarly comforting smells that always clung to her father's clothes and skin. And the rhythm of the milking saved her mind from wandering back to the awfulness of the previous afternoon. She had almost finished when she heard boots on the cobbled floor. Lorna froze. It was John Jo—he'd come back! But when they appeared on the other side of the cow, the boots were Paul's.

She hadn't heard the truck, and she hadn't had a moment to prepare. She'd have to apologize for John Jo's behavior. But how?

Until she could work that out, she would keep her head lowered and pretend not to have seen him.

Paul stood there for almost a full minute, but still Lorna did not lift her head.

"Your father told me to help you," he said finally.

Lorna searched those words for anger or upset, but Paul's tone was neutral, as if their last meeting had been nothing but everyday.

She could put it off no longer, so she looked up into Paul's eyes, or rather into his right eye. The left one was swollen completely shut. The scarred and shiny skin was puffed even tighter and had darkened into a dreadful red-and-purple bruise, making the rest of Paul's skin seem even paler.

"Oh my God, Paul, your eye!"

She leaped to her feet, the low milking stool toppling over with a bang.

Paul shrugged.

"It will mend quickly. My face has healed before."

He gave her a slight wry smile, clearly knowing she didn't believe a word.

"Did that happen when you fell? When John Jo pushed you . . . ?"

But that couldn't be right. He had banged the side of his head as he hit the ground, not his face.

Paul walked over to wash his hands at the sink. Lorna noticed a raw red patch of blood-matted hair just above his right ear and knew for sure that his swollen eye couldn't have been caused by the fall.

"He hit you, didn't he? My brother punched you. Tell me, that's what happened, wasn't it?"

He didn't respond, but put his hands under the spout to rinse off the carbolic soap lather.

"Paul, tell me!"

She grabbed his sleeve and tugged it hard enough to make him turn around and face her, his hands dripping. His silence told her she was right.

"Why didn't you fight back?" she demanded. "If it had been me, I would have punched him so hard . . ."

She balled her hands into fists as if to show him, and Paul took hold of them with wet fingers.

His knuckles were crowned with swollen and bloody grazes.

"Who says that I did not?" he said, gazing at her. "Your brother loves you. He wants to protect you, as he has spent years protecting his country from men like me. Remember, Lorna, he was trained to kill Germans. I am his enemy, so perhaps I was lucky to get from him only a blue eye."

"A *black* eye," Lorna corrected him tersely. "That git gave you a *black* eye."

"*Ein blaues Auge* in German, but a *black* eye in English. Interesting." Paul looked thoughtful, then shrugged again. "And I think that if your brother had seen you sitting as we were with any man, even a British man, then he would have given him a black or blue eye too."

He smiled, but then winced. "Do not be angry with him. If I found my little sister like that, I think I would do the same. We brothers are born with a job to do."

"What job?" asked Lorna. "To torture their sisters?"

"No, Lorna"—Paul's voice was wistful—"to stop you growing up. Because if you do, how can John ever protect you again?"

Lorna didn't want to listen to his words. They made the guilt of her fight with John Jo even more painful.

"But he's been away for more than four years now—that's not what I call protecting me!"

Paul shook his head and sighed.

"To me, when my sister is at home with my mother, she is

safe. Protected. That is why I can do my job and not worry about her."

Lorna put her hand softly on his arm.

"But you do worry about Lilli, don't you? And about your mother. Don't you wish you could go back to Dresden to see them?"

Sadness flashed in Paul's face, and he looked away as if trying to hide it. Lorna immediately regretted the question.

"I would love to see them, more than anything. *Almost* anything," Paul eventually replied, his smile gone. "But do you think the Third Reich would let me go home? If I escaped from this country and returned to Germany, they would make me be a soldier again, and I do not want to do that."

Lorna lifted her hand to Paul's twice-damaged face and gently cradled the side of his head where the bloody bruise bulged. With her other hand, she covered his swollen eye, so sorry to have been the cause of this pain.

Paul took her hands and pressed them to his chest.

"I am not a coward, Lorna, but I will not fight for a government I do not believe in. So I will wait and when the war is over, I will go home, and I will see my family again. As your brothers will."

Paul hesitated, then bent toward Lorna.

"Until then, I will stay in the most beautiful place in the world"—his lips almost touched her, his voice just a breath—"I will stay here, in Aberlady, with you."

Then he kissed her, warm lips upon her cheek.

Lorna swayed, but Paul drew her into an embrace of such gentleness that a shiver ran through her whole body.

Could Paul feel her trembling under his hands as they traced delicate patterns across her shoulders? And when he rested his palm there—oh, yes, there!—warm and indulgent, in the small of her back as he had done when they'd waltzed? Then Paul's lips were against her hair, her ear, her neck. His breath brushed her throat just before his lips did.

Lorna had to work to release the air from her lungs, letting it out slowly and softly. Paul must have felt it play against his skin, as she had felt his, because his lips hesitated, just for a second or two, before continuing their slow path along her jawline.

Suddenly, Lorna knew she could not wait any longer. She turned her face toward him until her mouth found his. She pressed her lips onto his, and they parted thrillingly under her pressure and followed where she led.

Paul's hand was in her hair then, and on her back, and at her waist, and . . . and Lorna could not think or breathe or do anything else but lean her body against his, and kiss him and kiss him and kiss him.

A while later, as Paul stepped back and Lorna could see his face, his smile reappeared and his undamaged eye sparkled.

"And when I do get home, I will certainly punch the eye of any man I catch doing *that* with my little sister."

Nineteen

"So has he kissed you yet?"

"Oh my goodness, Lorna, of course he has!"

"Well, with him being the minister's son, I just wondered . . ."

Iris swiped at Lorna with her white cotton gloves.

"That doesn't make him a nun, you know."

"That's a shame; I can quite see your William in a black and white frock." Lorna pulled off her scarf and draped it over her hair like a nun's veil. "Very fetching, don't you think?"

Iris stuffed her gloves into her pocket and put her hands, palms together, in front of her as if in prayer. Turning her face heavenward, she warbled an off-key "Ave Maria."

"Do you remember Deanna Durbin singing that in, oh,

what was the picture?" Lorna asked. "I know, *Mad about Music*! We went to see it for my tenth birthday, at the Palace. Remember?"

"Yes!" Iris clapped her hands. "My mum took us up on the train and we had tea at Mackie's afterward. *Mmmm!* What I wouldn't give for one of those chocolate cakes right now!"

They were walking back to the farm for dinner after the Good Friday service, and Lorna felt closer to Iris than she had done in ages. With everything that had happened with the dance, with John Jo, and of course, with Paul, she'd missed being able to talk to Iris—this Iris, *her* Iris—so much.

"I gave up chocolate cake for Lent, don't you know?" said Iris, pasting a pious expression onto her face and putting her hands back into the prayer position.

"No," said Lorna, "I think you'll find that *we all* gave up chocolate cake for *rationing*!"

"Oh, that's right, I forgot! Though perhaps, not *all* of us had to give it up entirely." Iris winked at Lorna. "*Some* of us had handsome American airmen feeding us chocolate cake as we danced, didn't we?"

The laughter died in Lorna's throat, but Iris didn't seem to notice.

"Well, *did* your American feed you chocolate cake," asked Iris, "as he waltzed you around the floor?"

Lorna tried to ignore the nausea Iris's questions were causing, and fought to keep the smile on her face.

"Hmm? Am I right? Hmm?" Iris was clearly determined to get a response, so Lorna swallowed the bile burning the back of her throat and searched her mind for the sort of sarcastic answer Iris would be expecting.

"No, he didn't have to," she managed at last, "because, if you remember, I learned to feed myself at quite an early age. I was very advanced like that.

"And anyway," she added quietly, "we didn't waltz."

But Iris had bent down to wipe some dust from her shiny leather shoe and didn't appear to have heard. Standing up again, she looked at Lorna inquiringly.

"Sorry, what did you say?"

Instead of answering, Lorna tugged at Iris's arm, casting around for a topic she knew would keep her friend distracted for some time.

"So," Lorna said, with only a little dread, "tell me about being in love with Silly Billy Urquhart."

And sure enough, it was at least another five minutes before Lorna needed to speak again.

As they walked through the gates into the farmyard, Iris was still chattering about how hard she was finding bridge lessons with William's mother, since she could never remember which of the black cards were clubs and which were spades.

"I think Mrs. Urquhart is starting to get rather annoyed with me, but William thinks it's sweet, or at least that's what he said as he walked me . . ."

Lorna heard no more. Paul had come out of the milking parlor and was heading across the yard toward the Glebe field. His head was down and he was concentrating on something in his hand.

Her heart jumped at seeing him, and she could feel his lips on hers all over again. Had it only been a few hours since he had kissed her? And since she had so willingly kissed him back? It felt like days, but then again, perhaps only minutes. Through all of the hymns and prayers, and through Reverend Urquhart's interminable sermon, Lorna had held on to the feeling of his soft dry lips pressing on hers. She had surreptitiously pressed her chilly hands to her burning cheeks as she remembered how she had opened her mouth without pause to his sweet kisses. And how the tip of his tongue had sought hers, insistent but not demanding. And how its touch had twisted her insides and sent her head spinning.

Just as the sight of him was doing to her again.

"Oh Lorna, you have no idea what it feels like to be in love!"

Paul had paused by the corner of the house, working at the object in his hand. Although he was still wearing Sandy's coveralls over his uniform, he had tied the arms around his hips and had rolled his shirtsleeves above the elbow, so his strong forearms were bare in the early spring sunshine.

"And how wonderful it feels to be kissed by a boy . . ."

The newly developed muscles on his back, chest, and arms were straining at the cloth of the shirt as his hands worked to break or separate the thing he was holding..

". . . I mean, to be kissed by a *man*. I'm sorry, Lorna, I don't want to upset you because I know you always had a fancy for my William, but I wish you could know how it feels when he kisses you. I mean, when he kisses me. Oh, you get what I mean, don't you?"

Lorna's fingers tingled at the thought of running her hands over Paul's shoulders, that chest, of how she could smooth the soft, short hair at the nape of his neck . . .

"Lorna! Are you even listening to me?"

. . . and lay her head again on his chest so she could hear his heart beating beneath her ear as he held her . . .

"*Lorna!* What is wrong with you?"

And then Iris was there, standing in front of her, hands on hips, forcing Lorna to look at her instead of Paul.

"Here's me, spilling all these juicy secrets," said Iris with a huff, "of how it feels to be in love, and you're not even listening. You're too busy staring off into space to pay attention to me, too busy . . ."

But Lorna couldn't keep her eyes from Paul for more than a few seconds.

Iris followed Lorna's gaze, seeing Paul for the first time.

". . . too busy looking at *him*."

Iris looked back at Lorna.

Lorna fiddled with the top buttons on her coat. Why had it suddenly got so much warmer?

"Lorna, you are blushing!" Iris said. "Why are you blushing?"

Paul had either won his battle with the thing in his hand or had given up on it, because he stuffed the object into the back pocket of his coveralls and disappeared around the corner, apparently unaware he'd had an audience.

"Oh my God, Lorna!" Iris pulled Lorna closer, talking

in a whisper virtually as loud as her normal speaking voice. "You fancy him, don't you? You do. You fancy that German chap."

Lorna opened her mouth, but no words came.

"Don't you dare deny it. I can see it in your face. Your eyes went all funny, and you've gone all pink." Iris stepped back and pressed her hands to her mouth. "Oh my God, Lorna, what is wrong with you? He's a *German*!"

Still Lorna could find no words—she had not planned to share her secret with anyone. But Iris had known her a long time, too long for Lorna to hide anything from her, at least when Iris chose to look.

"Tell me, *tell me*!" Iris pleaded, and then groaned as Lorna shrugged. "Come on, it's me. Tell me! Have you even talked to him yet?

"I mean, I'm not saying you ever should, because, well, you know . . ." Iris was clearly torn between being shocked and titillated. "And I'm not saying he wouldn't have been quite handsome if he hadn't been so . . . em, you know . . ."

Iris was still struggling for words, so she waved her hand around her face, putting on an expression to show what awfulness she was seeing in her mind.

"You know . . . *burned*."

Iris glanced behind her as if she was worried that Paul might hear, then back at Lorna.

"What I'm trying to say is that even if he weren't a German, which he is, but if he weren't, then it's not like you could actually fancy him, is it? I mean, because, after all, he *is* a German, and anyway, he looks like *that*."

Lorna felt curiously removed from her friend's panicked chattering. It was almost as if she were sitting at the pictures, watching it on the big screen. Iris was talking to her, and about her, but Lorna wasn't really there. Why couldn't Paul be handsome? Of course he was handsome, he was gorgeous. And kind and funny. The burns didn't get in the way of that for Lorna, so why on earth couldn't Iris see past them?

Lorna's annoyance pulled her back to the conversation.

"Why not?"

To Iris's astonishment, and her own for that matter, Lorna had asked the question because she truly didn't understand what Iris meant.

"Well, first, because he's . . . a *German*," Iris repeated hesitantly. "And you couldn't ever actually like a German, could you? That just wouldn't be right."

"Why not?" The question came again, but this time, Lorna didn't wait for Iris to answer. "If he was just a man, like any other man who happened to come visit, then perhaps I could."

Iris was staring at her, and Lorna couldn't stop the words now.

"And if he was kind and friendly and funny, and if he told you about places so beautiful that you wanted to go with him to see them, and if he listened to you talk like he actually cared about what you were saying? And if he tried to protect you when other people tried to tell you what to do, as if they owned you? And if he has the handsomest face you've ever seen, no matter if the skin has been damaged, because he's just lovely even so?"

As she talked, Lorna grabbed Iris's hands. Suddenly they were twelve again, sharing their special secrets.

"And when he touches your face with his fingers, and then he plays with your hair—"

"Lorna"—Iris looked almost scared now—"I really don't think—"

"But Iris," Lorna pressed on, "think about the way you feel when your William touches your face, and your hair—"

"But that's William. That's not—"

"And when he kisses you—"

"But—"

"And kisses you—"

"Oh my God, stop," whispered Iris.

"And kisses you again, and again, and again, until you think you'll faint and—"

And suddenly, though she had seemed so shocked, Iris couldn't fight Lorna's magic spell any longer.

"I know, I know, I know!" she squealed, throwing her arms around Lorna.

The two girls shook with delight and hugged each other tight.

After a few breathless moments, they drew apart, still laughing.

"But why didn't you tell me?" Iris playfully smacked Lorna's arm again. "And I'm not saying I approve, but oh my God, when did he first kiss you?"

Lorna lifted her wrist as if to look at the watch she wasn't wearing.

"About four hours ago."

Iris squealed again.

"I can't believe you kept something as huge as this a secret."

"Well, I wasn't really sure myself, and of course, I knew you wouldn't approve." Lorna grinned at her friend. "He is *German*, after all."

"Oh, Lorna"—Iris sounded long-suffering now—"what am I going to do with you?"

Lorna hugged Iris again, and they walked on toward the house. Before they'd gone too far, however, Iris slowed to a stop, a frown shadowing her face.

"What's wrong?" asked Lorna.

"Well, it's just"—Iris hesitated—"William will not be at all happy about this. And neither will his parents."

"But you can't tell them!" said Lorna immediately, remembering how badly Iris kept secrets. "You mustn't tell anyone. Promise me, Iris! No one can know about this. Paul could get into trouble at the camp if they found out, and you know what would happen if my dad heard about it. He'd hit the bloody roof."

Memories of John Jo's angry face flashed into Lorna's mind.

"But . . ." Iris looked doubtful.

"You must promise me! Paul could be punished and sent away. I'd never see him again. God! I should never have told you. Iris, you're my best friend, so please, promise me."

"But William . . . ?"

"What about William?"

"I've never lied to William, and you shouldn't ask me to lie to him either." Iris's mouth was pursed in its usual fashion when she was heading into prim and proper.

"But I'm not asking you to lie to him," said Lorna. "I'm just asking you not to tell him. That's not the same. Honestly it's not."

"But it *is* the same, Lorna," Iris said. "If William asks what you and me did after church this morning, and I don't tell him that we had this conversation, then I would be lying to him about what we did, wouldn't I? William and I have already pledged total honesty with each other, a pledge that I like to think of as a first step toward the pledge we'll make when we get married—"

"Get married to William? You're not serious," Lorna said, but Iris wasn't listening.

"So you really can't ask me to break such an important pledge over this. You're my friend, so it wouldn't be right." Iris's smile was apologetic. "But of course, he might not actually ask me. And in that case, I won't have to tell him."

Lorna was stunned by this warped logic.

"So if William doesn't ask you directly what you and me talked about this morning as we walked home from the church, then you'll keep my secret?"

"Of course!" said Iris brightly. "That's what best friends do!"

Iris smiled at Lorna, as if that should have been obvious, and Lorna's heart sank. She loved Iris dearly, but the chances of Iris keeping her mouth shut about this lay somewhere between slim and none. And once William knew, then his mother would know, and his father, and on and on how far? Who else would be invited to judge and condemn?

She and Paul had shared only one kiss, but suddenly Lorna knew that the whole world—or at least, *her* whole world— would soon be determined to make sure they would never share another.

Twenty

Lorna was right to worry. Only two days later, before she had even reached the church for the Easter Sunday service, she knew what Iris had done.

She knew as soon as she saw that Iris wasn't waiting for her at their usual meeting place under the budding boughs of the sycamore at the corner where the kirkyard met Coffin Lane.

Iris was instead standing near William and his mother, who were both offering haughty welcomes to the arriving congregation. She was twisting her white gloves in her hands and alternately staring down at her shoes and glancing up toward their usual meeting place.

When Iris spotted Lorna, she jumped. She actually jumped in shock, like Charlie Chaplin or Harold Lloyd. It was so comical that Lorna might have laughed, had the sick knot of dread not squeezed tight within her at the exact same time.

William, perhaps hearing Iris gasp, also looked toward Lorna, his expression changing in an instant from sanctimonious and smug to contemptuous. Without taking his eyes from her, William said something to his mother, and Lorna could imagine the sneer in his voice simply by the way his upper lip lifted at one side.

But of course, William looking contemptuous was not a sure signal of Iris's betrayal, nor was Mrs. Urquhart scowling down her nose at Lorna. The confirmation that Iris had blabbed came from the way that all the women talking to or standing near Mrs. Urquhart—Mrs. Harris, Mrs. McCready, Mrs. Patterson, and both Old Mrs. Guy and Young Mrs. Guy—turned and stared at Lorna. And then the group standing next to them stared, and the couple beyond them stared too, and so on until time itself froze. Even the children running past in a last-ditch game of tag before their incarceration in Sunday school sensed that something was up and stopped to see whatever it was that the grown-ups were looking at.

Suddenly Lorna was viewing the Aberlady Parish Church congregation as a medieval fresco painted across the stone wall of the church. Every pair of eyes was on Lorna. Except one.

Iris was studying her shoes.

Then, on some silent signal, everyone moved, and the

nudging and muttering, head shaking and tutting began, building into a cacophony of judgment rolling across the kirkyard at Lorna. Still Iris did not look up, even when she was nudged hard by Esther Bell, who had moved to stand beside her. Only when Esther nudged Iris a third time, and gestured toward Lorna, did Iris look up.

Iris's mouth pursed. It was a familiar expression for Iris, but what did it mean? Guilt, regret, or judgment?

Before Lorna could decide, William blocked her view, taking Iris by the arm and stewarding her and his mother into the church. The other women followed, each one casting a furious scowl at Lorna as they went.

Would everyone react like this to her from now on? Had she really done something so wrong? What if she had drunkenly kissed the American, if she'd allowed Ed to do whatever he wanted? Would that have been more palatable for Mrs. Urquhart than a sober and chaste—almost chaste—kiss with a kind and caring German? Perhaps it would.

It was so unfair that Iris should be *encouraged*—well, perhaps not encouraged exactly, but at least *allowed*—to kiss William, yet Lorna was being cast out by the village like a stranger for doing the exact same thing.

As the organ music rose into the opening Call to Worship, Lorna walked back down Coffin Lane toward Craigielaw.

And how would Mrs. Mack and Nellie react when word reached them, as it undoubtedly would? Or had it already? And what about her father? He would never allow Paul back on the farm again. In fact, she hadn't seen Paul this morning, she hadn't even heard the truck arrive to drop him off. So what if . . . ? What if . . . ?

Oh God! Dad wouldn't have, he couldn't have . . .

Lorna ran. She had to find Paul. She had to make sure. . . .

But there he was, just outside the barn, crouched beside the old Fordson tractor, with a large screwdriver in his hand and a collection of other tools at his feet. Lorna slowed, letting relief funnel new air into her tight lungs. Paul scratched the back of his head with the screwdriver and stood up, stretching his back and shaking his head.

As she approached, Paul glanced up. Though the bruise across his eye was still purple, the swelling had gone down.

"The engine of a watch is not like the engine of a tractor," he said. "So I think I must ask Fräulein Nellie to look at this old lady. She will not start for me."

He patted the hood almost as if it were the neck of a plow horse and then frowned at Lorna.

"But you are back early. In Germany, *am Ostersonntag*," he said, "on Easter Sunday, we must stay in church a long time before we may eat the eggs of the *Osterhase*—does the Easter Rabbit visit Scotland too?"

"They know about us," Lorna blurted. "That little cow, Iris, told everyone in the village."

Paul's smile faltered just for a moment, before he seemed to force it wide again.

"Told them what?"

"Told them about us," said Lorna, "told them that we've been . . . you know."

"Oh, I see," said Paul, his smile fading, "and how did Iris know that we have been . . ."

"Because I told her."

"Ah."

"But I only told her because I was so happy, and she promised not to tell anyone that we'd kissed, not even that oaf William, but she's never been any good at keeping secrets, and I shouldn't have trusted her, and I'm so, so—"

"You were happy that I kissed you?" Paul said.

"Of course I was happy, it was . . . it was . . ." She couldn't find the right words. "It was very nice."

"Very nice?" Paul looked serious and concerned, but his eyes were sparkling. "Only 'very nice'?"

"I mean . . . oh, stop, you know what I mean." Lorna allowed herself to smile and took another step toward him. "I liked kissing you. In fact, it turns out that it might be one of my favorite things to do in all the world."

Paul was smiling again, and he took her hand in his.

"Well, that is a lucky chance, because kissing you is—"

He lifted her hand toward his mouth, but as he went to kiss it, Lorna pulled away. Paul froze.

"Paul, no, you mustn't. Someone will see. You'd get into so much trouble, and so would I, and then they'd stop letting you come here, or they'd send you away, and I'd never see you again."

"You are right, Lorna, and I'm sorry," Paul said, seriousness darkening his expression. "I should not have tried to kiss you. And I will not try again."

"But that's not what—"

"Lorna, I understand the problem. It would not be good for other people to see us together."

Lorna swallowed hard.

Paul bent down and picked up the tools at his feet, then he walked into the barn.

At the bottom of the ladder up to the hayloft, he hesitated before turning back to her, a crooked smile playing on his lips.

"Of course," he said, "if we were somewhere other people could not see us . . ."

Paul set off up the ladder and soon disappeared through the floor of the loft.

Lorna watched him go. What would Mrs. Urquhart say? Or John Jo?

But they weren't here, were they? No one was here, except her and Paul. And anyway, what business was it of anyone else's?

The first rung creaked under Lorna's shiny black shoe, then the second.

"Happy Easter, Aberlady!" Lorna muttered as she climbed. "And to hell with you all!"

Twenty-One

"And then she spat at me. It was awful."

A week or so later, Lorna was standing wiping furiously at the remains of the mess on her skirt with a damp cloth as Mrs. Mack bustled around the kitchen. "And in front of everyone. It was so humiliating."

"Och, I'm sure it was nothing."

"But she spat at me in front of the whole school."

"The whole school?"

"Well, quite a few people, anyway. And who the hell is Nancy Bell anyway? If it had been her sister, I might have understood, because Esther's just plain nasty, but Nancy is only about twelve."

"But other than that, have you had a happy birthday so far?" called Mrs. Mack from the pantry.

"Oh simply super!" Lorna knew she sounded mean, even though Mrs. Mack was trying to be nice.

"And did Iris wish you a happy birthday?"

"Why would I even listen to Iris? She should have kept her mouth shut in the first place. I can't believe she told William I had . . . well, that she told him anything at all. She knew he would just go and tell the whole damn village."

Lorna saw Mrs. Mack frown. "Sorry, I mean, the whole village."

Mrs. Mack handed Lorna the bread basket and a jar of mustard, and Lorna tossed both onto the table, slumping down into the nearest chair.

"God! Iris is no better than Esther bloody Bell."

"Lorna!"

"Sorry."

"As I've been telling you all week"—Mrs. Mack's patience was clearly wearing thin—"you've only yourself to blame. I've nothing against the lad, in fact, I like him, but really, could you not both see you were asking for trouble?"

"But—"

"But nothing! You've no choice but to let the gossips do their worst. I don't know who I'm more annoyed with, you or them. As if people haven't enough to blather about right now, you have to hand them your silly head on a silver platter."

Lorna humphed but didn't reply. No point, because Mrs. Mack was right.

Lorna picked up the scrap of paper from the table on which Nellie had scrawled *Happy Birthday, Lorna!!!* She screwed it up and tossed it into the fire.

Some birthday! That note had been the only birthday greeting she'd had all day. Her dad had been away before she'd got up, and her classmates were either ignoring her or had forgotten. And Mrs. Murray had been too annoyed with Lorna for being late again to mention it.

And why had Lorna been late? Because her search for Paul had been fruitless, and therefore Lorna had spent her eighteenth birthday being tortured at school without even the hint of a sweet birthday kiss to see her through.

And now, she had to smile through this blasted birthday tea party.

Mrs. Mack had promised Lorna a birthday feast. In spite of the rationing restrictions, the housekeeper hinted that she'd been saving something special. Certainly, the smells that filled the house were mouthwatering. Even so, Lorna clung on to her filthy mood.

With no Iris, no John Jo, and no Sandy, and with an exhausted Dad and a still-sickly Nellie, what kind of party was it going to be, cake or no cake?

"Stick the kettle on, Lorna," said Mrs. Mack, picking up the egg basket, "while I pop down to see if the girls have left me any nice eggs to boil."

Almost as soon as she went out through the scullery door, Nellie appeared through the door from the yard. For someone who had always been a shimmering light around the farm, chattering and laughing and singing, Nellie now looked like death warmed up.

Her poorly stomach was still hanging around, Lorna knew, for she had found Nellie most mornings doing the milking with two pails in front of her, one for the milk and one in case she vomited. Lorna had nagged at Nellie to go to the nurse in the village, or even to the doctor's office in Gullane, to get some tonic to stop the sickness, but Nellie had only finally agreed to go that afternoon.

Nellie's face was ashen, her cheeks gaunt, and she walked like a woman fifty years older, trudging and reluctant. She sat down heavily and dropped her head onto the one corner of the table that wasn't covered with plates and bowls, protected under a muslin cloth. She looked totally drained.

Lorna put a glass of water in front of her.

"Did you see the nurse? Did she give you something to make you feel better?"

Suddenly an enormous sob shook Nellie, and she began to bawl. Instinctively, Lorna glanced at the door, desperately hoping that her father wouldn't come in. Nellie was a hard worker, if a bit silly sometimes, but her repeated sickness was pushing him to the limit.

Knowing he and Mrs. Mack would be coming in soon, Lorna laid her hand on Nellie's arm.

"Come upstairs and tell me all about it. Maybe I can help."

Nellie let Lorna lead her upstairs, but Lorna didn't want to go into Nellie's bedroom. It was still decorated with reminders of Sandy from when it had been his room, so she led Nellie to her own room and sat her down on the bed.

Nellie continued to cry, so Lorna gently rubbed her back as Mrs. Mack had so often done for her as a child. After a few minutes, Lorna fetched a fresh white handkerchief from her top drawer and Nellie blew her nose into it, loud and wet.

"It's over. He's dumped me." Nellie gulped and croaked. "My Charlie. Chuck. My American."

"When?" Lorna didn't understand. "I thought you went to the doctor's this afternoon, not to see Chuck."

"Well, you see, he's been a bit funny lately, a bit sulky, not like he was at first, all fun and flirting. And we had an argy-bargy last week before I got sick, you know, an argument. He said I was being clingy and demanding. 'It's not like we're in love or anything,' he said."

She turned her red puffy eyes toward Lorna.

"But you see, I thought that we were," Nellie sniffed. "At least, I was head over heels for him, and I thought I could tell that he loved me too."

Lorna nodded. What could she say?

Nellie scrunched up the wet hankie in her fist.

"We'd not seen each other since the argument, and then I got sick," Nellie said, hiccuping. "And today, I did go to see the nurse, but then I went up to the air base to talk to him. The guard wasn't happy about it, but I moaned at him so long, he sent someone to get Chuck.

"Oh, Lorna, the way he looked at me! It was like I was nobody to him. But I told him straight that I was sorry we'd had that fight, and that I loved him, and once the war's over, him and me should be together.

"'In fact,' I told him, 'you and me are going to have to get together even before the war is over, because . . .'"

Nellie fell silent, and Lorna knew what she was about to say. All the pieces of the jigsaw fell into place—the sickness, the exhaustion, the weeping.

"Nellie, you're pregnant," Lorna whispered, and Nellie nodded.

"'Chuck,' I said to him, 'I'm carrying your baby and we should get married as soon as we can find a vicar to do it.' And do you know what he says to me?"

Lorna shook her head, not wanting to hear what was coming.

"He says, 'How can I marry you when I've already got a wife back in Tennessee?'"

Nellie buried her face in her hands. "Oh, I've been so foolish."

Lorna put her hand again on her friend's back. "Nellie, I am so sorry. But surely he can't just leave you like that. He must do something to help."

She realized that she sounded like her dad, which gave her an idea.

"Maybe I could ask Dad to talk to Chuck's commanding officer—"

Nellie leaped off the bed.

"No, no! Your dad mustn't know I'm expecting. He would be so angry, and he would throw me off the farm, and the Land Army would sack me. I don't want to leave Craigielaw. I love it here, and anyway if I went back to London, my old man—my dad, that is—would do worse than throw me right back out on my ear again."

"Worse?" said Lorna.

"Oh, he'd beat me senseless. Always one to lecture with his fists, my dad. My mum put up with it only so long and then turned her face to the wall and died, just to escape him. And I couldn't blame her. I got out of there the very day I was old enough for the Land Army so I wouldn't have to count my bruises every morning."

Nellie laughed, though entirely without humor.

"You have no idea how lucky you are. Your dad is such a lovely, lovely man. A bit grumpy perhaps, but deep down, a lovely man." Nellie chewed on a fingernail. "But promise me you won't tell him about my . . . problem. Just give me a little while more to think what would be best."

"But it won't stay a secret for long." Lorna pointed at Nellie's belly. "How far along are you? Was it, em, the night of the dance?"

Nellie looked even more miserable.

"I think it was a bit before that."

"So it'll start showing soon. And you shouldn't be doing any heavy lifting from now on."

"I know, I know. But just give me a couple of weeks, please. I need to think carefully."

Lorna wasn't sure what to say.

"Promise me, Lorna, please."

Reluctantly, she nodded. "Fine, I promise, but in return, you must promise to tell Dad soon." Lorna hugged Nellie.

"And you know I'll be there for you, don't you?"

"I know, duckie. You're like the perfect little sister I never had."

At that moment, Mrs. Mack called from downstairs. Nellie stood up and patted Lorna's arm.

"Let me wash my face so I don't look such a fright, and then I'll be down, all right?"

"Are you sure you can face it? I'm not even sure that I can, and it's *my* birthday."

"We'll both be fine, and Mrs. Mack always talks enough for both of us."

Nellie went through to her own room, leaving Lorna to paste a deliberate smile onto her face.

"Coming!" she shouted.

Mrs. Mack had indeed kept something special up her sleeve. Ham sandwiches, boiled eggs, sausages, homemade chutney, slices of fresh bread with actual butter, and oatcakes lying next to a small block of cheese. On the dresser stood a crystal bowl of red jelly, scones oozing strawberry jam, and a small yellow sponge cake with four candles on top, as well as a clear bottle marked *Elderflower Cordial—Summer 1944* in Mrs. Mack's handwriting, a green bottle of ginger ale, and four brown bottles of beer.

Lorna stood, her mouth agape. In spite of herself, she let this wonderful sight break through her doldrums.

"Mrs. Mack, how did you do it? Did you steal the whole village's ration books?"

"You know me, Lorna, I have my ways and means." The housekeeper winked. "I thought we could all do with a wee party to cheer us up."

"Wee party? You could feed the Fifty-First Highland Division with that lot," said Lorna's father as he rose from his chair by the fire and laid a friendly arm around Mrs. Mack's shoulders. "A rare spread indeed, Edna, given that there's only the four of us."

Mrs. Mack cleared her throat and looked uncharacteristically sheepish.

"Well, no, not four. You see, I mentioned to young Iris that we'd be celebrating, and suggested she might like to join—"

"Iris? You didn't! You know I'm not talking to Iris after she—"

Lorna was silenced by a glance from Mrs. Mack. As yet, Lorna's father had still said nothing about whether he had heard the gossip in the village.

"Well, you're only eighteen the once," continued Mrs. Mack, "and you two've been friends for such a long time."

Lorna fought to keep a scowl on her face, though inside she was feeling hopeful and excited. In spite of what Iris had done, she still missed her.

"So that's five. And I thought it would be nice for the lad to join us, given he's probably not seen his own sister's birthday party in a few years."

Mrs. Mack gave Lorna a conspiratorial wink, then looked at Lorna's father.

Lorna was sure her dad would refuse to have the German

prisoner in the house, but he just nodded. He'd always had difficulty refusing Mrs. Mack anything. She had, after all, kept his family clothed, fed, and healthy since his wife had died fifteen years previously. Lorna knew he didn't pick fights with Mrs. Mack without very good reason and not unless he knew he could win.

"Aye, let him have a quick bite," Lorna's dad said, sitting back down by the fire, "but then there's weeding still to be done over the way before nightfall."

Lorna felt emotion bubbling inside her. Maybe this party was worth some excitement after all.

Right on cue, there was a tentative tapping at the kitchen door.

"Go on then, lassie," the housekeeper said with a broad smile. "Let your guest in."

Lorna rushed to open the door. Paul was there, smiling, and Lorna's heart skipped as he gave her a wink.

Suddenly she remembered her manners.

"Would you like to come in, Paul," she said, "and have a cup of tea?"

For goodness' sake, she'd turned into a waitress in Skeane's Tea Rooms, Lorna thought, and a giggle burst out before she could stop it.

Her father looked up from the newspaper, at Lorna, at Paul and back again, but then went back to his paper and said nothing.

At that moment, Nellie burst into the room, very effectively appearing to be her old self again. Her blond curls were bouncing and her lips had been painted with her trademark red lipstick. Immediately, she was chatting and laughing, squealing with delight, and almost unrecognizable from ten minutes before.

But Lorna noticed when it came time to fill their plates, Nellie paled and drew a breath, clearly concentrating on keeping her hands steady. She took a bit of everything, chatting all the while, but Lorna noticed that she scarcely ate more than one bite of each thing.

Mrs. Mack was also watching Nellie, obviously unconvinced by the act, but thankfully she didn't say anything.

Between them, Nellie and Mrs. Mack kept the conversation lively, but Lorna was all too aware that there had still been no second knock at the door by the time the desserts were brought out. Iris had not come after all.

Mrs. Mack lit the candles on the cake, and Lorna hesitated only long enough to make a wish—*let the war be over tomorrow, let John Jo and Sandy come home safe, and let Paul stay forever*—thinking it so quickly that perhaps it wouldn't count as three different wishes. For a second, she wondered if she should include Iris in her wish somehow, but no, Iris could do whatever she wanted to do. Then Lorna took a deep breath and blew.

As the flames vanished and four fine streams of smoke swirled up toward the ceiling, Nellie squealed. "Birthday presents!"

Within minutes, Lorna was hugging Mrs. Mack and

Nellie, delighted with the beautiful blue hand-crocheted scarf and hat, and with the powder compact and lipstick, thankfully a pale pink, not the bright red Nellie herself wore.

Then Lorna saw her father lift down a thick package, wrapped in brown paper, from the mantelpiece.

That would be the books, as it always was.

Each birthday and Christmas, Lorna's dad ordered books from James Thin Booksellers in Edinburgh. He didn't read many books himself, he always told her, and so he wouldn't know what to choose. Instead, he ordered a selection to interest a girl of eight, or twelve, or this year, eighteen, and Lorna was always happy with what they sent. Sure enough, this parcel included both a new Agatha Christie mystery and a collection of Kipling poetry.

A small cough made Lorna look up from her books. Paul was holding a small flat roll of linen, the same off-white fabric from the workbench in the hayloft. It was tied with a cross of fine brown twine. Lorna smiled at him, moved to think that he had brought something for her.

"You didn't have to bring me a present. Really."

Paul handed the packet to Lorna. "The camp store does not sell many gifts, so I wanted to make you something myself."

Before she could even pull on the twine, however, there was a sharp rap on the kitchen door.

Iris! She'd come after all. But then a man's voice shouted from outside.

"Mr. Anderson, are you there?"

Lorna's father strode across the kitchen and opened the door.

Derek Milne hobbled into the kitchen, sweaty and uncomfortable in his post office uniform. He looked nervous, rubbing at the withered leg that had exempted him from war service, not meeting anyone's eye.

Although Derek had been coming to Craigielaw for years, both as one of John Jo's school friends and more recently every morning as the Aberlady mailman, this visit was different and everyone knew it. Having a mailman knock on the door at five thirty in the afternoon could only mean one thing, one terrible thing.

And there it was, clutched in his hand. The delivery every family dreaded. A telegram.

Twenty-Two

It lay open on the table where Lorna's father had dropped it, still bent at its folds.

Minutes ago, Lorna's father had taken it from Derek, his face grave, and he'd broken the seal and read the contents. Though his expression did not change, the color had drained from his face, and without speaking, he'd dropped the telegram and strode out of the house, leaving the door wide open.

Finally, Lorna gathered what was left of her courage, and picked up the paper with shaking fingers.

At first the grainy gray type meant nothing. It was just random words. She shut her eyes tight, focusing her thoughts, and when she opened her them again the words had formed into staccato sentences she could read aloud.

```
    PRIORITY
    TO JOHN ANDERSON CRAIGIELAW FARM ABERLADY
EAST LOTHIAN
    FROM MINISTRY OF WAR
    9 APRIL 1945 REGRET TO INFORM YOU 934810
SERGEANT JOHN JOSEPH ELLIOTT ANDERSON DID
NOT RETURN FROM OPERATIONS THIS MORNING STOP
MISSING STOP ANY FURTHER INFORMATION RECEIVED
WILL BE COMMUNICATED IMMEDIATELY STOP SHOULD
ANY INFORMATION REACH YOU PLEASE INFORM THIS
DEPARTMENT STOP UNDER SECRETARY OF STATE
```

Lorna was barely able to whisper the last few words. She stood holding the telegram, unable to put it down, unable to move.

John Jo was missing.

John Jo might be dead.

John Jo had left home with her spiteful words ringing in his ears. He had left home thinking Lorna hated him and now he was missing, perhaps dead, and it was all her fault.

A screeching noise shattered the silence as Nellie pushed a wooden chair under Mrs. Mack's sagging frame. Once Nellie had helped her sit down, Mrs. Mack pulled out her handkerchief and held it to her mouth.

Why was Mrs. Mack weeping? Yes, the housekeeper had been like a mother to all three children for the past fifteen years. But had she sent John Jo to his death with her vicious bile? Had she told John Jo not to come back? No, of course she hadn't. So what did she have to cry about?

In that instant, Lorna despised herself, totally and utterly.

She also knew why her father had walked away. He must know that it was Lorna's fault and been unable to bear another moment in the same room as her. He was blaming her for John Jo's death. And John Jo was dead, she was sure of it, because this was punishment for her wickedness, her lies, her selfishness, her anger and . . . for loving an enemy soldier.

She had forgotten Paul was there as she'd read the telegram out loud, but now she found him, standing silently to one side.

There might have been concern in Paul's eyes, but Lorna would not see it. He was the reason for her pain. His damaged face, and the jagged red scars under his shirt, were reminders of her treachery. Even the remnants of the purple bruise around his eye, now yellowing at the edges, accused her of betrayal.

If Paul hadn't come to Aberlady, she would never have wanted to kiss him. John Jo wouldn't have found them together and been so angry. She would never have said what she had.

If Paul hadn't been here, John Jo would be safe, her father would still love her, and she would not hate herself as truly, as deeply, and as entirely as she did.

Paul was to blame for John Jo's disappearance, and she hated him for it.

Paul opened his mouth. "Lorna, I am sorry." He stepped

forward. "But your brother is brave and strong. I am sure they will find him."

Lorna stared at Paul for a second or two, a small part of her wanting to believe him, but then his reassurance was engulfed in a fire of her fury, of her contempt and her guilt. Lorna lashed out. Finding his gift still in her hand, she threw it at him. He caught it cleanly, but right then she wouldn't have cared if it had smashed to pieces on the floor.

"Get out! Get out of my house! John Jo is dead and it's your fault."

"But Lorna—"

She shoved her fists hard against his chest, pushing him against the wall beside the fireplace. Chimes rang out as he crashed against the horse brasses hanging there. Paul grunted in pain and twisted away. The fleeting echo of a light switch speared her spine, and sweaty hands clawed at her thigh. A red fog smothered her mind and her soul. Lorna was raging now. She screamed at Paul and beat her fists against him again and again, wherever she could make contact.

Paul blocked her blows with his forearms and hands, even the one still clutching the linen packet, but he didn't hit back, didn't try to stop her. He allowed her to hit him, though he leaned backward to protect his already bruised face.

"Lorna, stop, please" was all he said.

Suddenly, Nellie grabbed her, pinning her arms to her sides. Though Lorna's body wanted to resist, the spotlight of fury had been snapped off and the red fog was subsiding.

"Paul, I think you'd best go." Nellie's voice was low but

insistent, and when he hesitated, she repeated, "Go now. I'll take care of her. She's in shock, that's all."

Shock, that's all? Really? And what about the guilt and the hatred and the despair?

Suddenly Lorna was as weak as the newborn lambs Paul had nursed. Her legs buckled, and she slumped into a chair beside Mrs. Mack. She buried her face in her hands but still heard the click of the latch as Paul left without another word.

"Lorna," said Nellie, "it's not Paul's fault your brother is missing."

"No," Lorna agreed. "It's mine."

When the truck from Gosford arrived early next morning, Lorna was holding her damp washcloth across her sore and puffy eyes, not caring that it still dripped down her nightdress.

She heard the truck door slam and then the distinctive accent of the sergeant. "Your other bloke's in the sick bay, so you've got this lump of lard instead."

Lorna edged aside the curtain and looked down into the yard. An older prisoner, fat, balding, and unhealthy-looking, stood on the flatbed, clearly considering how he could navigate the drop to the ground without a stepladder.

Paul was sick? Lorna wanted to run down and ask the driver what was wrong with him. But of course, she knew. Paul was avoiding Craigielaw, avoiding her. And who could blame him?

Just as the prisoner stumbled to the ground, Caddy sped into the yard. She gave him no more than a vague sniff before circling the truck in search of her beloved Paul. Not finding him, she barked at the truck, calling for him.

Another day, Lorna might have felt as anxious as the little dog, but right now, she couldn't deny her relief at not having to face Paul.

Leaving her bedroom, she glanced into her father's room. She hadn't heard him come back last night, but the bed had clearly been slept in.

She trudged slowly downstairs, her stomach aching, though whether from the unusually rich food or from her overwhelming misery, she wasn't sure. Either way, she couldn't think of eating, but she hoped there was a pot of tea already steeping.

Sure enough, there it was. Lorna poured herself a cup, watching the rich brown liquid spiral through the milk. Mrs. Mack appeared from the pantry, carrying a loaf of bread and an almost empty pot of her gooseberry jam. Her eyes were swollen, but at least she wasn't still crying. Lorna couldn't have handled that.

"I'm not going to school today," Lorna said to her. "I couldn't bear it. So don't tell me I have to go, because I won't. And neither you nor Dad can make me."

She crossed her arms and waited for Mrs. Mack to argue with her.

But Mrs. Mack didn't respond at all; she just sat down, cradling the loaf on her lap.

"I'm sorry," Lorna said, "I didn't mean it like that. But please, don't make me go. I just want to stay home today."

Mrs. Mack pulled out her hankie and blew her nose.

"You couldn't go to school today, dear, even if you wanted to." She was struggling to speak. "Your class won't be at school tomorrow either, not until they've found a substitute teacher to take over."

"Take over? But where's Mrs. Murray? Why can't she teach us?"

Mrs. Mack's large bosom heaved.

"Mrs. Murray won't be teaching you for a wee while, my dear." A fresh tear escaped and rolled down Mrs. Mack's cheek. "She received a telegram last evening as well, and she's been given a leave of absence from the school."

"Oh, no!" Lorna gasped.

Poor Mrs. Murray! It hadn't occurred to Lorna that other families might also have received bad news.

"Is Gregor missing too?"

"No, Lorna, dear," Mrs. Mack said softly. "Gregor is dead."

Twenty-Three

Sandy came home that weekend, arriving early on Saturday morning, still rumpled from the overnight train from London. He said the trip to Edinburgh was on War Office business, but Lorna was sure that he'd pulled strings to get home as soon as he had heard the news about John Jo and Gregor.

Lorna hugged her brother like she would never let him go, and Sandy seemed happy to let her. He'd brought her a silk scarf from Liberty's for her birthday, and they spent all that morning together, talking and talking. She and Sandy could always tell each other anything, but somehow, Lorna couldn't tell him about Paul, or about her fight with John Jo.

Paul had still not returned. It had been four days and still the truck dropped off the "lump of lard." His English was so poor that when Lorna asked him where Paul was, he simply shook his head. She dreaded seeing Paul again, but she also missed him and was desperate to apologize.

So Sandy's arrival was a wonderful distraction. Mrs. Mack was always so busy, and Nellie had other things on her mind. And Lorna had barely seen her father since the telegram had arrived. He'd withdrawn into himself, staying behind his own dark shadows. He seemed to have nothing to say to anyone.

But then, Sandy arrived.

On Saturday afternoon, Sandy and their father left the house to walk around the farm, heads bent together, and Lorna would have given anything to go with them. That evening, however, when Sandy persuaded their dad to go with him to the Gowff, Lorna was glad to stay home. She had no wish to be seen around the village any more than she had to.

Next morning, Sandy was watching her intently as she added salt and milk to their porridge and placed the bowls on the table beside their cups of tea. He stubbed out his cigarette in the ashtray and picked up his spoon.

"Not going to church then?" asked Sandy, eyeing the old skirt and torn sweater that Lorna had put on.

"Not today," she replied. She would rather swim across the Forth in winter than spend another Sunday morning being whispered about or openly scorned. "I thought we could do something together after my chores are finished."

"I'd go to church with you," Sandy said, his studied innocence suggesting he'd heard something about her. But what? And from Dad, or in the pub?

"No, really, I'd rather not."

"Do you want to tell me about it?"

"Nothing to tell." Lorna tried to sound bright. "The beach is all covered in barbed wire these days, but we could follow the Peffer Burn and see if the redshanks have nested yet, or the wheatears."

Sandy smiled. "Yes, let's do that. And perhaps we can talk as we walk."

It was bright and warm for April, and Aberlady Bay sparkled in the sunshine. Even the ugly concrete tank traps shone silver in a regimented line along the shore.

"So, tell me about this chap Paul." Sandy put a match to his cigarette, using both hands to shield the flame from the blustery breeze.

"Paul?" Lorna tried to match her brother's nonchalance. "Oh, the German? He's sick, apparently, but Dad and Nellie will be glad to have him back. The other bloke's no use at all."

Lorna risked a glance at Sandy. His blue eyes were scanning her face, so she shrugged to emphasize her disinterest.

"Sounds like a useful addition to the farm with me and John away," said Sandy. "Nellie seems efficient enough, but Dad says she can't do any heavy lifting."

"It's her back, I think," said Lorna, hoping that tied in with Nellie's story. "She's great with the livestock, though. The cows are producing lots more milk now. And the chickens too."

"Really?" Sandy looked impressed. "She must be good. I've never seen anyone get milk from a chicken before."

Lorna swiped at him.

"You know what I mean. She's not as good with the sheep, though."

"Ah, yes, I heard about that."

"At her first birthing . . ." Lorna mimed Nellie's dead faint. "You know, with the blood and everything, so Paul looked after the sheep instead. But Nellie's fun to have around, and Dad won't be happy to lose her once John Jo gets back."

If John Jo came back.

Lorna clapped her hand over her mouth as if she might actually utter those awful words aloud.

Sandy pulled her to face him.

"Lorna, he'll come back, you know he will. A whole brigade of panzers couldn't bring that bruiser down."

Lorna leaned her head against Sandy's shoulder.

After a while, they started walking again.

"So," Sandy said, lighting another cigarette, "about Paul? What do we know of him?"

Lorna knew he was digging for more than Paul's name, rank, and serial number, but after what had happened with John Jo, she wasn't going to risk giving it to him.

"Not much," she replied. "Worked on his uncle's sheep farm, and he can drive a tractor."

Sandy nodded. "But I hear he got himself shot up a bit."

Who'd been telling Sandy all this, and how much more was there?

"Burns," she said, fighting the temptation to shrug again, "on D-Day, I think. And shrapnel, but he's recovered now, other than the scarring. And, well, that's about it."

Sandy stayed silent, but what else could she tell him without giving herself away? He knew his sister too well.

The pretty girl in the photograph by Paul's bed in the hayloft came to Lorna's mind.

"He has a sister. A bit younger than me. Lilli."

How had Lilli reacted to the news that Paul had been injured and taken prisoner? Had she exploded with rage, lashing out at the nearest target? Lorna doubted it. Lilli would certainly never have told her brother to go back to the war and not come back.

Sandy squinted at Lorna through the cigarette smoke.

"His father died in the war," Lorna stumbled on. "But his mother is alive, and his sister is almost the same age as me—"

"Lilli."

"Oh, yes, I told you, Lilli. They're in Dresden."

Sandy stopped walking.

"Dresden? Oh, that's a bad show."

"What is?"

"Nasty business, Dresden. The RAF and the Yanks had a go at it back in, when was it, February, maybe? Blew it apart, from what we heard, turned it into an enormous fireball. 'Blanket bombing,' they called it. The RAF boys went back for recon pictures, and they said it was unrecognizable, totally obliterated. Even the Blitz couldn't compare."

Lorna felt nauseous. She'd remembered hearing something about Dresden, but she couldn't believe she'd missed a story like this.

"What about the people living there?"

What about Paul's mother and sister?

Sandy flicked his cigarette into the muddy water.

"Like I said, nasty business." He put an arm around Lorna's shoulders and pulled her close. "But Paul was lucky to have missed it."

Lorna pulled away.

"Lucky?" She hadn't meant to screech. "He's stuck here not knowing if our planes firebombed his family. How is that lucky?"

"In the same way that I'm bloody lucky to still be alive after his mates spent months bombing the arse of London, that's how!" Sandy's face was now pink under his freckles, and he took a deep breath before continuing. "Look, we've all been through things that no one should ever be expected to go through. And hopefully, sometime soon, it'll be over and we can get back to some sort of normal life. But in the meantime, we are still at war, so don't you forget that."

"I'm not likely to forget—"

"Well, that's not quite the way I heard it."

God! Not Sandy too!

"Don't start telling me who I can be friends with, Sandy, I'm not having that again. Not from John Jo and not from you."

Lorna turned for home, but within a few strides, Sandy caught up.

"Come on, don't be like that," he said, as ever the peacemaker among the sulking Andersons. "You can be friends with anyone you want. But perhaps be a tad more circumspect about this friendship, that's all. Come on, Lorna, wait a second."

Lorna stopped so suddenly, Sandy walked into the back of her.

"Did you hear me?" he said. "Be Paul's . . . er . . . friend by all means, but be careful. For Dad's sake."

Er . . . friend? She didn't like the way Sandy had hesitated on that word.

"Why? Because Dad would hate the idea of me being Paul's . . . er . . . friend because he's a German?"

And now she was hesitating over that word as well. Sandy had read her like a bloody book. Just like he always could.

"You're wrong. I think Dad would hate the idea of you being Paul's '*er . . . friend*'"—the way Sandy was saying it now was so suggestive that Lorna's cheeks burned—"not because he's a Jerry, but because he's a man. Dad isn't going to be thrilled with any man you might have as your 'er . . . friend,' now, is he?"

That was what Paul had said about John Jo.

Sandy continued to waggle his eyebrows at her lewdly, and eventually Lorna couldn't hold back a smile.

"Well, I'm glad Paul's my friend." Lorna looked up defiantly into Sandy's teasing face. "And I'm especially glad he's my 'er . . . friend' too. No matter what John Jo thinks."

But, of course, she had neither John Jo nor Paul anymore.

"None of it matters anyway." Lorna's smile faltered. "I was

so horrible to Paul after we got the telegram, he'll never want to see me again, let alone be my friend."

"You mean your 'er . . . friend,'" said Sandy, winking at her. "And once I'm back in London, you'll need to keep me *abreast* of any developments between the two of you."

He nudged her elbow and gave a filthy chuckle, but this time Lorna couldn't laugh along.

She followed her brother into the house with a tug of dread. She had to say good-bye to Sandy tomorrow, and who knew for how long this time?

"You never told me your brother could speak German," Nellie said the next morning through a mouthful of bread.

"German?" Lorna glanced up from studying her porridge. "No, Sandy speaks French."

"And German," insisted Nellie. "He's out there now chatting away all in German. I hadn't a clue what they were saying."

"Who?" Lorna was puzzled. "What who were saying?"

"What your Sandy was saying to our Paul." Nellie talked slowly, as if Lorna was being particularly dense. "I didn't have a clue 'cause it was all in *German*."

Sandy was talking German? To Paul?

Wait! Paul was back?

Lorna ran to the kitchen door and peered out.

Paul was back!

He was standing across the yard with Sandy, who was

leaning against the low wall talking earnestly. When Sandy lifted his cigarette to his mouth, he left it there to free up both hands to illustrate in the air whatever he was explaining.

Paul's hands were pushed deep into his pockets, his head bowed as if studying the toe caps of his boots, but he was clearly listening intently.

Finally, when Sandy stopped talking to take a drag on the cigarette, Paul said something. As he spoke, he pulled a piece of folded paper out of his shirt pocket. He opened it up and handed it to Sandy, who studied it carefully, nodding, face serious.

Might that be the same piece of newspaper Paul had torn from *The Scotsman* a few weeks before?

Paul scratched the back of his head, then swiped his hand across one eye and then the other.

Lorna's heart tightened.

What were they talking about?

Sandy placed a hand on Paul's shoulder, and Paul looked up. After another few seconds of conversation, the two men shook hands and Paul walked away round the corner. Sandy took another pull on his cigarette before grinding it into the cobbles with his shoe. Blowing out a long stream of smoke, he walked over to where Lorna was standing at the kitchen door.

"He wanted to know if I knew any more about Dresden than this," Sandy said, handing Lorna the piece of newspaper as he walked past her into the house.

The page was from *The Scotsman*, dated Thursday, 15 February 1945, and it was soft and well handled, splitting slightly along its folds. The newsprint was smudged, particularly down one long thin middle column, the black type leaking gray shadows as if a finger had followed each tiny line.

ALLIED AIRCRAFT HELP RUSSIANS
Three heavy attacks on Dresden

Dresden was attacked by 450 heavy bombers of the American Eighth Air Force yesterday after 800 heavy bombers of the RAF had struck at the city twice during Tuesday night.

In the first attack on Dresden, which began soon after 10 o'clock, there was cloud over the target, though the sky was clear along the route. By the time the second force reached the city, over three hours later, the cloud had gone (a meteorological officer suggested that the heat of the fires caused by the first attack may have been responsible), and the crews were able to see the effect of the first attack.

Nearly 650,000 incendiaries, together with 8,000-lb. high explosive bombs and hundreds of 4,000-pounders, were dropped on the city. Air crews reported that smoke was rising to a height of 15,000 feet. When the Americans arrived about 12.30 yesterday, they saw fires still burning and there was a layer of smoke over the whole city.

The German military spokesman quoted by the German News Agency stated that the RAF "hit exclusively the very heart of the city. The world-famous Zwinger Picture Gallery, the Palace, and the Opera House were destroyed in the attack."

There was a photograph of Dresden. The caption mentioned the palace and the opera house, the two bridges spanning the river. This was Dresden as Paul remembered it, as it had been before the bombing. But it wasn't Dresden anymore. Paul's Dresden was gone.

Lorna leaned against the door frame. She wanted to go after Paul, to make things right between them, but now was not the time. At best, he needed time to think about what Sandy had told him. At the very worst, he would be raging against the Allies and their bombs, blaming every British citizen for the pain that must be tearing apart his heart.

He might blame Lorna, just as she had blamed him.

The irony wasn't lost on her. How angry she'd been, never thinking how he'd been suffering this whole time. How could she have been so selfish as to think hers was the only loss that mattered?

She had to apologize to Paul. Perhaps not now, but definitely later. She had to tell him how very, very sorry she was, and how wrong she'd been.

And she would have to hope that he would forgive her.

Twenty-Four

As if letting Paul walk away from her wasn't hard enough, Lorna had to say good-bye to Sandy. He promised he'd come back to see her as soon as he could get more leave.

After they parted on Monday morning, Lorna sprinted all the way to school, trying to outrun the demons nipping at her heels. She was therefore on time for once, and immediately wished she'd stayed home.

Mr. Wilks would be the substitute teacher for Mrs. Murray's class. A crotchety old man, he rattled along from Longniddry each morning on an old iron bike whenever another teacher was sick. Apparently, he'd once taught at one of the posh boys' schools in Edinburgh, and everyone knew his only delight was making his students as miserable as him. When Lorna arrived, he had everyone standing in lines outside the school door, even though a steady drizzle had set in.

"Precipitation never hurt anyone," he barked from the warm and dry front hallway.

Mean old git!

Beside Mr. Wilks stood William Urquhart—and Iris, Lorna noted—and William was taking an inordinate amount of time to ring the bell.

Eventually, as Lorna followed the dripping mass inside and past William, still swinging the handbell, Iris stepped forward. She had clearly heard the news about John Jo because her expression was torn and uncertain, so Lorna slowed to let her speak. They hadn't talked at all since Good Friday, but given the circumstances, Lorna might listen, just this once.

Suddenly, William banged the bell back onto its shelf and stepped between the two girls.

"Good morning, Lorna," he said, taking Iris by the elbow and ushering her toward the classroom door before Iris could say anything.

Lorna was dumbstruck. Iris had adored John Jo for most of her life, yet she couldn't even stand up to William long enough to say she was sorry to hear that he might be dead.

She was not Lorna's Iris anymore. That girl wasn't even Lorna's friend.

Lorna followed them, her woolen stockings squelching in her wet shoes. When they reached the classroom, William steered Iris inside but then he paused, looking back at Lorna.

"What?" Lorna hated the way he looked at her, as if she

were something stuck to the bottom of his shoe.

William shrugged and disappeared into the room.

The day got no better. Mr. Wilks made them all change desks so they were sitting in alphabetical order, meaning Lorna was now next to Esther Bell.

All morning, Esther would pull her desk a few inches away from Lorna's, as if Lorna smelled bad. Every time, Mr. Wilks made her move it back again, but Esther's desk would migrate again and again once his back was turned. This routine amused Esther, and apparently Craig Buchanan too. Lorna just wanted to go home.

Other than Esther and Craig, however, the class was unusually quiet. Five other telegrams had arrived in Aberlady on the afternoon of Lorna's birthday. Four had reported other soldiers from John Jo's regiment missing in action. The fifth had been delivered to Mrs. Murray. A shroud of grief lay over the school, the village, for these Scottish soldiers—these fathers, sons, and brothers of Aberlady—but still, Lorna's guilt-ridden thoughts could not help but seek out a German soldier instead.

At the end of school, Lorna bolted for the door. If Iris was trying to catch her attention, she didn't care. The damage was done and Iris had missed her chance to repair it.

Once she was away from the school, Lorna's mood lightened considerably. The rain had passed on, leaving a mild afternoon, so she carried her coat over her arm and hummed to herself as she hurried along.

She was going to find Paul, and she would apologize and

commiserate, and perhaps she would kiss him, if he would let her. It would be a kiss of comfort and of friendship, a kiss saying, *I understand*. Still, the idea of it sent a buzz of anticipation through her.

Gradually, Lorna become conscious of the tune she was humming. It was "John Anderson, My Jo," the song for which her brother had been named.

Mrs. Mack had always sworn that the poet Robert Burns had written it especially for Lorna's mother to sing to John Jo when he was a baby. Lorna had been almost eleven before she had discovered that Burns had died more than a century before her brother was born, but she'd never admitted to Mrs. Mack that she knew about the lie.

There had been a John Anderson in each generation of Lorna's family for centuries, and because her mother had loved the Burns song so much—and because "my jo" meant "my beloved" in the old Scots tongue—she had given her firstborn son the nickname John Jo.

John Jo Anderson. Beloved. Yet he had gone back to the war thinking that his only sister hated him.

Guilt pinched at Lorna again, and she let the melody trail off to nothing.

The hawthorn bushes along the path were coming into flower, the white petals and the new leaves lush after that morning's rain. In the field far beyond them, Nellie whistled and clapped to call in the cows for milking.

Lorna suddenly became aware of an aircraft's drone coming up the Forth from the east, drowning out Nellie's calls.

It had to be a fighter plane; the engine was pitched too high for the deep-throated American bombers from East Fortune.

Lorna could see it, silhouetted dark against the bright sky over Gullane Point. She shielded her eyes with her hand, squinting to make out the details.

A Spitfire? Or maybe a Hurricane? From RAF Drem, probably. No, the angle of the wings was too sharp. So, if it wasn't a Spitfire, then what . . . ?

Lorna recognized the tail strut and the blunt wings even before she could make out the fuselage. A maelstrom of grays, not greens. And there were no familiar RAF roundels on the wingtips, only menacing black Luftwaffe crosses.

The wail of the air-raid siren in the village rose over the shrieking engine.

Messerschmitt! A Messerschmitt 110 was streaking toward her.

Lorna ducked, crouching beside the brambles but not losing sight of the plane. One wing dipped slightly, shifting the plane's path so it wouldn't fly directly over her head, but still close enough. The engines screamed as the plane sank lower. Surely the pilot wasn't trying to land! The field beyond the house was open and wide, but certainly not long enough to land a plane on, plus it had a herd of dairy cows ambling across it, and Nellie.

Nellie!

At that moment, Nellie looked up. The plane was no more than two hundred yards from her now, but she didn't move, apparently transfixed, even as the cows around her scattered.

"Nellie! Get down!" Lorna shouted, though Nellie could never hear her over that ungodly engine.

Nellie mustn't have realized this plane wasn't friendly. RAF pilots frequently buzzed the farm as they returned to base, deliberately sweeping low and waggling their wings. Couldn't Nellie see that this was no RAF joyrider? Obviously not, and Lorna was powerless to warn her.

Nellie lifted her hand to wave just as the Messerschmitt pilot opened fire.

Crack-crack-crack-crack-crack-crack!

Crack-crack-crack-crack-crack-crack!

The red lights of the tracer bullets spat from the wings, slicing the air from plane to ground. Dirt spurted up in parallel lines as the bullets ripped across the field toward Nellie and the herd.

Crack-crack-crack-crack-crack-crack!

Lorna was on her feet, yelling. "NELLIE! NELLIE! GET DOWN!"

The Messerschmitt was level with Lorna now, passing so low she could see the pilot within the long glass dome of the cockpit. He leaned forward, his shoulders hunched in concentration.

Crack-crack-crack-crack-crack-crack!

The puffs of dirt had almost reached Nellie. The cows were scattering, panicked into bursts of heavy speed, and Nellie disappeared behind the heifers as they lumbered past her. Then the machine-gun bullets reached them.

One of the cows staggered. Her back legs crumpled, as a

slash of red scorched the dirty white of her hide. She dropped like a rock, her front legs still moving, tearing at the grass, desperate to escape this dreadful predator. Then she raised her head and bellowed.

A second cow fell just beyond and lay completely still, head torn back and contorted into a position no living cow could have endured. The others had stampeded to the farthest corners of the field and were gathering together in the lee of the hedgerow, instinctively trusting their safety to the herd.

But the Messerschmitt was already beyond them, the urgency of the engines fading as the pilot banked sharply to the north, lowering his right wing until it pointed almost directly at the ground. The shape of the plane's squared-off wings and elongated body was clear to Lorna now, exactly as if it were printed on that tattered Aeroplane Spotter card in Sandy's collection.

But where was Nellie? Lorna couldn't see her. She ran down the path but managed no more than ten yards before it came again.

Crack-crack-crack-crack-crack-crack!

More machine-gun fire crackled in the air as another plane screamed directly over Lorna, then a second, then a third.

Lorna threw herself on the ground, arms over her head, as if that would somehow protect her, and waited for more gunfire. When none came, she tentatively looked up, to find and then follow this trio of planes. Her terror was instantly diluted by relief. There were red, white, and blue roundels under the wings of the lead plane.

A Spitfire! Or rather, three Spitfires, snapping at the trespasser's heels, as Canny and Caddy would chase a fox off their land.

The Spitfires tore after the Messerschmitt, by then barely more than a smudge of black in the blue sky, as it headed north over Fife. Then it suddenly banked again to the east and disappeared over the North Sea, its sheepdogs not far behind.

Lorna clambered to her feet and ran. She could see the two cows. One was motionless, but the other still writhed and twitched, though its agonized bellows were growing fainter. But Lorna could not see Nellie.

Lorna was almost at the gate into the farmyard before she had a clear view past the cows to the bundle of brown sacking heaped on the grass. But Lorna knew that it was not sacking. That was Nellie in her Land Army uniform, and she wasn't moving.

Lorna threw her coat and bag to the ground and sprinted through the gate. The quickest route was through the yard, past the house, but the buildings would put Nellie out of her sight for a few seconds, so Lorna started shouting.

"Nellie, I'm coming. Nellie, hold on. Help, please, someone! Dad! Paul! Anyone! Please! Help us!"

Lorna flew round the corner of the house, her chest heaving, and there was Paul ahead of her, running to where

Nellie lay, flanked by the two cows. Not one of the three was moving.

Nellie was lying on her side, curled into a ball, with her knees up and her arms wrapped tightly around her chest. When Paul reached her, he crouched down and put his hand to Nellie's head, then her throat.

Thank God Paul was there so Lorna didn't have to do this on her own. But what if Nellie was already dead? "Please, God, no!"

Paul was talking quietly to Nellie as Lorna approached. That had to mean Nellie was alive, right? Paul wouldn't be talking to Nellie if he hadn't found a pulse, would he?

"Nellie, can you hear me?" His fingers were still pressed to Nellie's neck. "Nellie, it is Paul. Can you talk to me?"

There was no response, Paul looked up desperately at Lorna. Nellie remained absolutely motionless.

"Nellie, I know you are still with us," Paul continued. "I can feel your heart keeping you with us. Lorna is here too. Can you open your eyes so you can see her?"

He glanced back to the house and farm buildings.

"We need to—" Paul got no further for suddenly, Nellie groaned. Her whole body shuddered, and she vomited.

The vile yellow liquid spewed onto the grass, and Paul fell back out of its path. Nellie gasped. Then, as if a blast of pain were racking her body, she let out a terrible moan. She rolled onto her back as if that might stop the agony, and Lorna could see that Nellie's arms weren't wrapped around her chest

263

as she'd thought. They were wrapped around her belly.

And there was blood!

A deep red stain darkened Nellie's pants.

Lorna took an involuntary step back.

"Paul!" she croaked. "She's been hit. Nellie's bleeding! He shot Nellie!"

With a shaking finger, Lorna pointed at the dark stain.

"Oh my God, Paul! What do we do? What do we do?"

She could feel hysteria rising to choke her as Paul moved to see what Lorna was pointing at.

"Noooooo," Nellie groaned. "Not shot."

"But Nellie," said Paul. "You are bleeding, so—"

"Oh my God!" Lorna suddenly knew. "She's losing the baby!"

Paul's head snapped up to look at Lorna.

"Baby?"

"Nellie's pregnant. But now she's . . ." Lorna couldn't bring herself to say the word "miscarrying" but pointed to Nellie again and whispered, "Paul, it's the baby."

Paul seemed frozen.

"We need to help her," she pleaded. "We can't let her die."

At last, Paul nodded.

"Yes," he said, "we must get her warm and under cover. Quickly."

"The shed's closest. There's still straw in there, from the lambing, remember? The heat lamp is still in there, and I'll get some blankets."

Paul nodded. "But first, will you help me to lift her up?

Please steady her, so I do not give her more pain."

Nellie's eyes were still shut tight, her skin deathly white and her lips almost blue.

"Nellie, can you hear me?" Paul spoke slowly and clearly. "In a moment, I will lift you and carry you to where you will be warm and comfortable. Then we will fetch the doctor."

There was no outward sign that Nellie could hear, and Lorna wondered if she had passed out again, but Paul continued anyway.

"Tell me if I hurt you, Nellie. I will lift you up now."

With Lorna's help, Paul slid one arm under Nellie's shoulders and hooked his other arm under her knees. With some effort, he pushed himself up to standing, Nellie cradled against his chest.

Lorna laid her hand on Nellie's forehead. It was hot and clammy.

"Paul's got you safe," she whispered. "It'll be all right."

Still no response, so Paul took a couple of tentative steps toward the farm buildings. The grass was muddy and slick after the morning's rain, and Paul had to step carefully.

"I'll meet you in the shed in a minute," Lorna said to Paul. "Will you be all right with her?"

She waited long enough to see Paul nod, then raced across the field. Just before she reached the yard, she looked back. The deadweight of Nellie's body had sunk lower in Paul's arms, but still he plodded on.

Quickly Lorna gathered bedsheets and towels from the house, as well as a couple of thick blankets. Balancing the pile on one arm, she grabbed the kettle from the stove before hurrying back to the lambing shed. As she got there, Paul rounded the corner, mouth grimly set and muscles straining.

Lorna placed the kettle and bed linen between two of the pens and cut through the binding round a sheaf of hay. Laying it in a thick layer, she covered it with a blanket and two sheets.

Paul appeared at the door with Nellie and laid her carefully down onto the makeshift bed. Lorna covered her with the other blanket as Paul stood, rubbing the muscles of his arms.

Nellie was shivering, so Lorna lit the heat lamp and brought it to stand nearby.

"Can you stay with Nellie while I run to the village to telephone the doctor?"

"Of course," Paul said. "I will not leave her."

At the door of the shed, Lorna hesitated. The last few minutes—the plane, the guns, the cows, Nellie—had been so intense, so terrifying, that it was only now that Lorna remembered this was the first time she had been with Paul since she had shouted at him.

But now, there seemed to be no resentment, no anger.

"Paul?" she said. "I am so sorry. About everything."

Paul held her gaze for a moment.

"I know," he said, "but now you must go."

As she ran toward Aberlady, Lorna held on tight to Paul's forgiveness, again so grateful that he was there with her.

Twenty-Five

After spending almost an hour with Nellie, the doctor decided that she didn't require immediate hospitalization and that she could be moved to her own bed. He insisted, however, that Nellie stay in bed for at least a week, and he confined her to the house for even longer.

"She's a lucky young lady, Jock," said Dr. Mackenzie to Lorna's father, as Lorna handed them each a mug of tea. "Without the quick thinking of your Lorna and the German lad, she wouldn't have lasted more than half an hour in that field, and she certainly wouldn't have kept hold of her baby."

For Nellie's baby was still alive, he told them, against all the odds, and with rest, he saw no reason why Nellie wouldn't take the pregnancy to full term.

Lorna glanced at her dad, expecting an explosion at the

news that Nellie was carrying a baby, but he just nodded and muttered an "Aye, well." Soon the conversation turned to the weather and the chance of a late frost damaging the strawberry crop. When their mugs were empty, Lorna's dad thanked Dr. Mackenzie with a handshake and waved him off at the door.

"You knew Nellie was pregnant before today?" Lorna couldn't hold it back any longer.

Her father sighed.

"I'm the father to three children, the uncle and godfather to half a dozen more. And I'm a farmer. D'you not think I might know the signs that a lassie's carrying?"

"But you didn't say anything."

"No, because sometimes discretion is the better part of valor, and Nellie was still doing her work. But now, she'll have to go back to London so her own parents can deal with her. If nothing else, it'll save us any more gossip."

Lorna was shaken by her father saying "any more gossip," but she pressed on about Nellie.

"She can't go home. Her mum's dead and her father would beat her up and throw her out. We can't turn her away; she needs us. And since when do you care about what the gossipy old women think?"

"Perhaps I don't care. But I could do without the wrath of heaven that'll be brought down on us when word of this reaches Reverend Urquhart, or worse, his charming wife."

"Since when do you care about the wrath of any of them?" Lorna retorted. "You haven't set foot in that church since

Mum's . . . well, not for years. I'm surprised you can even remember the minister's name."

"You forget, Fat Bob Urquhart was at school with me. But whether I choose to sit through his dull sermons week after week is my business. This conversation is about a farmhand who can't work anymore. This is a farm, not a home for wayward lassies."

"Nellie's not a 'wayward lassie,' she's just . . ." Lorna wasn't sure how to put it. "She's just had bad luck."

Lorna's father only harrumphed in reply and scowled his way to his chair with his newspaper.

After a few days, Lorna's father finally agreed that Nellie could stay, though Lorna suspected his decision had more to do with Mrs. Mack threatening to quit than anything Lorna had said. Either way, Nellie could stay, at least until the baby was born.

"And then we'll see," he said. "I'm making no promises, mind."

He wrote to the Land Army to explain that while Nellie wasn't fit to work, he would be willing to keep her with board and lodging at the farm. He also requested they send two new Land Girls to Craigielaw for the summer. In the meantime, Lorna would cover Nellie's work.

Doing the early morning and afternoon milking, as well as her own schoolwork and chores, soon took their toll on Lorna. Gray circles underscored her eyes, and she was often too tired to eat but yearned to go to bed instead. She tried to find a few minutes to spend with Paul each day, when she took him his tea or collected his plates again, but she wasn't actually sure Paul wanted to see her anymore.

Once they'd known Nellie was safe, Lorna had tried to apologize again to Paul for what she'd said on her birthday, but he'd waved away her words.

"Lorna, do not apologize. Our countries are at war. That is how it is."

Lorna had held out her hand to him, but Paul had walked away with only a "Good night."

Over the two weeks since then, Paul had seemed happy to talk to her about the farm, the weather, or Nellie's recovery. But nothing else. And if, God forbid, Lorna tried to touch him, he'd immediately sped off to deal with something of vital importance.

Yet he seemed to have no problem being around Mrs. Mack and Nellie. Lorna had seen him going in or out of the house several times in one day. Sometimes Nellie would meet him at the door, or wave at him from the window, and he'd smile and wave back. But with Lorna, he'd barely even acknowledge her existence anymore.

Lorna didn't know whether to be hurt or angry, so she let herself be both. She yearned to talk to Iris about it all, to pour her sorry heart out to her best friend, but these days Iris was permanently wrapped round William Urquhart. And if Lorna caught her eye across the classroom, Iris would just look away.

One afternoon, Lorna decided she'd finally had enough.

She excused herself from Mr. Wilks's class with an upset stomach and walked home.

It was May now, and just walking in the sun helped clear some of the miserable fog clouding Lorna's mind. She came to a stop on the farmhouse doorstep, however, at the sound of voices in the kitchen. The words were muffled by the heavy oak door, but clearly two people were in conversation.

Then came Nellie's tinkling laugh, and for a moment, Lorna was pleased to hear her sound more like her old self than she had in weeks.

But suddenly Lorna knew who Nellie was flirting with, and her hand tightened on the handle.

How dare she? Just because Nellie didn't have Chuck anymore, it didn't mean she had to turn her attention to Paul.

Abruptly, the door to the kitchen opened. Paul was still talking to Nellie instead of looking where he was going, and in her surprise, Lorna couldn't get out of his way.

Before she knew what was happening, Lorna was falling backward. Her eyes shut instinctively, waiting for her head to slam against the stone, knowing there was absolutely nothing she could do to stop it.

And then Paul's arms were around her, catching her inches from the cobbles, and Lorna's hands were clinging to the sleeves of his sweater as if she were suspended over a cliff edge. Even after he'd lifted her onto her feet, she couldn't release her grip. Her heart was pounding, her knees wobbly, so she pressed her face hard against his shoulder to steady herself.

After a moment's hesitation, Paul relaxed a little and rested his cheek against her hair. He smelled wonderful. She had missed him so much.

But then Paul was pulling away, unlocking her hold.

"I apologize," he mumbled, and walked quickly across the yard, head down, hands in pockets.

Lorna's head swam. What had just happened?

He'd held her close, he'd almost kissed her hair, and then he'd gone. He'd chatted with Nellie, and laughed with her, but he couldn't even give Lorna a smile?

She just didn't understand.

There was a noise nearby, and Lorna looked up to see Nellie standing just inside the house, eyebrows raised, her mouth twitching as if she were trying to fight a smile. Not only was she trying to steal Paul from Lorna, but she was finding it funny too.

"And what are you laughing at?"

Nellie looked surprised by Lorna's tone, but instead of replying, she just went back into the house with a dismissive wave.

How dare she?

Lorna followed Nellie inside, slamming the door behind her.

"Nellie, I mean it. What do you and Paul find so hilarious?"

Nellie sat down in a chair by the fire and picked up a sock and a darning needle from her sewing bag. A sly smile crept across her face.

"Oh, you know, this and that," she said.

"Well, it's an awful lot of 'this and that,'" Lorna retorted, "considering all the time he spends in here."

She pulled a chair from the table and dropped down into it. In spite of her annoyance, it felt good to sit for a moment or two.

"And why would you be bothered if I spend time with a fellow farmhand, eh?" Nellie asked. "I can see the green tinge from here, duckie. If I didn't know any better, I'd say you're *a wee bit jealous, ma wee lassie*."

Nellie's attempt at a Scottish accent made Lorna cringe, though the usual flush was rising up her neck at Nellie's accusation.

"Jealous?" Lorna said. "Why would I care what you and Paul get up to?"

Nellie suddenly bent double, clasping her belly with one hand. Lorna dashed over to her.

"Nellie, what's wrong?"

But Nellie was laughing, her face bright pink.

"Oh, Lorna, you are so funny," she choked out, "saying 'why would I care?' So funny!"

It was good to see Nellie laughing again, but since Lorna was the butt of the joke, she refused to join in.

"I really don't see—"

"Oh my sweet girl," Nellie said fondly, wiping tears away with the sleeve of her cardigan. "You are clueless sometimes. Why would a lad like Paul look twice at me? In case you had forgotten, I am in the pudding club with some other bloke's baby."

Nellie held her hand out to Lorna, but Lorna ignored it.

"I do like talking to Paul, I'll admit that," Nellie said, "because he's a lovely fella. But do you want to know what we talk about mostly, Paul and me?"

Lorna shrugged, as if she wasn't desperate to know.

"We talk about you, Lorna. About what an amazing girl you are, helping me stay here till the baby's born. And about how clever you are, and about how you need to eat more. And we talk about how much your father and brothers love you and want to protect you."

She reached out her hand again, and this time Lorna took it, allowing Nellie to pull her down to kneel on the thick hearth rug at Nellie's feet. Nellie leaned toward Lorna.

"*And* we talk about how hard it is for Paul to keep his distance from the girl he loves, and how much he wishes he didn't have to."

"He said he—"

"He didn't need to. He has 'in love' written all over him, duckie, just like one of my old man's Navy tattoos." Nellie drew Lorna's hand onto her knee and traced her finger across Lorna's forearm as if following letters inked there. "And I'm sure you have 'in love' written all over you too."

Lorna stared at Nellie's finger as if she really were tattooing words onto her arm. How could Paul be telling Nellie such things while ignoring Lorna? She opened her mouth to ask, but Nellie seemed to understand.

"Paul is trying to protect you, in his own way. He doesn't want you to feel you have to choose between him and your brother, at least until you know that John is safe. But he still loves you."

Lorna drew in a long, slow breath and as she released it, she allowed herself to relax. She should go and find Paul. She'd be happy just to be his friend now that she understood, now she knew he loved her. She should go and tell him . . . but she found she could barely move. She was exhausted.

There were still so many things to worry about—John Jo, Sandy, Dad, Nellie and her baby, Iris, the war—but at least for tonight, one worry had evaporated. Paul loved her.

Laying her head down onto Nellie's knees, she let Nellie smooth her hair with a warm, gentle hand, and soon sleep stole every other worry away too.

Twenty-Six

A few days later, Lorna was carrying eggs back from the henhouse when the church bells rang out.

Nellie was sitting in the sun outside the scullery door, knitting something tiny in white wool. The two collies were stretched out close by. But now Nellie and the dogs were on their feet staring toward the church, toward the bells. And then more chimes floated like an echo through the mild afternoon air from the direction of Longniddry. The church bells of East Lothian, and all across the British Isles, had been silenced when war was declared in 1939. If the bells rang again, everyone knew, the Germans were invading.

But these bells couldn't mean an invasion; the Germans weren't capable of that anymore. Only a few days earlier, Lorna had listened to the slow, rich voice of a BBC newsreader announce to the world:

"This is London calling. This is a news flash. The German radio has just announced that Hitler is dead. I will repeat that. The German radio has just announced that Hitler is dead."

Finally, Lorna had let herself believe that the end was coming. And now, all these church bells ringing, just before three o'clock on Monday, May 7, 1945, could mean only one thing.

The war was over. Europe was at peace.

The resonant peals were almost drowned out by the clatter of boots as Lorna's father and Paul ran around the corner. Canny and Caddy began barking excitedly.

Her father was the first to find a voice.

"Is that it, then? Have the bloody Jerries surrendered?" he said, looking greedily toward the church bell tower.

Lorna grimaced as she caught Paul's eye, but he shook his head imperceptibly.

"Come on then, get the radio on," Lorna's father said as he strode inside.

"I'll get it," said Nellie. No longer hidden under her bulky uniform, her bump was already starting to show under the cotton of her summer dress.

Lorna's dad disappeared after Nellie, and Lorna followed, clutching the basket tight. As she went in, Lorna realized that Paul hadn't moved.

"Come and listen." Lorna beckoned. "It might all be over."

"Yes," he said, "it might."

The wireless burst to life inside and she could hear the

chimes of Big Ben strike once, twice, three times.

Paul started to follow her, so Lorna went inside. Nellie and her father were already seated, leaning toward the wireless set. A voice, the unmistakable growling bass of Prime Minister Winston Churchill, crackled around the kitchen.

"Yesterday morning at two forty-one a.m. at General Eisenhower's headquarters, General Jodl, the representative of the German High Command, and Grand Admiral Dönitz, the designated head of the German state, signed the act of unconditional surrender of all German land, sea, and air forces in Europe . . ."

Lorna clutched Nellie's chair for support, her knees suddenly weak. She bowed her head.

It was true then—the war was actually over.

Paul stood just inside the scullery door, listening intently. His muscles were tensed, as if he expected to have to run for his life, but his face was as expressionless as the first time Lorna had seen him. He'd withdrawn behind the protection of his mask. And Lorna could guess why.

The war was over, yet the future was still uncertain, particularly for a prisoner far from home. How long would it take for the POW camps to be disbanded, and the men sent home? And did Paul even have a home or family to go back to? Lorna didn't know. But she knew no letters had come through the Red Cross from his mother or his sister since before the bombing of Dresden in February.

Lorna shivered. What would that mean for her and Paul?

Lorna didn't know the answer to that either.

". . . Hostilities will end officially at one minute after midnight tonight, Tuesday, the eighth of May, but in the interests of saving lives the cease-fire began yesterday to be sounded all along the front, and our dear Channel Islands are also to be freed today. . . ."

Outside, the dogs were barking again, and Lorna opened the door just as Derek Milne propped his black iron-framed bike against the outside wall.

Lorna called Caddy out of the way as Derek almost tripped over her.

"D'you hear that, Lorna?" Derek wheezed. "It's over, it's all over!"

"Churchill's on the wireless right now," she said. "You didn't need to come all this way, though. We heard the bells."

The bright light vanished from Derek's face, and he dug his hand into his pocket.

"Actually, I was on my way up here anyway."

Derek pulled out a small brown envelope, but as Lorna went to take it, Derek held it back.

"It's addressed to your dad."

The memory of the last telegram, on the afternoon of her birthday, clutched at Lorna's heart. Derek clearly remembered it, too.

"Is he inside?"

Lorna nodded as a wave of burning acid rose in her gut. She stumbled aside so that Derek could come into the kitchen. Her dad stood to greet him.

Churchill was still talking. *"Advance, Britannia! Long live the cause of freedom! God save the King!"*

As it had done four weeks before, the blood drained from her father's face at the sight of the brown envelope in Derek's hand. After a moment's hesitation, he took it.

Everything froze. As the booming voice on the wireless dissipated into silence, there was only Lorna and her dad. And that envelope.

Lorna's father tried to tear the flap, but his hands were shaking, his fingers suddenly too clumsy for the fine paper.

Lorna took the envelope from her father, pulled out the single sheet, and handed it back to him. Holding the message at an angle away from Lorna, he read the message.

Suddenly, his chin dropped onto his chest, and his whole body sagged.

"Dad?" Lorna whispered. "Tell me."

He lifted his head. His dark brown pupils were awash, the skin around his eyes reddening as the first tear trickled into the graying stubble of his cheek.

How could bad news be dropped on them so quickly on the tail of such good news? It wasn't fair, it wasn't right.

But even as Lorna's own tears brimmed over, the corners of her father's mouth lifted.

"He's alive, Lorna. My lad is alive."

He held out the telegram, and as she took it, he sat down hard in his chair, dropping his head into his hands. His shoulders shook, and for the first time in her life, Lorna saw her dad sob.

As before, Lorna struggled to understand the message, to

make sense of the contradiction of her father's words and his tears. But sure enough, Sergeant John Joseph Anderson had been found in a prisoner-of-war camp in Germany. He was injured, it said, but alive.

Lorna dropped to her knees in front of her father. He wrapped strong arms around her, and she let his thick, warm shirt soak up her tears. She sniffed, and without letting her go, her father pulled a clean handkerchief from his pocket.

How many little-girl tears had been dried over the years by her dad's soft cotton hankie?

"Dad, I am so sorry! It was my fault that John Jo left." Lorna was powerless to stop the confession that had been choking her for weeks. "He was angry with me for talking to Paul, and we had a fight. I said I didn't care if he came back or not, and he punched Paul, and then he left. He didn't even say good-bye."

Lorna burrowed her face into her father's shoulder.

"And if he had been killed, it would have been my fault too."

Her father's arms stayed tight around her. Then he gently pushed her away. He took the handkerchief and wiped her cheeks and nose. Then he hugged her to him again.

"It's over. It's all over," he said softly into her hair. "And none of this was your fault. The war is over and our John is coming home."

"But Dad, I—"

"The war made all sorts of people do all sorts of stupid things, but now that it's over, we will have to work out how to make the best of the consequences."

Lorna's father laid his hand onto Nellie's arm. She was crying too, pressing her knitting to her face.

"Isn't that right, Miss Nellie? People make silly mistakes during wartime, but together we can work them out."

Nellie dropped her knitting into her lap and held out her hands to Lorna and her father.

"Mr. Anderson, I'm so happy that John is safe. And that the war's really over. But now," Nellie sniffed hard, "I'm scared about what's going to happen to me."

"Oh, lassie, don't you worry. You're part of this family now, so we'll be with you for whatever's coming." Lorna's father gestured toward Nellie's belly. "And something tells me it'll be an adventure."

Lorna glanced up. Derek had gone, and so had Paul, and one of them had closed the door behind them.

Her father patted his pocket. Failing to find another handkerchief, he used his shirtsleeve instead and stood up.

"Right!" he said, his voice cracking. "This calls for a celebration. Nellie, get some glasses down, and I'll get the beer. I'm sure a wee drop of stout will do that baby of yours no end of good."

He strode across the room, but at the pantry door, he looked back.

"And Lorna, go and bring back that young man of yours. We don't have any of that fine German beer he was telling me about, but I am sure Belhaven's will suit him just as well."

Had he really called Paul *that young man of yours*? He

knew? And he wasn't angry?

Lorna's father reappeared from the pantry, bottles in his hands. Seeing Lorna's astonishment, he laughed out loud. Wonderfully loud.

"Lorna Jane, do you honestly think that your old man can't spot the flush of a young girl's cheek and the bounce in a young man's step? For all that he's a Jerry, Paul's a good lad. He's suffered enough for a boy of his age, so you might as well enjoy each other's company while you can.

"But learn this lesson well," he said, shaking his finger in mock admonition. "I have eyes in the back of my head. So wherever you go and whatever you do, you can assume I will know about it."

He kissed her forehead.

"Now, get that boy in here before I change my mind and chase him off my farm with a pitchfork."

He set the bottles down and flipped off the first cap with his penknife. Lorna hesitated only a moment longer before she did as she was told.

She had gone several steps when she sensed something behind her and turned. Paul was standing by the wall outside the door, head tilted back. He looked drained, exhausted, lost.

Would Paul still want to keep a distance between them now? Because she didn't. She couldn't.

Crossing the space between them, Lorna laid her hand against his cheek. His eyes opened, though they didn't focus on her immediately, as if he were somewhere very far away.

"Paul," she whispered. "I'm here."

She slid her hand into the short hair at the back of his neck and drew his face down so she could kiss the soft skin of his forehead, then his cheeks, then along his jaw. Finally, she kissed his lips, tenderly, to reassure him that they could be together now, and that everything would be fine.

It wasn't long before Paul's mouth responded with reassurances of his own.

Twenty-Seven

Paul was opening another bottle of Belhaven's when the door burst open and Mrs. Mack barreled in, flushed and breathing hard.

"Oh my . . . thank you, dear . . . goodness!" Mrs. Mack panted. "Isn't it . . . marvelous? The news . . . about the war, and about . . . our John too. . . . Derek came straight to tell me . . . about . . . the telegram. So I headed right . . . back!"

Lorna took Mrs. Mack's carpetbag and shopping basket, while the housekeeper flopped into a chair, drawing in long breaths and fanning herself with her coat collar.

"Oh, I shouldn't be dashing around at my age . . . but it's such wonderful news, isn't it?"

Finally, she stopped talking and looked at the amused faces around her.

"Did I interrupt something?"

Lorna bent down to hug Mrs. Mack, and her father squeezed his old friend's shoulder.

"Not at all, Edna," he said. "And yes, it is wonderful, isn't it? Thank you for coming back. Can I get you a glass of beer to celebrate, or a dram?"

"Oh no, dear, not whisky, but a wee cup of tea would be perfect." She struggled to her feet. "Let me put the kettle on, and there's a wee bit of cake in the pantry."

Lorna gently pressed her back into the chair.

"You get your breath back. I'll get the tea."

As Lorna walked past her father, he looked pointedly at his watch.

"Once you've done that," he said to her, "those heifers aren't going to milk themselves now, are they?"

Paul put his glass down on the table.

"I am happy to milk the cows, Mr. Anderson. But before I go"—Paul hesitated—"there is something else I would like to do."

As Paul drew a white linen wrapping out of his pocket, there was a knock on the door.

"I'll get it," said Nellie, already walking over to open it.

"Is Lorna home?"

Lorna immediately lost track of what Paul had in his hand. That was Iris's voice.

"I'd like to talk to her, if she's here," Iris continued, "if she'll speak to me."

In two steps Lorna was across the room, throwing the door wide open.

"Of course I'll speak to you, Iris, you ninny!"

With a cry, Iris rushed into the room, letting Lorna enfold her in a hug.

"I been wanting to tell you how sorry I am," said Iris, "about John Jo, and about—"

"It's fine." Lorna squeezed her harder.

"And I didn't *not* want to talk to you, but William said I shouldn't. And I wouldn't blame you if you never want to talk to me ever again, after what I said to William about you and—"

Iris stopped talking suddenly. She was staring at Paul as if he were a growling dog, terrified but fascinated.

"Oh! I didn't expect . . ."

Paul nodded to Iris, smiling slightly, and put whatever it was back in his pocket.

"Look who it is!" said Lorna's father, walking toward Iris. "Young Miss Robertson. It's been a long while since we saw you. And you're just in time for a cup of tea."

"Oh, thank you," Iris stammered, dragging her eyes away from Paul. "It's wonderful news about John Jo. . . . Derek stopped by to tell us."

"Yes, indeed, a very special day. One we'll remember for a while yet. Come on, Lorna, what about that kettle?"

"Now, Lorna, I'll be getting that," said Mrs. Mack, pushing herself out of her chair and walking stiffly over to the stove, "so you girls can have a natter."

As Mrs. Mack picked up the kettle and headed into the scullery, there was another knock at the door.

"Who's this now?" said Lorna's father, with a chuckle. "It's like Sauchiehall Street on a Saturday night."

Nellie was still beside the open door.

"Hello," she said to the new arrival. "Come to join the party, have you, duckie?"

"Is Mrs. McMurdough here?"

Iris froze.

"Who?" said Nellie, sounding puzzled. "Oh, Mrs. Mack!"

"Yes, Mrs. Mack. Is she here? My mother needs to speak to her."

"William?" Iris gasped like a child caught doing something naughty, and grabbed Lorna's hand.

William came into the kitchen, frowning.

"Iris, what are you doing here? I thought you were helping your mother with the bunting."

"Oh, well, yes, I was," said Iris, "but then, I decided that I had to talk to Lorna—"

"*Had* to talk to Lorna?" His tone was snide. "What did you *have* to talk to Lorna about so suddenly?"

Lorna waited for Iris to crumple, to lower her head and apologize, but instead, Iris lifted her chin and squared her shoulders.

"Actually, I *wanted* to talk to Lorna," she said, "and why is that so strange? Today is a historic day and we've been best friends a long time."

"But you promised not to come up here unsupervised." William was talking to Iris as if no one were listening. "For your own safety, of course."

Nellie snorted with laughter. "Safety, my arse," she muttered, but William didn't seem to hear.

Lorna was about to tell William to get lost when Iris let Lorna's hand drop and took a step toward him.

"Yes, I know I promised, but that was then." Iris seemed to have grown at least an inch. "But I wanted to come because the war is over now, and John Jo is safe, and frankly, we should be celebrating that. And anyway, Lorna's my friend and I simply wanted to see her. I'm sorry if it slipped my mind to ask your permission to talk to my best friend."

Was that sarcasm? Good for Iris!

Lorna didn't bother to hide her smile at William's startled expression, though he quickly rearranged it back into one of superiority and disdain.

"Of course you don't need my permission, but—" he said.

"Well that's fine then," Iris interrupted, clearly enjoying her newfound gumption. "And why were you asking for Mrs. Mack?"

"Mrs. Mack?" he said. "Oh, yes, Mrs. Mack. Yes, I came to make sure that she knew about the tea tomorrow for the Victory in Europe celebration, for VE Day."

William scanned the kitchen for Mrs. Mack. Instead he found Paul, and again his expression faltered.

Paul stood perfectly still, watching William. Again, the mask had come down, and Lorna could see the rounded muscles in his shoulders tense beneath his once-white cotton shirt, but this time Paul didn't look like he would run. He looked like he might fight.

Lorna's father stepped in front of Paul.

"Victory celebration tomorrow? Excellent." He rubbed his hands together, almost gleefully. "So what'll you be asking Mrs. Mack for then?"

"My mother asked me to tell Mrs. McMurdough that she will be requiring at least three sponge cakes for the afternoon tea, and as many scones as Mrs. Mack can provide for the bonfire party in the evening. With jam, strawberry, if possible."

Lorna's father studied William. "Your mother *requires* that, does she?"

His tone was loaded, and William shifted from one foot to the other.

"That is, my mother *expects* Mrs. McMurdough to bring . . . I mean, she would *like* Mrs. McMurdough to bring—"

"That's a bit more like it," Lorna's father said, before turning toward the scullery. "Mrs. McMurdough, have you a moment?"

Mrs. Mack came in, still wearing her coat, and seeing William, she raised her eyebrows.

"Can I help you, son?"

William glanced first at Lorna's father, then uncertainly at Iris. To Lorna's annoyance, Iris moved beside William, tucking herself slightly behind his shoulder as if to bolster him against a strong wind.

William immediately looked bolder and stood straighter.

"Mrs. McMurdough, my mother sent me to ask you whether you would be"—William's glance at Lorna's father was almost imperceptible—"*kind enough* to contribute some of your delicious baking for the Victory celebration party tomorrow. On the Sea Green. Tomorrow. To celebrate the victory. In Europe."

Before Mrs. Mack could respond, Lorna's dad slapped his hand onto William's back, making William flinch.

"A Victory party, Edna," Lorna's father declared. "But it won't be much of a party without some of your legendary cakes, I'd say."

Mrs. Mack chuckled.

"I don't know about the 'legendary' bit, but aye, son, go tell your mother I'll do what I can." She looked up at the clock on the mantelpiece and grimaced. "And I'd better get on with it."

She headed for the door, suddenly remembering that in her hand was the kettle, not her bag.

"I'll forget my head one of these days," she said, handing the kettle to Lorna and picking up her carpetbag from the chair. "Now, there's cold tongue and tatties in the pantry for your tea, Lorna, since I'd better be getting home to make these cakes for Lady Muck . . ."

She glanced, only a little sheepishly, at William.

". . . I mean, for Mrs. Urquhart."

As she left, Lorna's dad turned to Paul.

"Aye, and if there's to be some slacking off for a party tomorrow, you and me had better get some work done today then, laddie."

Lorna's father gestured for Paul to follow Mrs. Mack out of the door, then winked at Lorna.

"And if you ever get round to making that cup of tea, lassie, we'll have ours out there."

As the door clicked into place behind the two men, William coughed.

"And we should go, Iris?"

"Actually," Iris said, "I'm going to stay here with Lorna for a while."

The temptation to cheer was almost too much for Lorna. Iris sounded so self-assured.

For a second or two, William looked dazed, as if he'd just woken up from a sleep and had no idea where he was.

Iris stepped forward and gave him a kiss on the cheek.

"But you can come back later, if you like, to walk me home."

"But Mother needs me to—"

Lorna couldn't keep out of it any longer.

"Of course your mother needs you, William," she said, mimicking Iris's kindly tone, "so Iris will have to find her own way back. But don't worry, I think she knows the way by now. And if she's worried, I can always ask our farmhand, Paul, to walk her home."

Iris giggled at this—actually giggled—and then pinched Lorna's arm, as if they were six again. Lorna shoved her away, laughing. Iris was back—*her* Iris—for a while, at least.

William looked furious, but short of dragging Iris down the road by the arm, he seemed to realize there wasn't a lot he could do. He turned on his heel and left.

Lorna copied Iris, fondly waving to him from the stoop, but Iris smacked her friend's hand down.

"Stop it, Lorna, we mustn't tease him."

"Why not? He deserves to be teased. He's a pompous ass, and I don't know how you don't want to tease him all the time."

Iris stopped laughing.

"I don't tease him," she said, "because I love him."

Lorna groaned, but Iris took hold of her arm.

"But I do. I really do. I know he can be a bit silly sometimes, and a bit pompous, but underneath, he really is very sweet. He wants me to be safe, that's all."

"And why wouldn't you be safe when you're with me?" Lorna asked. "And don't tell me it's because of Paul. William's been trying to get between you and me for months now. And he's managed it."

"But remember, Lorna, he's an only child and his mother has treated him like a little prince all his life. You and me learned to share because we had brothers and sisters, but William, well, William got to keep all his toys to himself."

"Is that what you are to him?" snorted Lorna. "A toy that he won't share with anyone else?"

"Oh, Lorna, you know I don't mean that. I was being, you know, metaphorical."

"Metaphorical?" Lorna snorted. "Or 'ridiculous'? I don't know how you put up with him. He split us up, and you just let him. How could you do that?"

Iris's face was so sad that Lorna almost wished she hadn't spoken. Except that it had to be said. Lorna had to make Iris understand how hurt she had been.

She went into the kitchen and Iris followed her inside a few moments later.

"I did it because I was in love," Iris said. "And because all I could think of was William. And because, well, because I suppose I took it for granted that you would always be there for me, no matter what."

Iris was looking at the ground now, her voice quiet.

"And I know what I did was wrong, and that I hurt you by telling . . . by doing what I did. But please don't judge me, Lorna." Iris lifted glistening eyes. "Because I think you know how easy it is to do something you regret, because you've fallen in love with someone."

"But William is so . . ." Which word should she use?

"Are you really going to lecture me about falling in love with the wrong boy?" Iris asked, with unexpected fire.

Suddenly, Iris was standing up to Lorna in the same way she'd stood up to William.

"And don't you think that you hurt me sometimes too?" Iris continued, "the way you always put William down, the way you ridicule me for liking him? That's not what friends do, Lorna."

Lorna bowed her head. How could she have been so mean

about William, and still expect Iris to be on her side about Paul?

"Iris, I'm sorry. I didn't think . . ."

There was a moment's pause.

"I know," Iris replied, "me neither."

Then the two girls hugged each other tight, as if it would make up for all those weeks apart. And in a way it did.

When Lorna stepped back, she saw Iris differently, and not just because of her tears.

"Please tell me we are best friends again. Proper best friends, who won't let all this other stuff get between us ever again."

"Of course we are," whispered Iris. "We always have been, but we forgot to remind each other about it along the way."

Lorna hugged Iris again. "I've missed you," she said.

Lorna felt like a load had been lifted from her back. The war was over, not just the war in Europe, but the one between her and Iris too. And that was certainly reason to celebrate.

"Actually, can I tell you something?" asked Iris after a few minutes. "Something about after school, you know, the future."

"The future?" Lorna gave a mock shudder. "I've been avoiding thinking about that."

She tried to sound like she was joking, but really, what had she planned? Not much. Actually, nothing at all.

"But I thought you and William were rushing off to get married," Lorna said. "Oh God! That's not what you're going to tell me, is it?"

"No! Well, not yet anyway."

"Thank goodness for that! But won't you work with your mum, doing the old seamstressing thing? That's what you're best at. How does your mum put it? 'Clothing coupons won't be here forever . . .'"

"'. . . but fashion will be,'" Iris finished off with a roll of her eyes. "That was Mum's plan, but Mrs. Murray had another idea, you know, before Gregor . . . She pushed me to be more ambitious."

"More ambitious? How?"

"She thinks I could be a real fashion designer, or at least, work in the fashion industry. She helped me put my dress designs into a portfolio and write the application."

"You applied somewhere?"

A huge grin spread across Iris's face.

"To the Edinburgh College of Art! And I got in!"

"Oh my God, that's wonderful!" cried Lorna. "Why didn't you tell me?"

"I didn't want to jinx it, and then you and I . . ." Iris coughed. "And I didn't think I'd be good enough, but last week they offered me a place in the fashion course after the summer."

"You're brilliant, Iris! Congratulations! And William must be pleased for you?"

"Actually, I haven't told him yet." Iris looked shamefaced. "I haven't told anyone, other than Mum and Dad, and Mrs. Murray, and now you."

"But surely he'll be as thrilled for you as I am," said Lorna.

"Hmmm, I hope you're right. I'll just have to find the right time to tell him, somewhere quiet where we won't be disturbed. Yes, I'm sure he'll be fine about it."

Iris took Lorna's hand. "So what about you?"

"What about me?"

"What are you going to do next?"

"Oh, who knows? I've refused to think about it. But I should start or I'll end up stuck here for the rest of my life."

"There are worse places," said Iris.

"Oh, I know, but I want to see the world. Mrs. Murray's been working on me too, pushing me to read English at the university. But how could I even think about doing that when Dad needs me at home? Except, maybe it's different now the war's over."

The kettle was whistling, so Lorna poured the boiling water into the teapot.

"Mrs. Murray gave me some leaflets about a secretarial school," she continued as she splashed milk into the cups, "so that might be an option, because other than farming, what can I do? I suppose I'm good at arithmetic. And I can bake a cake and knit a scarf."

Iris pulled a face.

"Well, sort of. And thanks to the Red Cross, I can wrap a tight bandage and seal a sucking chest wound with a powder compact. But other than that? Not much, except make a cup of tea."

"So be a nurse," said Iris, taking Lorna's joke seriously. "They're always looking for trainee nurses, aren't they? You'd be wonderful, you know you would. And perhaps that would let you travel."

Nursing? That might be worth a thought.

Lorna passed a teacup to Iris and picked up the tin mugs to take out to her father and Paul.

"What was that line of Scarlett's, right at the end of *Gone with the Wind*?" Iris asked, out of nowhere. "I know. 'Tomorrow is another day.' That's what she said. Don't you think we should say that too?"

And Lorna realized that Iris might well be right—corny, but right. Tomorrow really could be, for her, for Iris, for Paul, another day.

Twenty-Eight

Lorna was sure she could smell the peace in the warm spring air as she came out of Mrs. Mack's cottage carrying a tin box full of of jars of chutney and jam. School was closed for the VE Day holiday, and all of Mrs. Mack's grandchildren were frantic with excitement about missing school.

Lorna had arrived early at Mrs. Mack's with some of that morning's milk, fresh eggs, and butter so she could help bake scones, shortbread, and sponge cakes. Neighbors from around the village had gathered up what flour, sugar, and powdered egg were left from last week's rations so Mrs. Mack could work her magic. Rationing would not be over anytime soon, but this wasn't a day to scrimp and save.

They'd left some of the baking in the cottage, to be picked up before the bonfire that evening, but Mrs. Mack's daughter

Sheena now handed each of her children a basket or cardboard box full of goodies for the afternoon tea party, with strict instructions on how to carry them.

"No swinging, banging, or shoogling," she said. "Granny has worked very hard, so carry it gently. We'll give it to Mrs. Urquhart down in the big tent, and maybe, *maybe*, if you're very good, nice Mrs. Urquhart will let you have one of the biscuits when we get there."

Sheena made a face at Lorna that said, *Or more likely the old bat won't.*

They set off down to the Sea Green, where the Boy Scouts had erected an ancient tent in one corner of the wide-open grassy field by the beach. The tent was patched and stained, retaining a depressingly dour appearance, even with red, white, and blue bunting hung around it.

Bunting had appeared overnight in crisscrossing strings throughout the village, the triangular flags fluttering in the light breeze. It must have been in storage since King George's coronation in 1937, for there had been little to celebrate since then. It looked festive, though, with all the Union Jacks and the photos of the king and queen hanging on front doors and in windows. Someone had even wrapped a flag around the mercat cross.

Aberlady had been shaken out of its torpor by the news of the German surrender. Everyone was out on the streets, chatting, hanging decorations, or carrying furniture and baskets down to the Sea Green. It was as if the sun had come out for the first time in almost six years. Everyone was happy.

Or almost everyone. Mrs. Murray's little white-walled cottage on Sea Wynd lay silent and bare of decoration. The heavy curtains remained pulled tight, as they had been for almost a month. Her own very private blackout.

"Do you think we should knock?" Lorna asked Mrs. Mack as they walked by.

"No, dear, I think not. It'll be hard enough for her knowing that the end of the war came just too late for young Gregor, so let's give her a wee bit more time. Mrs. Hastie's been keeping an eye on her, and I popped in to see her yesterday. She's doing as well as we can expect, but for now, let's leave her be."

The Sea Green was already awash with children dashing around, and adults unfolding chairs and tables, stacking pallets near the tent, and generally contributing to the chaos.

Lorna approached the tent with some caution, letting Sheena herd the children inside first. Just because Iris seemed to have forgiven Lorna for befriending a German, it didn't mean that the rest of the village had.

She was surprised, however, to be greeted with no more than a few nudges and whispers by the ladies in the tea tent. Peace seemed to have brought with it a certain spirit of forgiveness, though Lorna doubted it would last much longer than the cakes and scones. Scottish people were not quick to forget a slight, she knew.

Out on the field, a raucous game of British Bulldogs was just finishing, the younger children in a frenzy, stirred up by the older ones, just as John Jo, Gregor, and Derek had done to Lorna and her pals at the annual Sunday School picnics before the war.

She had always loved being with the older boys for those games. For Lorna, the more rough-and-tumble the better, even—perhaps, especially—when Gregor Murray had tickled her into submission with painful giggles and joyful tears.

Gregor. So lovely, so handsome, and so much fun. What a waste!

Setting down the tin box where Sheena pointed, Lorna looked to see if Iris had arrived already and found her sitting with some of the little girls, making necklaces from the early daisies.

Iris glanced up and waved to Lorna, beckoning her to come make daisy chains, but Lorna shook her head. She didn't want to make daisy chains; in fact, she didn't want to be here at the party much at all, she realized. She wanted to be back at Craigielaw with Paul.

But she'd promised to help with the teas, so she pointed back into the tent and mimed being a teapot. Iris waved her amused understanding, and Lorna went to find Mrs. Mack.

To one side of the tent, on the makeshift pallet stage, stood William. He was also looking toward Iris, but then he found Lorna. She gave him a sarcastic smile and wave, hoping that Iris wasn't watching.

Just then a whistle blew, loud and insistent. All the children cheered and pelted toward the tea tent, yelling and elbowing one another aside. Even the little girls with the daisy chains came tearing over the grass, screaming like banshees.

As the ravenous mob tore past Mrs. Urquhart, standing with the whistle in her hand, she threw her arms up as if that might stop her being trampled. Luckily, no child came close to touching her, which was just as well. Mrs. Urquhart was so delicate and brittle, like a china doll, Lorna suspected she would have shattered at the slightest bump.

Mrs. Urquhart pursed her perfectly lipsticked mouth. "You'd think they'd never been fed!" she muttered as the last little girl stumbled past.

Then she caught sight of Lorna, and a disapproving wrinkle creased her forehead.

"Come along then," Mrs. Urquhart snapped. "These children need to be fed and watered. Don't expect the grown-ups to do all the work just so you can spend the afternoon gallivanting."

But the ladies of the village already had every child seated at a table with a paper napkin in front of him or her, piled up with a sandwich and a sausage roll, a fairy cake and a piece of shortbread. Paper cups of rich and sticky orange squash were already being refilled from big jugs by Sheena and the other young mothers. As fast as they could fill them, the sweaty children gulped them down. The noisy chatter rose and fell around each delicious mouthful. For the first time in most of these children's lives, rationing didn't exist.

Mrs. Urquhart was tutting again, but this time it was at William. As he approached his mother, her nose wrinkled as if she'd stepped in something.

"William Robert Urquhart!" she said, loud enough that

everyone could hear. "What do you look like? We have standards, you know."

Lorna couldn't see any dirt on him at all. William looked as conspicuously well-groomed as ever. Even so, he was desperately brushing at nonexistent stains on his pants.

"Go back to the Manse right now and change," Mrs. Urquhart continued without a breath. "No son of mine will parade around like a ragamuffin. There's even dirt on your face."

Mrs. Urquhart pulled a crisp white handkerchief from her sleeve and folded it over her finger. Licking it with the very tip of her tongue, she advanced on William and dabbed furiously at an imagined smudge on his cheekbone. Even though he towered over her, William squirmed away from his mother's viselike grip like a toddler.

"Mother!" William whined. "Stop. You can't do this. I'm not a child."

She held his chin between her bony fingers and inspected his face.

"While you are living under my roof, you are my child and you will do what you are told."

Lorna knew she should be laughing at this spectacle, especially since it was happening to William, but it was just too humiliating for that.

"Now, go home and change immediately!"

Mrs. Urquhart strode into the tent.

William looked dazed, but when he realized that a

number of his classmates had witnessed the scene, his pale cheeks flushed pink.

"What the hell is it to you?" he snarled.

Everyone else followed Mrs. Urquhart into the tent, but Lorna stayed put.

She was trying to imagine how Iris could find anything to respect in that vile woman, and her pathetic son. They would both destroy whatever spirit Iris had left inside. It was just so awful to contemplate.

When the others had gone, William glared at Lorna, his vexed scowl an exact replica of his mother's.

"And you can shut up, Lorna Anderson!"

"I didn't say any—"

"You shouldn't even be at this party. Among decent people."

"Look, just because your mother—"

"Don't you dare talk about my mother, or about Iris. In fact, I don't want you ever talking to Iris again."

Lorna was stunned. All right, he didn't like her, but what had she done to provoke this?

"I know you've been turning Iris against me." William was almost spitting. "But it won't work. Iris is too good for you, you little German whore!"

Lorna's heart stopped, then a fierce fury burst inside her.

How dare he?

She took a step toward him, but then remembered what Iris had said yesterday, and how much it would mean to her

305

if Lorna did not rip William's head off right now. So very calmly, or at least, trying to appear calm while staving off the shakes that rippled down to her fists, Lorna drew herself up and looked William Urquhart squarely in the eye.

"I think, for Iris's sake, you had better take that back. Did your darling mother never teach you that if you can't say something nice, say nothing?"

"I told you not to talk about my—"

"And I don't need to turn Iris against you, William. You are managing to do that all by yourself, simply by being the nasty, vindictive so-and-so you are. I need do nothing but stand back and watch you go down in flames. Now are you going to take that comment back? Or shall I ask Iris to come over for a chat? I doubt that she'd agree with you that I'm a little German—"

Before she could finish—thankfully, because Lorna wasn't sure she could even say *that* word—William furiously shoved past her and sprinted along the side of the tent. Within seconds he was at the top of Sea Wynd heading toward the Manse, and then he was gone.

Now Lorna's heart was pounding as if she'd been running the mile. Who had been listening? Who had heard what William had called her? She really didn't want to know, so instead of going into the tent, she went in the other direction, toward the sea and the road to Craigielaw.

Twenty-Nine

The kettle was whistling, but Lorna couldn't quite bring herself to stand up. She and Paul were sitting in her dad's carver chair by the kitchen table, Lorna nestled snugly on Paul's lap, her head resting on his shoulder. He smelled of carbolic soap and hay, and of the early strawberries he had been picking.

Paul had been nervous at first of coming into the house with Lorna, but she had whined and wheedled and bribed him with the promise of tea. When that hadn't worked, she had kissed him, and then kissed him again, after which he had allowed her to lead him uncomplaining into the kitchen.

Lorna needed Paul close; his security and his strength mattered to her, especially after what had happened on the Sea Green. No matter how she formed the words in her head, however, Lorna couldn't bring herself to tell Paul about what William had said to her. Anyway, Paul didn't need to know. Telling him would upset him; it would spoil this perfect moment. So she cuddled against him, knowing nothing would induce her to move.

Then Lorna's dad opened the door and stamped into the kitchen, and Lorna was out of Paul's lap like a scalded cat. Paul rose too, though with more dignity.

Lorna's dad looked at each of them in turn.

"Eyes in the back of my head," he said. "I warned you two about that, didn't I?"

Before Lorna could decide whether he was joking, her father pointed toward the singing kettle.

"So are we listening to that racket as part of a music appreciation lesson, or are you likely to make a cup of tea at any point?"

Reddening, Lorna pulled the kettle off the heat and gathered the teapot and cups together.

"I will go back to the fruit, now I have brought in the strawberries Mrs. Mack asked for," said Paul, as if expecting Lorna's father to believe that was the only reason he was there.

Lorna's dad snorted.

"The strawbs'll be fine for a wee while longer, so sit yourself back down, lad, and enjoy your cuppa."

Paul hesitated and then sat back down, though not in the big chair they had been cuddling in. Instead he sat in the chair on the other side of the table. For a moment or two he gazed thoughtfully at his fingers.

"Mr. Anderson," Paul said at last, "may I ask you a question?"

"Aye, lad, ask away," said Lorna's dad as he took back possession of his own big chair.

"I would like to know more about your watch," Paul said. "It is a very fine German piece, but I am surprised to find it outside my own country. I hope you do not mind that I am asking."

Slowly, Lorna's father undid the buckle on the watch and laid it flat on the arm of his chair before standing and reaching up to the high mantelpiece above him. Lorna thought he would pick up the photograph of Lorna's mother, but instead, he lifted down the photograph next to it, the one of her grandfather with his four sons. He ran his thumb gently over a smudge on the frame as he handed the photograph to Paul.

"The watch belonged to my father," he said, pointing at the older man in the center of the group. "Before that, it belonged to a German soldier."

Lorna was surprised. She knew nothing of that.

"This is Frank," said her father, pointing at the tall young man to the far left of the photograph. "He was the eldest and then there was Billy, then me, and then Harry. Frank and Billy both went off to the Great War in 1916. Neither of them came back."

"I am sorry to hear that," said Paul.

"It was a long time ago, but they were Royal Scots, same

as our John." He stood taller suddenly. "'First of foot, right of the line . . .'"

"'. . . and the pride of the British Army,'" Lorna quietly finished the recitation.

"Aye, that's right. And they were the pride of the British Army, fine boys, and brave. But that did them no good. My parents received two telegrams on the same afternoon. They said that both boys had been killed in the battle for the Somme. Most of their battalion, the Sixteenth, was lost in the one offensive.

"My mother never recovered from the shock. And even though me and Harry were still at home, being too young to join up, I don't think Mother ever really looked at either of us again."

Lorna's father lifted the watch into his palm.

"In due course, my parents received a letter from the company padre, returning the few things that Frank and Billy had left behind. He said my brothers had died as heroes, as if that would console my mother."

There was bitterness in his voice.

"Then in 1919, a few months after the Armistice," Lorna's father continued, "another letter arrived, from a German soldier called Heinrich Wolf, addressed to 'Mr. and Mrs. Anderson, Aberlady, Scotland.' In the letter, which was written in fine English, I might add, Wolf told how he met had Frank in a bomb crater in no-man's-land.

"Wolf's company went over the top of their trench and he was hit in the leg by machine-gun fire, high in the thigh. He was bleeding badly and crawled toward a shell-hole to find shelter from the cross fire, but the pain was so intense, he couldn't quite get there.

"But then someone, a British soldier, grabbed his uniform and pulled him down into the crater. That soldier was also badly wounded, his hands bloody, and he kept them pressed against his chest."

Lorna's father paused.

"That British soldier was my brother Frank."

Lorna had lived with that photograph her whole life, but, she realized shamefully now, she'd never once asked to hear more about her uncles.

"From what the German told us," her father continued, "they passed the night in that damned hole talking about their homes and their lives before the war. He said Frank told him all about Craigielaw Farm and Aberlady as if they were meeting in a pub, not bleeding in a shell-hole.

"Frank was worried about his younger brother, who had gone over the top beside him. He had no idea if Billy was alive, or wounded, or . . ."

Lorna's father's voice faded away to nothing, and it took him some moments before he could continue.

"Frank had shared the water in his canteen with Wolf, and he had unwrapped the cloth puttees from his own boots to bind Wolf's thigh wound to stop the bleeding. At some point, Wolf fell asleep, and when he woke up, my brother was dead."

Lorna's father ran his thumb across the face of the watch and swallowed.

"The German stretcher bearers rescued Wolf during a cease-fire soon after dawn, but the doctors had to take his leg off to stop the gangrene. They said that Frank's tourniquet had saved Wolf's life, if not his leg. Wolf was sent home to Germany and survived the war, unlike so many other young men on both sides.

"In that letter, he said he owed Frank his life, and as a token of his gratitude, Wolf sent my parents this watch, which had been a twenty-first birthday gift from his father. He wanted it to mark the sacrifice made by a man who had shown compassion and comradeship to an enemy stranger when they met on the battlefield of hell. And he said that he hoped that Billy had made it home safely."

Lorna's father slowly placed the watch back onto his wrist and did up the buckle.

"My father wore this watch for almost twenty years. And from the day he died, it never left my wrist. Not until it found its way into the hands of another German soldier, who gave it the care and attention it needed."

He stood up and held his right hand out to Paul. "You did a grand repair on it, lad, so I thank you for that."

"Mr. Anderson," replied Paul as he tentatively returned the handshake, "I am honored to have worked on such a watch."

The two men stood facing each other, hands grasped for a few moments more. Then Lorna's father stepped away, clearing his throat.

"Now, what about this service at the kirk then?" he said.

It took Lorna a moment to work through what her father

was talking about.

"The church service?"

"Aye, there's a thanksgiving service at six o'clock. By my reckoning, we've just enough time to get ourselves cleaned up, so we can wander along to that. And as long as Fat Bob, I mean, Reverend Urquhart, doesn't gab too much, we'll get the lad back here right on time for his pickup."

What was he talking about?

"Dad, you don't mean you want Paul to go with us." Lorna was shocked.

"Why not?"

"Why not?" she almost screeched. "Because we've only been at peace since yesterday, so no one in the village will suddenly open their arms wide to an enemy soldier, will they? Paul, you agree, don't you?"

"What nonsense!" Lorna's dad replied. "The war's over, so now Paul's not really a prisoner anymore, he's more of a . . . a *guest*. And I am sure he feels he has a thing or two to be thankful for, even though this war has harmed him more than some."

"But Dad"—Lorna changed tack—"you never come to church, so why today?"

"Am I wrong to want to go to the kirk with my only daughter to mark such a historic day, and to give thanks that my boys have both come through alive, if not unscathed?"

Lorna knew she was losing the battle; her dad's mind was set. And even though the idea of walking up Coffin Lane with Paul at her side held a perverse appeal, she still had to have one more go.

"But what will people say? I mean, the Urquharts and the Bells and people like that, you know they'll be horrible."

Lorna's dad took her gently by the shoulders.

"Will having Mrs. Urquhart's approval govern every decision you make in your life?"

"No, of course not."

"Then go and change your frock." He guided her toward the hall door. "The lad and I will get washed up, and perhaps you'll tell Nellie that we're away as you pass her door."

"But Dad, no—"

There was a light cough behind Lorna.

"May I say something?" Paul said, smiling wryly.

Lorna's face warmed as she realized they had both been talking about Paul as if he weren't there.

"Oh yes, of course. Sorry."

"I do not want to cause trouble, for you or for myself. But I am honored that you might consider me now your guest, when I have been here as your enemy. And you are right, Mr. Anderson, this war has caused so much damage to me and to many others on both sides. So I would like to walk you to the kirk—or *zur Kirche* in my language. It is because of you, and Mrs. Mack and Nellie . . ."

Paul swallowed before he could continue.

"And of course, because of Lorna, that I still have so much to be thankful for."

Thirty

The bells were ringing again as they approached the kirkyard, passing under the fresh green leaves of the sycamore
beside the gap in the wall onto Coffin Lane.

At the foot of the bell tower, Mrs. Mack and Sheena stood
with what looked like the entire village. Children were chasing one another around nearby gravestones, none of them
showing any sign of exhaustion from the earlier party.

Lorna scanned the crowd for Iris, but she couldn't see her.
She had hoped to talk to Iris before the service, to apologize
for leaving the party without explanation. Not that she would
be telling Iris the truth about her conversation with William,
but still, Lorna wanted to say sorry.

The cacophony of the bells was suddenly silenced, though
the echo rolled around the kirkyard for some seconds more.

Everyone knew this was a sign that the service was about to start and began to make their way to the doors.

When Mrs. Mack caught sight of Lorna, or rather, when she caught sight of Lorna's father and Paul, the crease between her eyebrows grew deeper than usual. But a second later she smiled and waved. That hesitation, however, set the hornets buzzing in Lorna's stomach. If Mrs. Mack couldn't find an immediate smile, something was wrong.

Mrs. Mack nudged Sheena and pointed in their direction. Sheena's gaze followed her mother's finger, and one by one, every other face in the crowd turned toward the sycamore. It was the medieval fresco all over again.

Self-consciously, Lorna brushed at the skirt of her summer dress and glanced at Paul, slowing her steps. But Lorna's father strode purposefully forward. And after a moment Paul followed, his head held high, although he walked with less assurance than Lorna's father.

The path was narrow, so Lorna and Paul had to walk close together, and Lorna wanted to take Paul's hand, to hold it tight for reassurance—hers and his—but she didn't dare.

A silence crept over the crowd around the door as the three of them approached. Once they were closer, however, she could hear the whispering and muttering. Lorna was glad that Nellie had not come with them because her bump would have just been another target for the loudmouthed gossips. As it was, Paul's arrival was causing enough of a stir.

"It's disgraceful, that's what it is!" came a voice. "What right has Jock to bring one of *them* here?"

"And today of all days," said someone else.

"Exactly! It's not right."

"Look at the state of his face! It's dreadful."

"Enough to make the children cry."

"Go get the minister. He'll sort this out."

Lorna glanced at Mrs. Mack. There was still a smile on her face, but it was now set hard, as if it was painted on. While she had clearly been taken aback by Paul's arrival at the church, she was determined not to show it.

Lorna's father stopped a yard or two away from the gawping crowd and waited for Paul and Lorna to catch up. He stood legs apart and arms folded across his chest as if bracing himself against some invisible force. His eyes never left the people in front of him, his steady expression a challenge to anyone who dared come up against him.

Paul had again withdrawn behind his mask and was looking intently at Mrs. Mack as if she were his sanctuary.

"Take him back, Jock!" a man shouted. "He's not welcome here."

There were several cries of agreement, but Lorna's father did not move.

"And that girl of yours'll want to watch out as well." A woman this time. "We've all heard what the Jerries do to the lassies in France and Belgium. Nasty devils, they are!"

The memory of Ed's grasp and stench tore at Lorna's calm. She wanted to shout back, *And what about the Yanks? D'you think they're all bloody angels?* But she knew that would never help, and anyway, she didn't think her voice would work.

But still, she could show them they were wrong, she could show them how safe she felt with Paul.

Lorna took hold of Paul's hand and held it tight. Paul did not immediately respond, though Lorna was sure he must have been surprised at her touch. After a moment, his fingers folded around hers and he let out a long, slow breath. She almost didn't hear it beneath the hiss and murmur of the crowd, which had grown considerably in the minute or two they'd been standing there. People were coming back out of the church to see what was happening.

Suddenly Mrs. Mack walked out from the crowd to stand in front of Paul.

"Good for you, son. I'm glad to see you here," she said, louder than was necessary, her words aimed at those behind her. "And you too, Jock."

Paul gave her one of his curt nods, and as Mrs. Mack moved to stand next to Lorna, facing the other villagers, Lorna wished she could tell her how good it felt to have her on their side.

Then Lorna saw that Iris had come to stand at the front of the crowd. Iris lifted her foot from the ground as if she was about to step forward to join them, but suddenly William materialized beside her and took hold of her arm. Iris started at William's touch, and she didn't step forward. She just stood silently and did nothing.

"Now, what's all this?" The plummy voice of Reverend Urquhart rose above the hubbub as he pushed through the crowd. "What's the fuss? We really do need to get on with the service."

Mrs. Urquhart followed behind him, her hard-edged purse swinging neatly from her bent elbow, looking more like a lethal weapon than a handbag.

"Oh, I say!" Reverend Urquhart muttered as he noticed Paul. He stopped beside William, who leaned toward his father and whispered something that Lorna couldn't hear. Without acknowledging that William had spoken, Reverend Urquhart drew in a deep breath, the way he did as he started every sermon, and took up his usual oratory stance with feet wide apart, shoulders back. As he opened his mouth to speak, he forced an unconvincing smile onto his flabby face.

"Anderson—I mean, Jock—it is a welcome surprise to see you here on this historic evening." The minister's bright tone was conciliatory as he looked up at Lorna's father, his shiny bald head barely reaching the big farmer's chin.

Lorna's father stood silent, his expression unchanged.

"And of course," the minister continued, glancing to each side of him, "we warmly embrace each and every soul who comes here to praise the Lord. But in the circumstances, I'm not quite sure that your, em, your companion . . ."

He paused. His mouth was still smiling, but there were tight stress lines wrinkling his forehead and around his eyes. He suddenly seemed unsure of where his sentence was going.

"Do something, Robert!" Mrs. Urquhart hissed in his

ear. "This is a disgrace, and you must do something about it. Right now!"

She prodded his arm with a sharp finger and he stepped forward, on the pretext of having more to say, but more probably to escape his wife's jabbing nails.

"After all, does the camp commander know he's here?" the minister asked. "There are still rules for these chaps, you know. Or at least, I'm sure there must be—"

"Bugger the camp commander!" said Lorna's father, and a rippling wave of gasps and giggles swept around the crowd. "The war's over. I've come to give thanks in the kirk that my family has been part of for more than a hundred and fifty years, and the lad is coming in with me to do the same. Or are you planning to stop me?"

Lorna's father looked around the crowd in challenge.

The minister looked shaken. "Now, Jock, I have no doubt that there will be a time and a place for reconciliation with our enemies . . . em . . . I mean, *former* enemies. However, I think I can speak for everyone in the village when I say this moment might not be the best one. So I really must ask you to escort the young, em, gentleman back—"

"You're not speaking for me," said Mrs. Mack sharply from beside Paul, and the muttering rose in volume again.

"Nor me!" Sheena pushed past Iris and William and went to stand next to her mother, gesturing to her children to follow her.

As Sheena passed, Iris pulled her arm purposefully out of William's grip, and Lorna's heart sang.

But as Iris took a step away from him, William was suddenly shoved forward by people behind him. The crowd was splitting down the middle, opening up a path for someone coming through.

"You would not be speaking for me either," came a woman's voice from the widening gap.

There was a murmur as people realized who it was.

"And in my opinion, Reverend Urquhart, this is *exactly* the best time and place," Mrs. Murray said as she walked to the front. "What better place could there ever be for reconciliation than within the house of the Lord?"

Mrs. Murray was wearing a black coat and a rather old-fashioned black hat pinned to her hair. Her face was gray and drawn, but her eyes were sparking.

"But Mrs. Murray . . . Peggy . . . I don't know what to say," blustered the minister. "You of all people should understand how inappropriate it is to have a German soldier among us today."

Mrs. Murray fixed him with a stare that Lorna knew all too well, and Reverend Urquhart looked like he wanted to dive for cover. His wife, however, appeared still to be pressing sharp nails into his back, so he was forced to stand his ground.

"Of all the people in this village"—Mrs. Murray's voice bounced off the kirkyard walls like chips of ice against a window—"I am one who is best placed to understand how much we should be thanking the Lord for ending this war. And while we are here, we should also thank him for sparing this boy's life, and the lives of so many other thousands of mothers' sons.

"Gregor will never come home to me, to Aberlady. But we should send this young man home to *his* mother with our songs of praise ringing in his ears to bless them both. And with our prayers, we should be thanking the Lord for bringing wisdom at last to the men who have put us through these six years of hell."

The minister spluttered.

"Yes, Mr. Urquhart, this *hell*! So please step aside, because I would like to take my usual seat in the church, and I hope that the Andersons and their young friend will sit with me."

Mrs. Murray turned and tried to walk back toward the church door, only to find that people had closed in behind her, blocking her path. With the same sweeping hand gesture she used in the school yard when ushering small children back to the classroom, she shooed the assembled throng out of her way.

Lorna's father offered Mrs. Murray his arm in an unusually gallant gesture, and she took it elegantly as they moved through the crowd. Mrs. Mack ushered her family after them, the green feather in her best hat bobbing as she walked with her nose in the air and defiance in each step.

Beside Lorna, Paul hesitated.

At first, he seemed unsure as to whether he should follow, but as he held out his hand in front of her, she realized that he was in no doubt at all. He was simply indicating that she should go first. But Lorna felt a strong need to protect Paul's back and shook her head.

"No, you go first," she said, glancing around. "Please."

Paul waited only a moment more and then did as she asked without argument, though she noticed that he kept his head turning, just enough for him to see any trouble that might break out around them.

Though the crowd had parted to let Mrs. Murray and her father through, it was quickly closing in again, and Lorna could see that Mrs. Mack was having to hold her elbows wide to stop people jostling her. Lorna went quickly after Paul, keeping close to him. The breach in the crowd had narrowed even further, and Paul was struggling to get through.

Suddenly he stumbled, held up only by the bodies pressing on either side. Lorna too almost tripped over the boot that had been stuck out into their path. She looked up to find that the foot in the boot belonged to Craig Buchanan. Esther Bell was pressed close behind him, her tiny green eyes set deep in her flabby pink face, snorting scornfully.

"Get lost, Craig!" someone hissed from behind Lorna. "Go away and crawl back under your rock! And you, Esther!"

It was Iris, and her hand was on Lorna's shoulder, helping her push through the throng.

As Mrs. Murray and her father led them into the cool, echoing stillness of the church, Lorna fought to find the same calm within herself. But all she could think about was beating the living daylights out of Craig Buchanan. And out of Esther Bell, for that matter.

Toward the front, Mrs. Murray went into her usual pew,

immediately on the other side of the aisle from the Urquharts, and Lorna's father shuffled along to sit next to her. Paul followed, but Lorna turned to Iris.

"Thank you," she said.

"For what?"

"For standing with us. At least, I saw you try to."

Iris shrugged. "I think maybe I should have done that a long while ago."

"Come and sit here with us then? We can all budge up. And you and me can share the kneeling cushion like we used to."

Iris looked tempted, but then William grabbed her elbow, his fury ill disguised under a layer of serenity. He bent close to Iris's ear. "I don't know what that was about," he said quietly, "but come and sit where you belong beside me and Mother. You're making a show of yourself."

Lorna wanted to slap his hand away and tell him to mind his own business, but before she could, Iris gently pulled her arm from William's grasp for a second time, smiling sweetly as she did so. Then she kissed him on the cheek.

"You are so right, William, thank you for reminding me," Iris said in a voice loud enough for even the gawpers at the back to hear. "I would like to be where I belong on this special day, so I'll go and sit with Mum and Dad, thanks."

She gave Lorna a peck on the cheek as well.

"And I'll see you at the bonfire tonight."

With that, Iris walked to where Mr. and Mrs. Robertson were sitting a few pews back. She squeezed in beside her father and began riffling through the hymnbook.

Lorna followed Iris's example, smiling sweetly at William and sitting down between Paul and her father.

"Did I miss something?" Paul asked in a low voice.

"I'm not entirely sure," said Lorna, "but I think Iris just made a very important decision."

Thirty-One

In his sermon, Reverend Urquhart waxed lyrical about the need for new thinking in this hard-won time of peace, for rebuilding, for reconciliation, and for forgiveness, all the while seeming to take care not to look in Paul's direction.

After the service, Lorna's father attempted to guide Mrs. Murray, Paul, and Lorna out of the church as quickly as possible. But to Lorna's surprise, a number of people stopped him, wanting to shake his hand or Mrs. Murray's, saying they were proud to see someone stand up to the minister. Several of them wanted to shake hands with Paul too.

Lorna bit back the obvious question, *So where were you when we needed you?* But better late than never, she supposed.

Out in the kirkyard, they huddled together.

"Bloody hypocrite!" Lorna's dad muttered about the

minister, then grimaced at Mrs. Murray. "Sorry, Peggy."

"Don't worry about me. I couldn't agree more." Mrs. Murray studied Paul for a few moments.

"I hope you'll get home to your family soon," she said, taking one of Paul's hands in hers, "because I'm sure your mother will have been praying for your safe return."

"Thank you," Paul said, his voice choked.

Lorna's eyes prickled. Here were two people who had lost so much to this war. Mrs. Murray was alone now, and who knew what Paul had lost? His home, his mother and sister, his city and his job, his whole life?

Lorna leaned against her dad and he put his arm around her. They were lucky. They had each other, and they had John Jo and Sandy, and now Nellie and soon her baby.

"Shall we walk you home, Peggy?" Lorna's dad asked, releasing Lorna and holding out his arm to Mrs. Murray. When she waved away the suggestion, he cleared his throat. "Well, perhaps, you'd like to come over to have some dinner with us on Sunday at Craigielaw? Nothing fancy, mind, but it would be lovely to share what we have with you."

"That would be lovely, Jock, thank you."

If Lorna hadn't known Mrs. Murray so well, she'd have sworn there was suddenly a flush on her pale cheeks, but before Lorna could look again, Mrs. Murray had set off alone toward the High Street.

Lorna looked up at her dad. Was there also a sudden pink warmth to his swarthy cheeks? Imagine that.

Lorna, her father, and Paul set off through the kirkyard,

and as soon as they were past the sycamore and onto Coffin Lane, Lorna's father lengthened his stride toward Craigielaw. He was quickly twenty yards ahead of Lorna and Paul.

When she was sure he was far enough away, and that they were also beyond sight of the church, Lorna slipped her hand into Paul's and slowed him to a stop.

"I'm sorry," she said.

Paul squeezed her hand but said nothing.

"Perhaps you shouldn't have come today," she said quietly. "You saw how people were."

"No. I am glad I went with you, to show respect for your father, and to be with you."

Lorna pushed up on her tiptoes and pulled down on Paul's shirt until his lips met hers.

Parp! Parp!

They broke apart, and both looked over the Glebe field to where the road wound to the farm. The familiar green army truck was bouncing along, though only partly visible over the hedges.

"I wish you could come to the bonfire tonight," Lorna said. "Can't they let you out, just for tonight?"

"I wish that they would too, but . . ."

"In fact, perhaps I'll stay home with Nellie instead. She's miserable at missing all the fun."

Paul took Lorna's hand again.

"But you must go to the party. This is a very big day, a day to tell your grandchildren about."

For a second, Lorna felt a stab of disappointment that Paul

had said *your grandchildren* and not *our grandchildren*, but she knew that was ridiculous.

Parp! Parp!

"I had better hurry," said Paul.

Lorna pulled back on his hand. "Wait!"

Paul hesitated and Lorna laid her hand on his damaged cheek, feeling its coolness against her warm palm.

Parp! Parp!

Paul sighed and leaned his face into her hand. "Really, I must go."

The truck was in the yard, the dogs barking frantically.

Paul bent to kiss Lorna again, no more than a light butterfly touch. "Enjoy the party. I am sure it will be a night you will always remember."

"And I'll see you tomorrow?"

"Yes, of course. I will see you tomorrow."

Parp! Parp! Parp! Parp!

Paul set off at a sprint toward the truck that would take him back to Gosford Camp. The same truck would bring him back again in barely twelve hours' time, and again the next morning, and the next . . . but for how many more mornings?

How much longer would Paul remain at Craigielaw with Lorna?

The huge bonfire on the Sea Green filled the twilight with orange light as if it were part of the sunset. Logs cracked and snapped, popping hot sap sparks across the surrounding grass, and onlookers jumped back, giggling in alarm. The coastal blackout restrictions were over, so the lamps had been lit all through the village, and burning torches illuminated the field.

The ropey old Scout tent was almost unrecognizable. All the stains and repairs were masked by the invitingly radiant glow of the Tilley lamps that hung from the sloping tent poles. The tea urns on the far tables had been joined by two wooden kegs of beer, and the villagers were holding nothing back in their enjoyment of either.

Nellie would have loved this.

"If you can't be good, be careful!" Nellie had called as Lorna and her dad had left the house. "And don't do anything I wouldn't do!"

"Well, that leaves us plenty of room for maneuver," Lorna's dad had said, and chuckled at his joke most of the way to the village.

And he was certainly having fun. Looking at him in the yellow lamplight, Lorna could see that years had dropped from her father's face. He threw his head back as he laughed with his friends, draining his pint glass and wiping his mouth on his sleeve. He looked relaxed and happy.

On the stage near the tea-and-beer tent sat the members of the old Aberlady ceilidh band, their heels beating out an echoing rhythm on the wooden boards as they played. The footsteps of the dancers hurling and burling in front of them, in contrast, were strangely muted by the grass on which they danced.

Paul would have loved this too.

As the band played the opening chords of the next dance, Sheena's eldest daughter, Agnes, sidled up to Lorna, clearly yearning to join in, but not brave enough to ask any of the boys her own age.

Lorna held out her hand to Agnes.

"Do you want to lead or will I?"

Agnes giggled. She was at least a foot shorter than Lorna, and clearly found the question silly. But she gratefully grabbed Lorna's arm and yanked her into the military two-step.

When the dance came to an end with one long chord, Lorna and Agnes bowed and curtsied to each other, and Lorna wiped her forehead on the sleeve of her dress. It had been fun to dance the whirling energy of the Scottish country dancing with Agnes, but Lorna ached to feel Paul's arms around her, for the intimacy of a waltz in a ballroom, or even in a barn. She just wanted to feel again his hand on her back, his cheek against hers, and the whisper of his breath in her ear.

Agnes grasped Lorna's hand again, but the musicians laid their instruments down and raised their empty glasses to the clapping crowd to signal a break.

Agnes muttered a quick "Never mind" and dashed off toward the refreshment tent. Realizing how thirsty she was, Lorna followed her.

Lorna picked up a paper cup of orange squash from a table and gulped it down. She picked up another, as crackling ballroom music burst from a shiny old wooden gramophone that sat on the corner of the stage, a black record rotating under its needle. It was playing "Bye Bye Blackbird," and immediately couples were spinning around the flattened grass with less finesse than the dancers she'd seen at the air base, but with just as much energy.

Where was Paul when she wanted him most? At Gosford, tucked up in bed. But perhaps he would be dreaming about dancing with Lorna too.

She flushed at the idea that Paul might be thinking of her as he lay in bed, and fanned her face with her hand.

In an attempt to distract herself, she looked around for Iris. She wanted to tell her how proud she was of her for standing up to William that afternoon, and how happy she was that Iris had finally seen the light about him.

Iris wasn't among the dancers, so perhaps she was sitting down having a drink.

The beer tent was packed, and Lorna had to squeeze past the group of older men clustered around her father. He was regaling them with some long, and probably tall, story from when they were all young, or were all in the Home Guard together, a story they had probably all heard countless times before.

Beyond the men, the chairs were filled with loudly chattering women, the tables littered with a variety of purses, glasses, and teacups.

But where was Iris?

Suddenly, the needle on the gramophone screeched as it was knocked from its groove, and the music was silenced. Somebody tapped something metal on a glass to call the crowd to attention. Everyone stood up or turned to see what was happening.

A roar of laughter and clapping rose outside the tent, but Lorna couldn't see past her father and his friends, so she grabbed a nearby chair to stand on.

When she was up high enough to look over their heads, Lorna finally found Iris, standing in the pool of yellow lamplight on the dance floor. Her head was lowered, and she was staring down at the boy who was on one knee in front of her.

William took Iris's hands in his. He kissed the back of each hand in turn and raised his eyes to look into hers. If Lorna hadn't known William so well, she might have believed the adoration was real.

"Iris"—William's voice was strong, making sure everyone could hear—"would you do me the very great honor of becoming my wife?"

Another cheer went up, and Lorna almost burst out laughing. Did William not realize he was too late, that his placid little girlfriend had become a strong and independent young woman?

In spite of herself, Lorna could almost pity William. Having your marriage proposal turned down in front of all these people would be a spectacular humiliation. But then, it couldn't happen to a nicer bloke.

The cheers quickly died down to a low buzz as everyone watched Iris expectantly. But as the seconds stretched out, and Iris continued to stare at William without giving him a response, soon even the buzz fell silent.

Iris looked up, searching the faces of the crowd. When she found Lorna, she seemed to be telling her something. But Lorna didn't understand what it was. Was Iris asking her for a sign of support before she dumped William in front of everyone? Did she need Lorna to intervene? Or was it . . . was she . . . ? Was that expression on Iris's face one of apology?

Iris looked back down at William, who was clearly feeling foolish for still being down on one knee after all this time.

"Iris?" he said, sounding desperate. "I asked if you would marry me."

And then, to Lorna's horror, Iris nodded her head.

"Yes," she said. "William, I would love to marry you."

Lorna's heart dropped like a brick as everyone cheered again. This could not be happening. Why would Iris throw her life away like this after all she'd said to him?

Then William glanced behind him, to where his mother stood, her face a portrait of dismay. She pressed a lace handkerchief to her mouth as if she was struggling not to scream at her son for his folly and his treachery.

And Lorna realized that this proposal wasn't about William showing Iris he loved her. This was William having his revenge on his mother. What sort of man had Iris said yes to?

William looked back to Iris and smiled with satisfaction. But before he could get to his feet, Iris held up one hand, signaling for more quiet.

"But . . . BUT." Iris had to raise her voice to get people to listen. "But not quite yet."

William staggered to his feet.

"Not yet?" he stammered. "Well, when then?"

Iris glanced around, as if she now wished everyone were looking in the other direction. They weren't.

"I mean, we should wait a bit. You'll be called up for National Service soon, and then there's university. And I have plans too."

"What plans?" William looked like he wanted to vomit.

"Well . . ." Iris was growing pinker, even in the yellow light, "I want to go to the Edinburgh College of Art to study fashion design. They've offered me a place for September. And I've already said I'll take it."

"But . . ." William looked confused. "Well, good, that's great, but . . . even so . . . you did say you'd marry me, didn't you?"

"Yes," cried Iris, now looking excited, "of course, I said yes!"

That was all William needed. He wrapped an arm around Iris's shoulders, holding the other aloft as if he were a Roman gladiator accepting the approbation of Caesar's mob.

Everyone followed his lead and cheered again, though there were a few puzzled frowns and shaking heads. William paraded Iris around, lapping up the calls of good wishes and congratulations. After a while, he looked up and saw Lorna. His smile didn't falter for one moment; it seemed to dare her to cry out an objection.

Not only revenge on his mother. This was also William Urquhart's revenge on Lorna.

"Dance!" someone shouted.

"Dance! Dance! Dance!" chanted the crowd, and the gramophone crackled as the needle was placed back into its groove. Everyone stepped back to form a wide circle around the happy couple, and Lorna jumped down from her chair to avoid being pushed off.

As the music began, William swept Iris into his arms, and she beamed as he spun her around and around the dance floor.

Someone nudged Lorna.

"Don't look so glum, lassie," said a gravelly voice. "It'll be your turn soon enough."

Lorna looked to see who had spoken, to put them right, but everyone near her was concentrating on William and Iris.

Suddenly, she felt very, very tired. All her joy on the first day of peace across Europe had vanished, leaving her hollow and strangely untethered. She had to escape.

As she walked across the grass and on to the Sea Wynd, she wondered what would happen now.

Germany might have surrendered, but Britain was still at war with Japan. And her brothers might be coming home, but Lorna knew they would not be the same as before. She'd seen how much John Jo had changed, and who knew what injuries he'd suffered? And Sandy might not even come home. Having Nellie at Craigielaw was wonderful, but would she stay once her baby was born? And then there was Paul.

Lorna couldn't bear the idea that he might be sent back to Germany. What would he go back to? The newspaper had been full of pictures of the wreckage of Europe, historic cities razed by fire and bombs, crater-pocked roads, and railway bridges tossed into rivers like broken matchsticks. And there were new reports that Allied soldiers had liberated prison camps in Poland and Germany in which, the reports said, hundreds of thousands of men and women, and children, had been killed. Hundreds of thousands? The scale of the death and destruction was unimaginable.

And there had been photographs of the survivors too. Streams of refugees, carrying all they owned in pockets or potato sacks, following whatever road would lead them west. So many displaced people, friendless and homeless. Were Paul's mother and sister among them? Or did they survive the inferno, only to find themselves trapped in Dresden by the advancing Russians? Paul would have no way of knowing.

Yes, Lorna was relieved that the war was over, but happiness and stability were still a long way off.

She was so wrapped up in the maelstrom of her thoughts, she didn't see the man in the shadows until he grabbed her by the arm, pulling her out of the torchlight and into the darkness.

Thirty-Two

"No!" Lorna gasped.

She tried to wrench back her arm, but his grip on her elbow held fast, and suddenly her mind was filled with sweat and tobacco, tearing satin and a stabbing light switch, sweet American lemonade and bitter yellow vomit.

"Let me go!" she croaked, unable to release enough air to find any volume. "Don't hurt me, please."

And the man did let her go.

He let go of her arm so suddenly that Lorna sprawled onto the road.

But quickly he was there again, lifting her to her feet.

"Lorna. I am so sorry."

He wrapped his arms around her, and Lorna was clinging

to him, pulling him closer, and burying her face into the soft cloth of his shirt.

"Paul!"

"I did not mean to frighten you," he said.

Paul had come after all.

Lorna lifted her lips to his and kissed him, softly and gratefully. Then she laid her head back against his chest.

"You came," she whispered. "Thank you."

Paul kissed the top of her head, her temple, her cheek.

"I could not lose any more time with you," Paul whispered. "I had to see you."

Lorna didn't want to hear Paul talk of lost time, she didn't want to talk at all, so she lifted her mouth to his once more.

After a while, Lorna realized that someone from the Sea Green might see them, so she took Paul's hand and pulled him down the shadowed pathway behind a hedge.

"But how did you get away?" she asked, gazing up at his handsome face.

"I had a quiet word with one of the guards and—"

"A quiet word?"

"Well, a quiet word and a shilling or two." Paul's eyes glinted in the faint light. "The guard did not want to be in the camp tonight either, so he was happy to take my money and look the other way so I could come to find you."

Lorna smiled. "I am so glad you did."

"Because there is something I need to give you." Paul put his hand in his pocket and drew out the little gift from her birthday, still wrapped in white linen, the twine cross binding it now a little more ragged and off center than it had once been.

Lorna let her fingers reach out to touch it, though she didn't take it. In her heart, she knew what this gift might mean if he were to give it to her here, now. It could mean good-bye.

"I want you to have it tonight," Paul continued, "so that if they send us away from—"

"No!" Lorna snatched her fingers back as if the gift had burned her. "Don't talk like that! Not tonight."

"Lorna, you know that at some time—"

"I don't want to hear that. Not tonight!"

"Lorna, I want you to have this so that—"

But Paul could say no more because Lorna had pressed her lips hard onto his, to silence him, to stop him from talking about—from even thinking about—ever leaving her.

With only a moment's hesitation, Paul responded. And then he was kissing her with an urgency she hadn't felt before, searching and hungry, and Lorna forgot about the gift. Paul's mouth opened on hers, compelling her lips to follow, and she could taste him then, salty and sweet. And his tongue touched hers, lightly, then with more purpose, and Lorna's whole body responded in kind. The taste, the feel, the smell of him sent sparking shocks through her.

Paul's hand found the small of her back, and its warmth on her skin through the fine cotton fabric of her dress made Lorna shiver. Without letting her lips leave his for even one second, she pushed him against the stone wall. Or did he pull her against him? Lorna didn't know, she didn't care, she didn't think, she just pressed herself against him, flattening her body to his.

And then it was her back against the wall and the weight of his body was pinning her to the cold stone. She shivered again, relishing the heat of his neck and his chest under her hands in contrast to the chill on her back. Every nerve ending fizzed. She heard a low groan and realized that it had come from her own throat.

One of Paul's hands was in her hair then, one round her waist, his long fingers cupping around her rib cage, as if he couldn't get enough of her, ravenous and desperate.

And then she heard the waltz. At first, she couldn't be sure if the music was real or in her head, but Paul began to move in time to the music too, gently swaying against her in three-four time. His lips left hers, and he kissed Lorna's fingers.

"This is not 'The Blue Danube Waltz,' but . . ." Paul drew her toward him. *"Möchtest du tanzen, Lorna?"* Paul laid her hand upon his shoulder, and they began to dance as the fiddle's haunting melody sailed over the rhythm of the other instruments. It was a tune Lorna knew well.

"This is a Robert Burns song," she whispered. "A Scottish waltz. It's called 'Ae Fond Kiss,' a song of love and farewell."

Lorna kissed Paul's neck, just below his ear, where the scar tissue melted into the perfect undamaged skin, and Paul shivered against her lips. She let the nail of one finger trace the line of Paul's chin and throat.

"'Had we never loved sae kindly,'" Lorna sang, "'Had we never loved sae blindly . . .'"

Lorna let her fingers slip into the front of Paul's shirt, between two buttons, until she could feel the soft hair on his chest.

"'Never met—or never parted, We had ne'er been broken-hearted.'"

BOOM!

The explosion came on the final beat of the song as if the devil himself were playing the drum.

While Lorna's rational brain knew she had heard the noise, she still struggled to process it. It was too far away to worry about; she wanted to dance, to sing, and to feel Paul's skin under her fingers. It had only been fireworks going off in her own head.

Paul whispered something she couldn't quite hear, perhaps in German, she couldn't tell.

BOOM!

This time they both heard it, and Paul pulled away from her.

"What was that?" she asked.

"I do not know. I will look."

Paul peered around the corner of the wall just as the police whistles sounded, so Lorna grabbed at his shirt and pulled him back into the shadow.

"No, they mustn't see you. Let me."

People were running from the Sea Green in every direction, casting anxious glances behind them, clearly expecting another explosion even nearer. The lamps in the beer tent were being extinguished, and all the torches around the field were being dowsed.

It was hypnotic to watch the little fires die one by one, but then she realized that they weren't the only fires she could see. The headland beyond the bay was silhouetted against an orange-and-red sky, even though it was hours until sunrise.

Then the whine of the air-raid siren sounded, a dreadful sound they had all thought, had all hoped, they would never hear again.

Lorna ran back to Paul, and they crouched down, listening for the drone of incoming bombers.

It didn't come.

Lorna pointed in the direction of the false sunrise.

"There's fire out at sea," she said. "Maybe on a ship, because it's not far north enough to be on land, but what caused it? I thought this was all over."

Paul shrugged, and even in the poor light, Lorna could see he was anxious.

"I heard no plane, did you?" he asked. "It might have been torpedoes from a U-boat, but why? Now there is no reason to attack ships anymore."

Another shrill whistle sounded, and there were sharp smacks on the cobbles as a man in boots ran toward them. Lorna pulled Paul close to her, but the man ran straight past.

"You must get back to the camp," she whispered. "If they catch you out here, they'll lock you up. Properly, this time. Please, Paul, go now! I need you safe, not in jail."

Paul laid his forehead against hers.

"I am sorry to have to go, Lorna."

"But you must," she said again. "Now!"

"But what about you?"

"I'll be fine, I promise. I'll go home. Now go!"

Paul stood up straight and Lorna wished she had time to tell him everything she couldn't find the words to say.

"But we'll have tomorrow," Paul said.

Lorna laid her hand over his damaged cheek, not covering it up, but caressing it.

"Yes, we will have tomorrow."

Paul leaned forward and kissed her once more on the mouth, gently, lovingly, longingly. Then he sprinted away, round by the beach, away from the village itself. If he ran all the way, he'd be back at the camp within ten minutes or so.

It was only once Paul had disappeared from view that Lorna realized that he hadn't given her his gift, the one in the little linen roll, the one he had wanted her to have before it was too late. She wished now that she hadn't stopped him, wished she could have seen it. But that was all right. Paul would give it to her tomorrow. They would see each other tomorrow.

Thirty-Three

Lorna gazed miserably out of the classroom window on Friday afternoon.

Nine sailors had been killed in the torpedo attack on two merchant navy ships by a German submarine on VE Day. The paper had said there was no official explanation about why the German U-boat commander had ignored orders from Berlin to surrender his submarine. Instead he had fired torpedoes at two ships in the Forth, one Canadian and one Norwegian.

The youngest sailor to die, according to today's *Scotsman*, had only been seventeen years old. Younger even than Lorna. The pointless death of this young sailor, a boy she had never even met, had lain heavily on Lorna as she walked to school that morning. She was so angry for him and for his family who must have thought—as she had about John Jo and Sandy—he'd be safe once peace was declared. But instead, he'd be buried today, far from home.

Most of all, she wanted to talk to Paul, but she had not seen him since Tuesday, the night of the bonfire. The POW camp at Gosford House had been off-limits for the last three days. No prisoners had been allowed out, not even those working as farmhands, and no visitors had been allowed in.

Nobody in the village seemed sure as to why the camp had been put on alert. Whatever the reason, the farmers needed the prisoners back at work, particularly the local fruit nurseries, which could not afford to lose their labor just as the summer berry crop was almost ready for harvesting.

Lorna had even waited around for Paul that morning until she was likely to be late again. When she eventually gave up, she'd left Caddy by the gates, staring down the road, ears pricked, clearly straining to hear anything coming from the village. She was probably still there, Lorna thought.

She had been late, and when she'd walked into the class-room, Esther Bell had applauded. But Lorna didn't care. What was the point?

Listening to the prime minister's announcement on Monday afternoon, everyone had been so excited, so expectant that life would now change for the better. But young sailors were still dying, prisoners of war—including *her* prisoner— were still locked up, and Esther Bell was still a miserable cow. So really, what the hell had even changed?

Well, one thing had changed: Mrs. Murray had returned

to her classroom at the end of the two-day Victory holiday. Still dressed all in black, she was no less strict than before.

They would be taking their Higher Leaving Certificate examinations in June, she said—as if they needed reminding—so it would be a crucial few weeks ahead, especially for those going to the university or to other training institutions, such as secretarial colleges. At this, Mrs. Murray looked pointedly at Lorna, who had looked away, embarrassed.

Lorna hadn't forgotten the suggestion that she'd made about secretarial college, but until her chat with Iris the other day, she had given no more thought to the letter and brochure from Dugdale's. She doubted she would even get her Leaving Certificate, because she was finding it so hard to concentrate, or even care about schoolwork. But perhaps they could talk about it, or about Iris's suggestion of nursing, when Mrs. Murray came to the farm for dinner on Sunday.

That had been an unexpected invitation from her father, but he was clearly excited about it, because he'd mentioned it to Lorna two or three times since. So had Mrs. Murray, checking the time and asking what she should bring. Lorna had always liked her teacher, strict though she was, and worried that she was looking so much smaller than she had done before Gregor was killed, paler and more fragile. So perhaps having some company over Sunday dinner might do her some good.

Lorna was ripped from her daydream suddenly when she heard the truck—no, more than one truck. Even through the thick glass of the school windows, Lorna could hear the parade of trucks making their way through the village. They were loud enough to make all the other students look up too. After six years of troops movements between the military bases and camps nearby, they all recognized the sound. But this week it meant something else. Were the trucks taking soldiers away from Aberlady? Or were they bringing soldiers—fathers, brothers, uncles, cousins—home from the war?

Chairs clattered and screeched as most of the class ran to the window to see, standing on tiptoes to peer over the high windowsills. Johnny Milne, Derek's younger brother, was the tallest in the class, and he said he could see an army convoy was heading up the High Street, but when Ross Miller stood up on his chair for a better look, Mrs. Murray shouted at him and he quickly got down again.

At that moment the door flew open, and Mrs. Mack burst in. Her face was bright red and she was struggling to catch a breath.

Why was Mrs. Mack there? What was wrong?

Mrs. Mack scanned the class of students until she found Lorna.

"Lorna, you must come," she panted. "It's them."

Mrs. Murray strode forward, clearly rattled by the sudden interruption.

"Mrs. McMurdough, can I help you?"

Mrs. Mack glanced at her.

"Sorry, Peggy, but Lorna has to come quick. It's an emergency." Mrs. Mack gasped as she tried to make Lorna understand. "It's the camp . . . the trucks, Lorna . . . come and look!" She pointed toward the window, the other hand pressed against her chest. "They're taking them away."

Lorna couldn't move. She couldn't understand, wouldn't understand. How could the Germans be leaving? Paul promised her they would have tomorrow.

Mrs. Mack grabbed Lorna's hand and pulled her toward the classroom door.

"Oh, for goodness' sake! Paul is leaving," Mrs. Mack hissed. "On one of yon trucks *right now*."

Lorna finally understood. She could not let him leave.

Her legs were moving without direction from her brain. She bolted from the classroom and was out of the main door, across the yard, and onto the sidewalk before she realized what she was doing. The green trucks rumbled across the junction in front of the church, and she pushed herself to run harder.

From behind her, Lorna could hear voices shouting after her, but she didn't listen. She wouldn't stop. By the time she got to the corner, in the cacophony of the huge engines, she could hear nothing else but the blood pounding in her ears.

The noise on the main road was bone-shaking. The trucks were enormous, much bigger than the one that brought Paul to Craigielaw, and they towered over Lorna. Looking down the High Street, she could see that perhaps a half dozen of them had already passed, with perhaps the same number still to come.

The last few trucks in the convoy were just entering the village, and they squealed as each driver applied the brakes.

The acrid stench of burning rubber caught in Lorna's throat, making her choke and cough, and she put her hand up to cover her mouth and nose.

What should she do? The convoy stretched all the way toward the far end of the village. Men were peering out of the trucks in front of her, and she strained to see if Paul was among them, but the farthest faces were blurred in a haze of exhaust fumes. Had he already gone by? And then the final truck passed her, with a young man perched on the end of the bench at the back. He was blond and dressed in the familiar uniform, but even as Lorna lifted her hand from her mouth to reach out to him, to wave, she saw it wasn't Paul. This man's face was pale and handsome, but undamaged.

But he must have thought she was waving to him, because he waved back.

"Auf Wiedersehen, Fräulein!" he shouted as the truck rolled on away from Lorna. "Good-bye, pretty Scottish girl!"

No, he wasn't Paul. But perhaps he might know which truck Paul was in.

"Is Paul Vogel in there?" Lorna cried, and ran after him. "Paul Vogel! Is Paul Vogel in there with you?"

The truck was pulling away from her. The man cupped his hand to his ear to show he hadn't heard her properly.

"Paul Vogel!" she shouted at the top of her voice, and he nodded and called back into the interior of the covered truck. Several other prisoners appeared beside him, a mix of faces and waving hands, but they weren't Paul either.

But, she realized, they weren't waving, they were signaling.

All of the hands were pointing farther up the convoy. By this time Lorna had run as far as the Gowff and could barely breathe. The dense fumes from the engines were stifling, and her heart was thumping, but the momentum of her panic kept her legs moving.

The trucks at the front had all slowed down before they turned right onto the Haddington Road. Sure enough, the truck at the back was slowing. She was gaining ground on it at last. She could hear the men calling to her, still pointing.

"Run faster, Fräulein"—she could hear them clearly—"run three trucks more."

Lorna counted the trucks in front of this one. One, two, three. But it was so far away, she would never catch it. But still she must try.

As that truck took the tight bend, Lorna caught sight of several men hanging out of the back. They were holding on to the metal frame, swinging precariously as the truck turned the corner. One of them waved, his wide mouth open in a shout, his whole body leaning forward as if to reach her. For a moment Lorna thought she could hear her name shouted over the thundering engines, but then he disappeared round the corner, the men waving from the next truck taking his place, then the next.

Lorna staggered to a stop beside the post office, lungs heaving as the last truck reached the corner. The young blond man who hadn't been Paul put his hand to his mouth and blew across his flat palm, sending her a kiss. Then he smiled and waved and was away.

The roaring in her ears was no more than a dull reverbera-tion. Footsteps approached from behind, but she didn't look to see who had caught up to her. She didn't care.

Lorna pressed her hands to her face and let the tears flow over her fingers. Her knees buckled, but she had neither the energy nor the desire to stop herself from crumpling to the ground. She had nothing left.

She felt someone crouch beside her and lifted her face to look into concerned eyes of her best friend as warm arms closed around her.

"He's gone, Iris," Lorna choked out. "Paul's gone without saying good-bye."

Thirty-Four

Lorna trudged home alone.

Iris had picked her up off the sidewalk and had held her tight until the sobbing subsided. She'd wanted to walk Lorna back to Craigielaw, but Lorna had said no. She'd rather go by herself.

Back in the yard, there was no little dog waiting sadly at the gate as Lorna had expected there would be. Instead, Caddy was sprawled on the warm cobblestones outside the lambing shed. Fickle creature! But her ears pricked as Lorna approached, and she was immediately on her feet, dashing toward Lorna, tail thrashing, nails skidding.

Lorna put her hand down to rub Caddy's head, but before she could touch her, the dog had run back to the door of the shed, where she gave a soft *wuff*.

"Silly dog!" Lorna muttered, and turned toward the kitchen door.

She hadn't gone more than a couple of paces when a wet nose nudged across her palm, and Caddy's soft head filled her hand as she sat at Lorna's feet.

"So you want a pat after all, do you?"

Caddy's deep-brown gaze seemed to understand Lorna was hurting as she crouched down and rubbed her hands through the rich black and bright white fur on the dog's head and back. Lorna's eyes were scratchy and dry after all her tears, so she let her face rest on the comfortingly soft and silky ruff around Caddy's neck. Her fingers rubbed the grubby, more-brown-than-white fluff under Caddy's belly, but when they were caught by the mass of tangles, burrs, and mud knots, she grimaced and withdrew them.

"You need a bath, Caddy-girl."

Caddy's tail thumped on the cobblestones.

"And I suppose I'll have to give it to you, since Paul's not here to do it."

Caddy jumped to her feet, wagging her tail madly at Paul's name, and Lorna felt a surge of annoyance at the dog's futile loyalty.

"He's gone, you know that, don't you? Paul's gone, and chances are, he's never coming back."

Lorna sighed and stood up. Caddy bounded away again to the other side of the yard and looked back at Lorna expectantly. But Lorna had had enough puppy play, so she went into the kitchen. God, she needed a cup of tea!

In the kitchen, Lorna filled the kettle and put it on to boil.

"You're home early. I thought you were Mrs. Mack when you came in," Nellie said from where she was sitting by the open window overlooking the garden. "She said she'd be a bit late this morning. Ooh, are you making a cuppa? Count me in."

She had a basket of pea pods on the windowsill beside her and was shelling the bright green peas into a bowl in her lap. Popping a couple into her mouth, she chewed them with obvious relish. "Mmmm, I love peas, don't you?"

So Nellie hadn't heard then, about the convoy taking all the prisoners away, about Paul. If she had, surely she wouldn't be sitting there smiling as if everything was wonderful.

Lorna worked the start of several sentences round her head, but could not find the words to tell Nellie that Paul had gone.

"And while I think about it, duckie"—Nellie waved a fat pea pod toward the table—"that there's for you."

The pea pod pointed at a small roll of linen, off-white and creased at the ends, bound with fine brown twine tied in a cross, its ends frayed and feathery.

Paul's gift.

But how . . . ?

"Paul was in with it earlier. Said that if he left it right there, you might actually get it this time. Said he'd tried a dozen times already, but something had always gotten in the way."

Lorna stared at the little parcel.

"Paul's been here? Today?"

"Yeah, he stuck his head round the door a couple of hours ago, just for a minute or two, but then he said he had to go."

Lorna could have cried all over again. Paul had been here, at Craigielaw, long enough to deliver this parcel, and she had been at school. Why hadn't she stayed home? Why hadn't she been here, even just for those two minutes?

Nellie put the bowl of peas onto the windowsill and walked to where Lorna was still staring at the gift.

"Well, get on with it then!" Nellie picked up the linen package and held it out to Lorna. "He left it for you to open. He said you shouldn't wait for him."

She shouldn't wait for him?

Lorna slowly took the parcel in trembling fingers.

"Aw, come on, Lorna, you're killing me!" Nellie tugged at the corner. "He told me what it is. Said he bought it off someone in the camp, but then he did some work on it to make it extra special, just for you."

"What is it?"

"Ha! Not telling. You'll have to open it."

Lorna fiddled with the twine. When the knot released, she unfolded the linen. Inside was a layer of finer fabric, a cotton handkerchief, and Lorna could feel something hard inside it.

Her fingers shook as she pulled aside the cotton.

"Ooh," cooed Nellie, "have you ever seen anything . . . ?"

On the white cotton lay a watch. A beautiful watch, glimmering with silver and copper highlights, its soft brown strap buffed to a silken sheen.

"Oh, Nellie, it's . . ."

But what words were there?

It was the most beautiful thing she had ever seen. Under the flat dome of glass, framed within a ring of silver, lay an exquisitely carved watch face. Rippling silver across the lower half, and above it an undulating line, lifted in relief and somehow edged with copper. The wavy line formed a shape that Lorna recognized only a second or two ahead of Nellie.

"Is that . . . ?" said Nellie, pointing gingerly at the watch face, clearly trying not to touch the spotless glass.

"Yes," Lorna could only whisper. "It's the shoreline of Aberlady Bay."

And there they were, the rolling hills of Fife on the left-hand side, cut across toward the center by the distinctive rise and fall of Gullane Point, sitting beyond the rippling sand of the bay as it would be at low tide. And hugging the nearest edge of the circle was the curving line of the Peffer Burn.

"And look, the birds . . . ," said Nellie. On the end of each hand hovered a tiny copper bird, its wings outlined against the silver of the sky and the hills. "It's like they're flying. But how . . . ?"

Nellie was obviously as stunned as Lorna.

"He made it for my birthday." Shameful tears pricked Lorna's eyes as she remembered. "And I wouldn't let him give it to me. I threw it back in his face. How could I have done that, Nellie? How could I?"

Nellie squeezed Lorna's arm.

"That was an awful day, and not one any of us want to remember. But Paul understood why you did that, you know he did."

Nellie held the watch to her ear.

"It even ticks beautifully. Sounds like a lullaby."

Nellie took the watch and, with deft fingers, did up the silver buckle so that the watch fitted snugly around Lorna's wrist.

Lorna studied the watch and then looked at Nellie, who was smiling.

How could Nellie be smiling now?

"Nellie," Lorna croaked through the tightness in her throat, "what am I going to do?"

"Well, you might want to say thank you as a start." Nellie winked.

How could Lorna say thank you if Paul was right now in an army truck being driven away from Aberlady, away from her?

"No, Nellie, I mean what am I going to do without Paul?"

"Without Paul?" Nellie sounded puzzled.

Of course, Nellie still didn't yet know about the convoy.

"He's gone, Nellie, Paul's gone. They've cleared all the prisoners out of Gosford. They've taken them all away."

Lorna sat down hard and pressed the watch tight against the desperate ache across her chest.

On the range, the kettle whistled to announce that it had boiled.

"Wait, Lorna—" began Nellie, but at that moment, heavy

boots came stamping up the stone steps, and the door to the yard banged open.

"Perfect timing as always," said Lorna's dad as he came in. "So who's making the tea then?"

Apparently oblivious to Lorna's tearstained face, he went into the scullery to wash his hands, whistling a random tune in competition with the kettle.

"I will in a minute," said Nellie. "But first, I need to tell Lorna—"

"Get on with it then," he said, coming back into the kitchen, drying his hands on a towel. "We're parched. And get that tin from the pantry. I promised the lad that we'd have some flapjack with our cuppa."

"In a second," said Nellie tersely. "I just need to explain—"

It had taken a moment for Lorna to process what her father had just said.

"'The lad'?" she asked, cutting across Nellie. "What lad?"

Her dad looked at her as if she'd suddenly started talking in Welsh.

"What do you mean, 'what lad'? I mean the lad. *Our* lad. What other lad would I be talking about? He's just finishing up with the whitewash in the shed, so after we've had our cup of tea, we can get on with—"

"Paul?"

"Aye, Paul."

"You mean Paul's here?" Lorna could hardly breathe. "But he can't be. Paul's gone. On the convoy. They've cleared the camp. Today. They've all gone."

Nellie was patting her shoulder.

"That's what I've been trying to tell you. Not all of them left. They've shifted some of them off to somewhere else, because of the overcrowding apparently, so—"

"Then Paul's here?"

"Did you not hear your dad?" Nellie was chuckling now. "Paul's in the shed mixing whitewash, and in minute or two, he'll be coming in for his—"

But Lorna wasn't there to hear more.

She ran through the door and jumped off the top step, her shoes sliding on the muddy cobbles as she landed. Then she sprinted, with Caddy's noisy and tangling escort, across the yard. At the door of the lambing shed, Lorna yanked herself to a skidding stop by grabbing hold of the door frame.

Paul looked up from the wide white tub, a long wooden spoon in his hand. Almost at once, he noticed the watch on her wrist and smiled.

"At last, you have your birthday present." He indicated the watch. "Very late, but I hope that you like it."

Not even a second passed before Lorna was pressing her lips to his and twisting her hands into the short hair on his neck. And before Paul was kissing her back.

There was a vague splash as the spoon dropped into the thick liquid, and then Paul's arms were around her so tightly, he almost lifted her off the floor.

When eventually she pulled back, she tilted her chin so she could gaze into those silver-gray eyes again.

"So I think perhaps you like your gift?" said Paul with a shy smile.

Lorna gently ran her thumb across a thick white smudge of whitewash that crossed the shiny pink scarring of his cheek.

"Quite the most beautiful thing I have ever seen in my life."

Paul's smile widened, and his hand cupped Lorna's face in reply.

"I know what you mean."

Lorna kissed the white-stained palm of his hand and then rested her face against her favorite place on his shoulder. Paul was here, with her.

"I thought I'd lost you," she said.

"You will never lose me." Paul kissed the top of her head. "And even if I have to leave, you must know that I will come back to you again. If you'll wait for me?"

Lorna nodded against his chest. "Of course I'll wait. I'll wait for you forever."

Paul's arms tightened around her, but then he chuckled.

"But before your father gets out his shotgun," he said, "perhaps I might be allowed to kiss you again?"

Lorna smiled and withdrew her arms from around Paul's back so she could look again at the beautiful watch on her wrist.

She lifted her mouth to meet his once more. Just as their lips touched, she whispered, "I think we have a little time."

Author's Note

When I was writing this book, I wanted to be truthful to the people of Aberlady in 1945. However, I did allow myself to take a few liberties with history. So, what was real and what wasn't?

There was a farm called Craigielaw exactly where I put it. Now Craigielaw Golf Club, the farm was then part of the Earl of Wemyss's Gosford Estate. So that the farm would reach the water, I also adopted the tract of land next door, which was, and still is, Kilspindie Golf Club.

Across Britain, German and Italian prisoners of war were sent to work on farms near their prison camps. One of those camps was at Gosford House. Although the prisoners signed papers promising not to fraternize with local people, in reality, the prisoners developed long-standing friendships and even love affairs. Many stayed in Scotland after the war, avoiding a return to homes in the Russian Zone, what was to become communist East Germany for the next few decades. The POWs often returned the kindnesses of the British people they met by making gifts by hand, as Paul does, such as jewelry, paintings, and wooden toys for the children.

Before the POWs arrived, farms around Britain were already "manned" by the Women's Land Army. Though some of the eighty thousand Land Girls were from the countryside, many, like Nellie, came from the big cities and had never even seen a cow before.

So if those are some truths, here are some liberties:

Aberlady School is actually a primary or elementary school. Older students like Lorna would have traveled to North Berwick High by bus each day.

The United States Army Air Force did not have bomber base in Scotland. However, East Fortune was a Royal Air Force training base from June 1940 to 1946. It is now the National Museum of Flight and hosts Scotland's National Air Show every July.

There was no attack by the German air force, the *Luftwaffe*, on East Lothian so late in the war, although there were German bases in Norway until 1945 and the Messerschmitt 110 fighters did have the range to reach Aberlady. East Lothian was, however, bombed in two attacks in 1942, on Haddington and RAF Drem.

The sinking of the two merchant navy ships, *Avondale Park* and *Sneland I*, actually took place on the night of May 7, not May 8, as I have it. Nine men died in torpedo attacks several hours after peace was declared, because the German submarine captain refused to believe the radio messages from Berlin telling him to surrender.

The Victory bonfire on Aberlady's Sea Green was actually on August 15, 1945, to celebrate VJ Day—Victory over Japan—rather than VE Day in May.

Since I finished writing *Wait for Me*, I have heard about several love stories between Gosford POWs and local girls, who met on farms during and immediately after the war. Some of these not-so-young lovers are still living in East Lothian. One email I received was from Effie Renton, the daughter of a Gosford POW, Rudi Franzel, who fell in love with and married Betty Young, a girl from Haddington. Effie told me:

> *My father was a POW in Gosford and worked on a local farm. He met and married my mum in 1948 while still officially a POW, and they celebrated their diamond wedding in 2008. Sadly, Mum died in 2013, but my dad is now ninety and still very much alive.*
>
> *[Your] story could have been about them, and I just wanted to let you know that they had a very happy life together.*
>
> *Regards, Effie Renton (nee Franzel)*

What wonderful reassurance that perhaps Lorna and Paul do get a happy ending after all.

Acknowledgments

This book is dedicated to my parents, Shirley and Jimmie Sibbald, who have always loved and supported me, and my sister, no matter what messes we got ourselves into (okay, Jane, the messes were mostly mine). They inspired my love of Scotland and my passion for reading and writing, and they shared with me their memories of World War II.

Mum was evacuated as a child from London in 1939 to a farm in Oxfordshire with her sister, Sylvia. Dad was called up at age eighteen in 1944 and followed his four brothers—Frank, Archie, Billy, and Eric—into the army. Sadly, Archie was killed by a German shell in North Africa on Christmas Day 1941.

In October 1939 in Port Seton, near Aberlady, Barbara Stevenson returned home from school to find two wringing-wet Germans drinking brandy in her kitchen. Shot down by RAF Spitfires while bombing Rosyth Naval Base, they were waiting for the army to arrive to arrest them. Barbara

Sibbald, as she is now, is my aunt, and I tried to sneak her story into *Wait for Me* but failed.

I began this story in 2010, during NaNoWriMo—National Novel Writing Month—racing my friend Mike Deacon to fifty thousand words. He won, and I still owe him a victor's pint. I owe more than a pint to Penny Linsenmayer, who loves historical fiction even more than I do, and who kept me believing.

Thanks also:

To my dear Welsh writer friend, Angharad Wynne, who first told me of a watch given in friendship by a prisoner of war. If you meet Angharad and her daughter Myfi out walking, you will also meet the real Caddy (or rather *Cadi*, in Welsh).

To my experts: Ian Malcolm from Aberlady Heritage, Liz Martin (and Bunty), Kennethmont Taylor and Jan Michaelis; to eastlothianatwar.com and to the *Scotsman* Archive for permission to use the Dresden article.

To my best friends, Rachel Dickson and Lara Powers, and to my critique group: Andrea White, Chris Cander, Tobey Forney, Mimi Vance, and Gretchen Mazziotti.

To Kathi Appelt, who mentored me as my priceless prize in the SCBWI Joan Lowery Nixon Prize in 2014. And to Clara Gifford Clark and Stephen Roos, my patient tutors at the Institute of Children's Literature.

To my wise SCBWI friends, Samantha Clark, Nikki Loftin, Cynthia Leitich Smith, Melissa Buron, and Sara Joiner, and to HarperCollins's Jocelyn Davies, who first gave me hope. And to all the Swanky 17s—other YA/MG authors debuting in 2017—who have kept me going.

To Alice Jerman, my fabulous editor at HarperCollins, who read ten pages as an RWA Emily Prize judge and immediately believed in my book. With Alice's insight and her smiley emojis, Lorna and Paul's story became stronger and leaner (and sexier). Also to all the team at HarperCollins, including Aurora Parlagreco, Alison Klapthor, Renée Cafiero, Elizabeth Ward, Sabrina Abballe, Gina Rizzo, and Jean McGinley, and also to Valerie Shea.

To Jackie Lindert and Joanna Volpe at New Leaf Literary & Media, who are leading me by the hand through the thrillingly scary mire that is publishing. Thanks too to Suzie Townsend and Danielle Barthel.

To Perryn, my husband, who told people I was a writer long before I could. He turned us upside down by moving us to Texas, which gave me time and space to write. I owe him so much.

And to my children—Jemma, you were this family's writer long before I was. You are an exceptional soul, with the fortitude and wisdom of the ancients. Kirsty, you constantly amaze me with your intelligence, your wit, and your extraordinary energy. Rory, you are so passionate and so talented, you shine on every stage. I wish I could keep all three of you in my arms forever, but I also can't wait to see what joy you will bring to the world.

And thanks to you, dear reader, for allowing Lorna and Paul's story to fly.